SPRING'S GREEN SHADOW

CECILY MACKWORTH

With an introduction by
Angela V. John

WELSH WOMEN'S CLASSICS

First published in 1952 by MacGibbon & Kee, London
First published by Honno in 2022.
'Ailsa Craig', Heol y Cawl, Dinas Powys, Wales. CF64 4AH

Introduction © Angela V. John, 2022

ISBN: 978-1-912905-53-9 (paperback)
ISBN: 978-1-912905-54-6 (ebook)

Printed with the financial support of the Books Council of Wales

Cover image: Pearl Falconer, from the original
1952 MacGibbon & Kee edition
Cover design: Graham Preston
Printed in the UK by Severnprint Ltd

Angela V. John lives in Pembrokeshire and is an Honorary Professor at Swansea University. For many years she was Professor of History at the University of Greenwich, London. She has published a dozen books. They include biographies of Elizabeth Robins, Lady Charlotte Guest, Henry Nevinson, Evelyn Sharp and Lady Rhondda. Her most recent studies are *The Actors' Crucible: Port Talbot and the Making of Burton, Hopkins, Sheen and All the Others* (Parthian, 2015) and *Rocking the Boat: Welsh Women who Championed Equality 1840-1990* (Parthian, 2018). She has also written Introductions to several reprints of Menna Gallie's novels in Honno's Welsh Women's Classics series.

ACKNOWLEDGEMENTS

I am grateful to have received a Writer's Bursary 2020 for my project 'A Free Spirit': The Life of Cecily Mackworth', funded by Literature Wales and The National Lottery through the Arts Council of Wales. I'm greatly indebted to Cecily's daughter, Pascale Donckier, for her conversations and for sharing Cecily Mackworth's autobiography and other papers. Many thanks too are due to Anne Bony and Geneviève Chabannes La Palice, for generous hospitality and access to family papers. I thank Ariane Banks for letting me use Inez Holden's diary and am grateful to her and to Kristin Bluemel for their assistance. Michael Gaum has been extremely helpful. Thanks also to Alison Chardel, Hedwige Chevrillon, Jessica Graham, Isobel Grundy, Dafydd Johnston, Richard Keen, Julia Mackworth, Martine Monacelli, Elizabeth Murray, Richard Rhys O'Brien, David N. Thomas, the late Frankie Webber, and Judith Zinsser. I'm grateful to the LSE Archives Division, University of Manchester Library, Cheltenham Ladies' College, the British Library and the University of Glasgow Archive Services. And I greatly appreciate the skills and support of Jane Aaron, Caroline Oakley and Honno Press.

Angela V. John

Introduction

ANGELA V. JOHN

'Mountains of paper are being covered' announced the Welsh writer Cecily Mackworth in August 1950 as she worked on her first novel, *Spring's Green Shadow*.[1] She and her friend Inez Holden[2] were on a fortnight's writing holiday in Brittany. They were both journalists and authors, independent women who challenged convention. Cecily lived in Paris and Holden in London. They had first met there in 1945, Holden's diary describing Cecily (who was in her thirties and eight years her junior) as 'a rather charming poetical minded girl.'

At the time of the Breton holiday Cecily was recovering from illness and a financial crisis of 'fearful proportions'. The two women spent their mornings and three hours each evening writing at their hotel in the village of Sainte-Marine. Holden had already published a string of novels but Cecily had, until now, concentrated on non-fiction and poetry. This new genre was, she wrote, 'very difficult and exciting'.[3]

Both novels were published in 1952. Holden's *The Owner* includes a character named Laura. The heroine of *Spring's Green Shadow* is Laura Gethryn. Its blurb declares that the author's 'view-point' is the same as Laura's. Given its powerful depiction of a dysfunctional family in the aftermath of war and a daughter who flouts conventions of acceptable sexual propriety, asserting her independence far from home, this was a bold claim for the time.

So, what was Cecily Mackworth's own story[4] and how might it help us understand this novel? Although decades later her French passport would claim that she had been born in 1914, Cecily Joan Mackworth's birth was on 15 August 1911 in the Mardy district of the rural parish of Llantilio Pertholey (Llandeilo Bertholau), two miles northeast of Abergavenny in south east Wales. Like the socialist thinker and writer Raymond Williams, also from this border country (but a very different background), the landscape had an indelible effect on her life and work.

Cecily's parents were both from respected Tory families. Dorothy Conran Lascelles (who had been born in Narberth, Pembrokeshire) had married Francis Julian Audley Mackworth in Llantilio Pertholey's St Teilo's Church in 1910. His father was one of the principal landowners of Monmouthshire. This branch of the distinguished Mackworth family produced soldiers and Cecily's father was a captain in the Royal Field Artillery, stationed at Camberley in Surrey. Cecily and her mother lived at Sunnyside, her widowed grandmother's home. There were three acres of land including a paddock that looked across to The Skirrid or Holy Mountain, rich in legends. A younger sister, Helen Margaret, was born in 1914.

Cecily's father was an early casualty of the First World War, killed on the Western Front on 1 November 1914, two days after becoming a major. He was a shadowy figure in his daughter's life though his medals and memory were carefully preserved at Sunnyside. Mrs Mackworth immersed herself in the war effort, helping to run Abergavenny's Voluntary Labour Bureau and organising work for women and girls in agriculture through the Ladies' Committee. As in the novel, mother and daughter were not close and Cecily's interests and ambitions seem to have puzzled Mrs Mackworth.

In 1916 the family, Granny included, moved to the picturesque Somerset village of North Cheriton where Cecily's uncle lived. Although she returned to Wales for holidays, the rest of her childhood was spent in the West Country. Six years later her mother remarried and they moved to Sidmouth in Devon. Cecily did not warm to her stepfather, the equine artist Charles Edward Gatehouse.

A succession of governesses was followed by two years at school in Burnham-on-Sea. Here the sister of her future friend, the poet and novelist Stevie Smith, taught Cecily English. She then boarded for two years at Sherborne School for Girls, followed by a brief spell at art college in Cheltenham where she was also a part-time student at Cheltenham Ladies' College, studying Literature.[5] She reluctantly attended a domestic science college in Malvern for one term to please her mother before her aunt proposed a much more enticing path: studying journalism at the London School of Economics.

This aunt was the 2nd Viscountess Rhondda from Llanwern near Newport. She had married, then divorced, Sir Humphrey Mackworth, Cecily's uncle (and best man at her parents' wedding). A former suffragette who had been imprisoned, renowned businesswoman and founder, owner and editor of the influential weekly *Time & Tide*, Lady Rhondda was one of Britain's best-known feminists.[6] The views and actions of the 'delinquent Aunt Margaret' were sufficient to earn the disapproval of Cecily's mother and for Cecily herself to view her as an appropriate role model. In *Spring's Green Shadow* Lady Wynn-Evans (married, as Lady Rhondda had been, to a Master of Foxhounds), understands Laura better than does her mother, intercedes on her behalf and is a catalyst for change. And it is she who helps Laura to appreciate some of the difficulties facing her mother. Cecily always remembered sitting on her aunt's lap as a small child, listening to her story about a dwarf who sailed down the River Usk on a rhubarb leaf. 'It was Aunt Margaret who changed my life' declared the elderly Cecily.

Although appendicitis had prevented Cecily from matriculating, she was accepted as an LSE student in 1929 (Lady Rhondda was later a governor there). Cecily lived in a hostel for female students. Her account of it is not unlike her description in *Spring's Green Shadow* of the International Home for Female Students in Paris.

Several sources erroneously suggest that Cecily failed to graduate and eloped from university. However, she never embarked on a degree, opting instead for a two-year diploma in journalism. The wide-ranging course included classes in Modern English Literature, International Relations and Practical Journalism. Cecily's tutors at this forward-thinking, modern university included distinguished scholars such as the sociologists T. H. Marshall and Morris Ginsberg and the Marxist political theorist and economist, Harold Laski. Cecily wrote in old age that she learned from Laski the art of being 'obediently disobedient.'[7]

She produced several commissioned reviews for Lady Rhondda's *Time & Tide*. They provided welcome cash as well as confidence and experience. Cecily would earn her living writing for British and French literary journals and newspapers for many decades. During the war, for example, she contributed (as did Holden) to Cyril Connolly's *Horizon*.

After gaining her diploma in 1931, Cecily helped her aunt to organise, with the novelist Winifred Holtby and the Old Vic Theatre, a dinner for the suffrage playwright Cecily Hamilton, author of the influential study *Marriage as a Trade*. Thanks to Lady Rhondda, Cecily found herself 'in a whirl of smart literary life', including Foyle's famed Literary Lunches where she met writers such as Rose Macaulay.

Lady Rhondda also gave Cecily money to travel. At the LSE she had met the Hungarian student, Nicholas Kaldor (later the eminent economist Lord Kaldor) and he appears to have been her first lover.[8] She went to Hungary where she was briefly employed to speak English to the daughters of a wealthy landowning family near Pécs, then stayed with Kaldor's family in Buda. The love affair did not last.

By early 1933 she was living in a Berlin pension. She did a German language course. Lacking money, she and a young English woman frequented a café where they would order coffee and eat their way through the entire sugar bowl. Cecily then secured lodgings with a Jewish widow, looking after her small son.

She watched political and economic tensions escalate. On the night the Reichstag was set on fire she saw the sky glowing red with flames. She heard but did not see Hitler and witnessed young Nazis parading. Her sympathies were with the Communists and she marched with them. She compared the atmosphere to the 'violence of a liberated steam cooker which had burst at last.'

Her landlady fled from Germany and Cecily returned to London, did some translation work, hawked electrical appliances and, recalling this period in her early nineties, added: 'Oh yes, that's it. I got married during this time.'[9] But that apparently casual note camouflaged a tragedy.

Léon Donckier de Donceel was a Belgian lawyer in his late twenties. Born in Liège into a distinguished family dating back to the fourteenth century, he had met Cecily in a Swiss sanatorium where, it seems, they were both recovering from tuberculosis. They married in 1935. She moved to Brussels and their daughter Pascale Léonie Juliette was born the following year. But, after just a few years of married life, Cecily's husband died from a recurrence of TB.

Just before this there had been another Mackworth tragedy, one conspicuous by its absence from Cecily's accounts of her life. Her younger sister Helen had been about to marry William McClintock from Donegal. A soldier, he had fractured his spine at a military point-to-point. His mother was apparently so distressed at her adored son becoming a paraplegic that six months later and two days before the wedding, she fatally shot him and herself. Helen promptly took her own life and was buried in her wedding gown. None of the Mackworth family attended the funeral in Ireland. By the age of 27, Cecily had lost her father, a Mackworth uncle also killed in war, her only sibling and her husband. Her tiny daughter was left, as Cecily had been, with just one parent.

After staying with her in-laws in Brussels, Cecily headed for Paris. It was especially alluring in the late 1930s for an adventurous, aspiring writer keen to mix with international artistic figures. The Welsh language poet and writer Eluned Phillips, the only woman to have twice won the National Eisteddfod crown, also lived in Paris in the 1930s. Like Cecily, she found it the antithesis of life back home, in her case 'sleepy Cenarth' in Carmarthenshire.[10]

Cecily rented a flat in the Rue du Moulin Vert in the 14th arrondissement. She taught English, attended Paul Valéry's classes in poetics at the Sorbonne and immersed herself in Left Bank society, meeting worldly-wise intellectuals. She gained an entrée to 18 Villa Seurat, in effect a cul-de-sac inhabited by artists and writers, just minutes from her flat. Here lived Henry Miller. He published *Eleven Poems*, Cecily's first poetry collection, as an offshoot from his notorious magazine, the *Booster*.[11]

Miller's circle included Lawrence Durrell, in his mid-twenties and fresh from Corfu. He was, Cecily wrote, 'Short and sturdy and so full of force that his whole body seemed to be charged with static electricity.' Keen to see her poems, he wrote on a scrap of paper left under her door: 'Send me everything in your jam cupboard.' Years later she published an influential essay on the neo-Romantic aspects of his *The Alexandria Quartet*.[12]

In retrospect she remarked that pre-war Montparnasse was 'nothing like the romantic Bohemia of so many memoirs.'[13] It was, after all, a refuge for those already afflicted by war, like her friend the writer Alfred Perlès, and for others now fleeing Nazi Germany. It nevertheless provided a heady mix whilst it lasted. But it ended abruptly, which partly explains why these times were later recalled in such vivid terms.

Cecily stayed on after war was declared, working for the Books for the Army scheme. The Jewish art dealer René Gimpel also volunteered and introduced Cecily to more artists and writers. By late spring, foreigners were increasingly unwelcome in Paris and, to avoid neighbours' suspicion, she moved to Jeanne Bucher's art gallery in the Boulevard Montparnasse, sleeping amongst surrealist paintings and tapestries. By early June 1940, just before Paris fell, she was a Red Cross volunteer at the Gare d'Austerlitz, helping thousands of refugees from Belgium and Holland and the north who arrived in the city daily as the Germans advanced. Rumours that they were about to enter Paris intensified the desperation. Cecily recalled being 'crushed among human flesh' as people panicked at the station. Her precious typewriter was lost: 'only the pressure of the crowd held me upright because I had no room to fall.'

Still wearing her white red cross uniform, she fled with friends in a battered car that kept breaking down. They aimed for Chartres, only to find that it had been bombed. After barely eating for five days, they reached Rennes to rescue the driver's family. Cecily struck out on her own but her suitcase, passport and papers were destroyed when the railway station was hit. She got lifts in a horse-drawn cart, on a motorbike and a workers' bus but much of the time she tramped south on foot in stifling heat. In old age she recalled:

Refugees beside me, behind me, before me. From above, we must have looked like a column of drugged ants. We trudged, shedding belongings by the roadside... When planes swept out of the sky, graceful as seagulls, to spray us with shrapnel, there was just time to throw ourselves into the ditch. Piled on top of the other, we ceased to be individual selves, and became just an amalgam of bodies, breath held too tight to scream. But afterwards patches of blood shone bright on parched grass.[14]

She slept in ditches, beneath hedges or wherever she could find shelter. At a makeshift refugee centre in Aubusson, she heard that the armistice had been signed with Germany. Clad in borrowed clothes with an oversized raincoat and tennis shoes, she reached Marseilles on a military train after securing, with difficulty, a Belgian passport. When she finally arrived at the Spanish border, she was accused of hiding something valuable in her corset. There was no corset. Cecily was so emaciated that her ribs were protruding. By the time she got to Barcelona, she had been on the road for more than a month. Eventually, after four weeks in Lisbon, she boarded a Japanese vessel, reaching Liverpool in mid-August. Her arrival coincided with the first bomb to hit the city.

Bombs aimed at London started soon after Cecily arrived there. She lived at Thames Bank House, Chiswick Mall with a couple of other women 'plus occasional male imports'. The town planner and Labour Party activist Monica Felton, who also lived there for a time, introduced Cecily to the publisher Routledge,[15] who commissioned a book about her harrowing escape. *I Came Out of France* (1941), with its vivid yet unsensational eyewitness account, deservedly gave Cecily her first critical success, winning plaudits from many, including T. S. Eliot. The narrative is powerful and as moving as Irène Némirovsky's 'Storm in June', written in the same year and eventually forming the first part of the posthumous novel, *Suite Française*.[16]

A short poem Cecily wrote about the flight from France was printed in *Poems for France*, a collection edited by the writer, translator, heiress and political campaigner Nancy Cunard (described by Cecily as having 'eyes like blue oysters' and uttering 'amazing obscenities'). It tells of weary people on the move beneath an indigo sky:

Incarnate summer's ultimate and proud display
Before she laid her corn and birds and flowers down in defeat.[17]

Inspired by de Gaulle's 'Call to Honour' appeal for French people to join him in London, Cecily worked briefly as a secretary to Admiral Meffre, head of security at the Free French headquarters in Carlton Gardens. Many years later, in an interview at the Imperial War Museum, she explained in detail how MI5 had recruited her. She used to steam open letters. Meffre's aides became suspicious – Cecily was not a competent typist – and her 'handler' warned her to leave immediately or face imprisonment. She dismissed her brief foray into the world of espionage as 'very slimy.'[18]

Cecily spent rather longer working for the Army Bureau of Current Affairs.[19] Tutors were given 10-minute scripts to prompt weekly group discussions on subjects such as parliamentary democracy, the possible fate of India and birth control. Most tutors held left-wing views and the organisation has been credited with helping to swing the popular vote towards the Labour Party in 1945. Cecily put it well: what she heard in these discussions was, she wrote, 'the sound of the crumbling of Britain's class system.'

She felt 'stiff with terror', facing her first class: Glaswegian soldiers fresh from Libya discussing 'Women: are they equal?'[20] She persevered and was assigned weekly classes in Wales where the organiser was Amabel Willams-Ellis. Cecily found the miners brimming with ideas and well versed in discussion. She joined them in the pub in the evenings. Her classes included young women working at Bridgend's ordnance factory and others making parachutes near Builth Wells.

She met the Swansea poet Vernon Watkins and he suggested that his friend Dylan Thomas visit her in Chiswick. Unsurprisingly, given all that she had been through and her propensity for burning the candle at both ends, Cecily was ill with chronic fatigue at the time. Thomas sat on the edge of her bed, hugging his knees: 'small and cherubic, snub-nosed' with 'curly daffodil-yellow hair and rather globulous [sic] light-brown eyes.'[21] His 'rich, fruity voice' had 'hardly a trace of a Welsh accent.' He gave her a volume of poetry. Nine months after *Spring's Green Shadow* appeared, Thomas was hailed as Britain's greatest living poet with the publication of his *Collected Poems*. Cecily later wrote about his work for the French literary and philosophical review *Critique*.[22]

She wrote two books about Czechoslovakia's tribulations. *Czechoslovakia Fights Back* (1942) told the story of its Nazi occupation. *Czechoslovakia* (1943) was written with the Czech lawyer and political activist Jan Stránský. Many of Cecily's friends were influential exiles from Eastern Europe, including Mihály Károlyi, former first president of Hungary. His wife Catherine had started the Free Hungarian Club in Connaught Square. Refugees and British sympathisers would 'listen to poetry readings or discuss Danubian economics while the walls rocked to the rhythm of falling bombs.'

Cecily also lectured for the Alliance Française on subjects such as Mallarmé and the Symbolists. She did occasional radio broadcasts, including a French programme on Van Gogh. She also worked in the research department at the Labour Party headquarters producing, inter alia, reports on the fishing industry, the government of New Zealand and the Savings Bank scare of 1931.

Cecily left Chiswick to live in Primrose Hill with a man called Géza. An artistic figure, he was engaged in medical research in a laboratory in the Midlands but spent a lot of time in London.[23] It transpired, however, that he was double-crossing Cecily and by the spring of 1945 he had disappeared to Paris. Although most of her extant diaries simply record appointments, a detailed journal does survive for 1944-5. It shows that although busy, she was seriously depressed, fearful for her mental state and for the future. The horrors of flying bombs and now war-weariness were accompanied by intense loneliness. On 30 December 1944 she wrote: 'I have come to a blank wall in my life and my own springs are sagging and I think I shall never get across it.' Her despondency had intensified by the spring. She admitted that she was 'in the grip of near moral collapse.'

Cecily moved back to Paris in the autumn of 1946, revelling in its freedom and intellectual stimulation, though transport, heating and money were in short supply. The following year her book *François Villon: A Study* was published. He had been an unscrupulous fifteenth century French criminal but a fine writer of poems and ballads. Cecily's book was the result of many hours of research in the British Library and Bibliothèque Nationale. A review by Holden emphasised how being a poet enhanced the author's understanding of her subject.[24]

A Mirror of French Poetry 1840-1940 also appeared in 1947. An anthology of French poems, accompanied by translations into English by British poets, including some of Cecily's own translations and five by Vernon Watkins, it reflected her wish for the French poets she valued to be appreciated beyond national boundaries, and for readers to understand the complex triangular relationship between themselves, the poet and translator.

Keen to travel – the French version of *Spring's Green Shadow* described her as a 'Grande Voyageuse' – she persuaded the French press (*L'Aube* and *Paris Presse*) as well as Routledge to fund an investigation of life in the Middle East. She spent a month in Palestine in 1947 then a year later returned as the British Mandate was ending. She left a few days before the creation of the State of Israel.

Cecily possessed the journalist's knack for being in places on the threshold of tumultuous change. She was, though, more interested in 'think pieces' than were most of the foreign correspondents residing with her in Jerusalem's Hotel Yasmina. She recalled a British General telling her: 'There, there, little lady, this is no place for you.' A female correspondent in Palestine was, Cecily wrote, 'a species practically unknown at the time.' The only other woman was Claire Hollingsworth, the *Daily Telegraph* war correspondent who had been the first British person to report the outbreak of the Second World War and would live to be 105. Hollingsworth gave Cecily useful tips.

Cecily interrogated Zionists, conscripted soldiers and Bedouin tribesmen. She interviewed Hebrew poets, the president of the Arab Women's Federation and even King Abdullah of Transjordan. Her French language accounts featured in newspapers and radio broadcasts and in a book called in English, *The Mouth of the Sword* (1949) dedicated to her daughter. It had a mixed reception being rather more popular in France than in the UK where some wariness was voiced about her pro-Jewish stance. Cecily's next book, however, provided very different perspectives. It was prompted by being given a copy of Isabelle Eberhardt's book *Dans l'Ombre Chaude de l'Islam.*

Cecily's biography *The Destiny of Isabelle Eberhardt* appeared in 1951 (with a French edition in 1956). It was her favourite publication. It isn't difficult to see why. Cecily's zest for adventure, disdain for order and the mundane, and belief that she too was an outsider, set apart from others and destined to plough her own furrow, attracted her to this extraordinary, true tale. Born in 1877, the daughter of a Russian nihilist, Eberhardt had fled to Algeria aged twenty after an unhappy childhood in Switzerland. A writer, she converted to Islam and became a mystic. She dressed as a man and lived the life of a nomad but was drowned aged twenty-seven during a flash flood in the Sahara. Eberhardt provided Cecily with an excuse to travel in her footsteps to Switzerland, then North Africa where she undertook her own intrepid journey across the desert.

Eberhardt later became something of a cult figure and the subject of a film, play and opera. There have been translations of her writings and research into her multiple identities and relationship to Islam, colonialism and feminism. Cecily's biography was reprinted in the United States in 1975 and as a paperback in the UK in the 1980s. When researching Eberhardt's life, she had confided in a journal that she shared with her the same mix of being 'an adventuress and sentimentally nostalgic' but conceded that her subject possessed 'a recklessness and purity that I lack.'

On New Year's Day 1950, reflecting on the past year, Cecily could see some positives: buying an apartment and the 'satisfaction of giving a home to Pascale… seeing her blossom & grown calm in her own shell.' Yet the few journals that survive suggest that Cecily remained a troubled soul who might appear to others to be in control yet believed (in November 1949) that 'I never had a moment of calm happiness in my life… Never, never the calm sureness I see in the eyes of other women.' She was well aware of the irony that her wartime experience of fleeing France and the heightened intensity of her life as a journalist had made her better equipped to deal with danger and privations than to relax and settle down in one place.

In February 1952 *Spring's Green Shadow* was published in the UK by MacGibbon & Kee. The drama and pace of Cecily's own life story already resembled a novel. She was a seasoned, international journalist and wide-ranging author who had witnessed shocking events that must have had an indelible effect on how she viewed humanity and her own destiny. Whereas many of her contemporaries sought a quiet life after the upheavals and horrors of the Second World War, this writer had opted instead for challenges and danger rather than domesticity or routine. Cecily has the elderly French philosopher in *Spring's Green Shadow* warn Laura that writing is 'a profession which demands terrible sacrifices… Writers are seldom happy people' (p. 136).[25]

Cecily had wandered far from her rural and privileged early life. Yet it was to this world that she chose to return in her novel. Nevertheless, despite the peaceful landscape that it depicted so well, its central character is one whose life is in turmoil. Written in the first person, the story had been gestating for some time and was mentioned in a letter Cecily wrote in December 1946.[26] At the start of the novel Laura is a small girl in the Welsh village of Pont-y-Gibby, based on Cecily's native village on the River Gavenny. Yet although the fictional Laura loves the Welsh countryside, this is no story of an idyllic childhood. It begins with a far from flattering description of Laura's mother, a no-nonsense, sporty and haughty woman who disparages books, had wanted a son and frequently expresses her disappointment with her sole child.

Laura has a vivid imagination and takes refuge in a secret garden perch high up in an oak tree, affording a privileged bird's eye view of her village. This new perspective fortifies her, providing a parallax view that reflects her distinctive vision of life that is so different from that of her family, and makes her feel more secure.

She is thrilled when the opportunity arises for private lessons with the grave North Walian schoolmaster Mr Howells (seen through the eyes of the young narrator, so shorn of a first name). He doesn't fit into the village and harbours secrets. He opens up a world of learning to her. A tormented soul, he and his precocious, musical daughter Mair and sullen, wayward son Idris, have a profound impact on the impressionable and lonely Laura. Her difficult relationship with her mother is mirrored by the complex father-son situation in the Howells family. Mr Howells is the antithesis of all that her mother stands for: he is from a different class, is Welsh speaking, a Methodist, erudite, caring and interested in ideas. He is slightly exotic: his mysterious past has even taken him to Paris.

This *bildungsroman* was clearly influenced by Cecily's own upbringing. It is set soon after the end of the First World War so coincides with her early memories. Laura's soldier father has returned home – she is seven when she first encounters him – but, broken in body and spirit, he might as well be absent like Cecily's own father who had been killed at the start of the war. Her novel powerfully portrays the insidious effects of war as an emasculated soldier comes home to an uncomprehending family and society. Rejection of a child by a mother when the father returns is a familiar trope in fiction but one that would have resonated with readers only too familiar with the scars from the Second World War.

Yet Cecily's novel should not be taken too literally.

Although attending the Sorbonne and an aspirant writer, Laura's experience of Paris seems to bear little relation to Cecily's life in that city. Comparisons can be drawn between her fictional representation of family life and her lived experience but we need to exercise caution.

Cecily continued to visit her mother in Devon (now living in Budleigh Salterton) at least once a year. After her ordeal in 1940, Cecily recuperated there and Pascale spent holidays with her grandmother. Duty and convenience account in part for Cecily's visits but on her mother's part at least there is evidence of caring. For example, in correspondence in the 1950s she addressed her daughter as 'Darling Girl.' Although the fictional mother was virulently anti-intellectual, flying into a rage when her daughter mentioned university, Cecily's mother had written a number of supportive letters to the LSE, urging her daughter's admission as a student.[27]

Nevertheless, the real mother and daughter led markedly different lives. They shared neither cultural interests nor political beliefs. Although Cecily could play the part of the dutiful daughter when required, she could never sustain it for long. And she chose to believe, even in her nineties, that 'My mother's disapproval of everything I said or thought had been total.' In the novel when her mother denounces Laura's wish to go to Paris and asks 'Why must you always cause trouble?', the young woman can take no more:

Suddenly I felt a hatred for my parents that astonished me. It was no longer the dull resentment, mingled with unwilling nostalgia, that I had known for so many years, but a fine fury, a liberating burst of rage (p. 85).

Laura screams that she will go wherever she likes, anywhere away from her parents. In an earlier draft of the novel her pent-up feelings are expressed even more graphically:

> A wave of fury & frustration swept over me. The years of odious repression seemed to reach a culminating, an insupportable point. For once the truth should be heard in this family where the most ignoble sentiments were wrapped in an advantageous disguise. I was so stifled with mounting rage that I hardly recognised the voice that accused my parents of hatred for their own child, that cried to them that neither of them could bare [sic] to see that child grow to a woman with life opening before her.

In the published novel Laura goes out to the hillside road where her outburst seems 'a little childish and indeed the whole scene ridiculous' (p. 85), but in the earlier version she dwelt on the reaction to her outburst and her mother's 'congested face, crimson in the firelight.'

When visiting England, Cecily would stay at Holden's flat in London's West End. After their Breton holiday in 1950 she spent two months there completing her novel. Holden had an English landed gentry background against which she had rebelled. She too had a difficult relationship with her mother who kept fifteen horses and was reputed to be one of the country's best horse-women. In the opening paragraph of *Spring's Green Shadow*, we learn that Laura's mother was said to be the best rider in Wales. Cecily may in part have been writing autobiographical fiction (with elements of what literary critics define as autobiografiction or autofiction) but she drew on a range of influences, a fertile imagination and personal memories.

Spring's Green Shadow recalls a number of Cecily's own experiences. For example, as a small child she had watched with fascination from her grandmother's garden as a man climbed the Skirrid Fawr and got smaller and smaller as he moved further away. The first chapter of Cecily's unpublished autobiography opens with this incident, describing it as her first memory. Cecily inserted it into the novel at the important point where Laura climbs the Sugar Loaf Mountain and encounters Idris.

The scene at the Eisteddfod in Carmarthen where Laura hears Mair Howells sing – and win her competition – is described as 'one of the days of my life, one of the staring, flaring days that not all the passing years would dim in memory' (p. 72). This is based on Cecily's memory of the National Eisteddfod in North Wales at Rhosllanerchrugog in August 1945. She covered this for the BBC's French Service. She told her friend Walter Strachan, poet, French translator and teacher, that 'it was heaven... one of the essential experiences of life.' She heard the Eisteddfod choir sing Bach's Mass in B minor 'and believe me it was the finest singing I have heard in all Europe.' [28]

Cecily's unusual yoking of the Welsh countryside and the European city reflected the two seminal locations in her own life. Interestingly, the British setting for the novel is not the West Country where she spent most of her childhood. When she describes a granite war memorial overlooking her Welsh village, she draws on but does not acknowledge the memorial that had been erected in North Cheriton, Somerset, opposite the church and at the top of the village. Here her uncle Ronald Lascelles and a member of the Gatehouse family were commemorated. [29] Similarly, her account of Laura astride the oak at home in Wales is based on the cedar that Cecily climbed in her Somerset garden.

Spring's Green Shadow is divided into four parts with parts 1 and 111 (slightly more than half of the story) set in Wales. The rest takes place in Paris, that classic symbol of escape, free love and freedom from restraint. Laura, however, soon discovers that living in the metropolis can be as lonely as her childhood home and a bewildering place for a young student from the Welsh countryside. There is little that is joyous in the way that her self-obsessed, nihilistic lover treats her. They eke out their frugal existence in suburban Montrouge.

Not surprisingly, the reader is guided expertly around Paris by an author who is keen to penetrate beyond the tourist's environs: Welsh villages are given fictitious names but French locations are real places and Cecily inserts some of her own haunts such as the Café Dôme. When the couple move to Montrouge it is early spring – the seasons play an important part in this novel – and at first it seems like a time of hope.

Yet this is no straightforward *rite de passage* novel. Laura finds that Paris lacks the freedom provided by the Welsh landscape in which she had earlier sought refuge. Her experience suggests the need to look beyond the images of gaiety and Bohemia so associated with the city. But it is in Paris that Laura eventually comes to understand the profound and unsettling influence upon her of the flawed, tragic figure of Mr Howells, with his youthful inner struggles between a Calvinistic upbringing and intellectual experimentation and eventual humiliation. She has experienced spring's shadow rather than its green shoots and needs to exorcise the shadow cast by the man who had appeared to offer her hope as a child, as well as by her family memories, before she can truly be free and enjoy her adulthood. At the core of the novel is an exploration of how the past impinges on the present, and the need to expunge it in order to enable a free and independent future, something Cecily grappled with in her own life.

Her book appeared at a time when much seemed to be changing. George V1 died that month and the press speculated as to what a New Elizabethan Age might herald. The previous summer the Festival of Britain had sought to harness a mid-century optimism and modernity. Yet although the war had ended in 1945, its legacy was omnipresent. Rationing was still in place and families were irrevocably affected by the toll that war had taken. The publishing trade had revived but remained overwhelmingly male.

The novel was extensively reviewed in Britain, France and beyond – from Johannesburg to Louisville – and the over-whelming response (of 37 reviews) was positive, praising Cecily's technical skill, tone and style as well as her per-ception and sensitivity.[30] Her 'bitter-sweet lyricism' that captured adolescence so well was praised in *Current Literature* as was her 'polished economy of phrase.'

Richard Church was especially impressed by the images Cecily created of Paris and 'her sensibility in the manner of Mauriac.' Several reviewers felt that only when the narrative moved to Paris did the story really get underway. Yet, John Betjeman argued in the *Daily Telegraph* that the author was at her strongest when writing about Wales and, in particular, depicting female characters.

Perhaps the most perceptive review appeared in the *Spectator.* It stressed that what really counted was the vision rather than the narrative in this 'profoundly able' novel. Descriptions of landscape, characterisation and exploring how and why people behaved as they did were paramount for her. Cecily's familiarity with France, French fiction and audiences enabled a *mentalité* that was refreshing for mid-twentieth century British readers.

Always open to new ideas, and appreciative of the French passion for philosophical debates, Cecily was attuned to 'Le nouveau roman.' Its practitioners sought to eschew traditional literary conventions of characterisation and plot in favour of more experimental and open-ended approaches. The former Cistercian abbey of Royaumont, north of Paris, had become a cultural centre frequented by writers such as Alain Robbe-Grillet. Cecily had been invited to participate in a conference there in 1949 where the theory and 'brilliance of presentation' impressed her. Delegates discussed subjects such as 'Will the Novel Survive?'. A number of visits followed. Cecily was amused to find how the terms 'signifier' and 'signified' were 'passed around like the coffee and brioche.'

A lack of sentimentality when writing about family, frankness in depicting Laura's relationships and the nature of the discussions between the lovers, marked Cecily out from contemporary English women novelists such as Barbara Pym whose popular and perceptive comedy of manners *Excellent Women* appeared at the same time as *Spring's Green Shadow*. Despite living in London, Pym's Miss Lathbury literally inhabits a parochial world but, unlike Laura, largely accepts her limited expectations.

However, 1952 also saw the first novel in Doris Lessing's series 'The Children of Violence'. *Martha Quest* was semi-autobiographical and set in the former British colony of Southern Rhodesia where Lessing had grown up. Like Cecily's novel it focused on an adolescent who feels alienated from her own family as she observes, like an outsider, the narrow world around her family on its African farm and, in this case, the troubling racial politics. She too breaks free, seeking a new life in the city.

The original jacket illustration for *Spring's Green Shadow* by the Scottish artist Pearl Falconer is reproduced in this Honno edition. It neatly suggests the divided self with its representation of the naïve country schoolgirl in plaits, back-to-back with the young woman of the world – complete with chignon – set against a Parisian scene. Here is Cecily's version of the country and the city, neither of which are quite as they might at first sight appear.

The novel was published in the United States in 1953 and translated into French by J. C. Pichon and C. Prost in Gallimard's prestigious series *Du Monde Entier* two years later as *Les Ombres Vertes du Printemps*. The French – but not the English – edition reproduced the well-known quotation from *Ecclesiastes* that opens with the line 'To every thing there is a season.'

Spring's Green Shadow was Cecily's only published work in which Wales was writ large. Although her background ensured that she sounded quintessentially English, she chose to identify and present herself as Welsh. One Mackworth relative remembers how she 'considered herself to be Welsh through and through.' In the biographical description accompanying the French edition of 1955 we are even told that Cecily divides her time between Wales where she was born and Paris.

Yet although she returned to England fairly often, there is no evidence that she spent much time in Wales (apart from her war work) and before long it would be Normandy that vied with Paris. The blurb for her biography of Isabelle Eberhardt states that the author is 'Welsh but has spent most of her life in France. She *came to England* in 1940 [my emphasis].[31] During the war she had published a few short stories from London under the pen name of Rhiannon in the monthly journal *People and Freedom*.

Cecily's identification with Wales could be dismissed as little more than a romantic gesture but is perhaps best appreciated in the context of a long, bifurcated life during which she straddled countries, cultures and languages (though she spoke no Welsh) with the advantages but also problems that this engendered. When she visited the 1945 Eisteddfod there was a dramatic moment – perfect for the journalist – when the Dolgellau Male Voice Choir was interrupted in full flow. The Archdruid rang a bell and announced from the stage that the Japanese had surrendered. There followed a prayer and everybody sang 'Cwm Rhondda.'

On returning to London Cecily bought a newspaper. Screaming out from the front page 'in big, aggressive black lettering' were the words 'SECOND DAY OF THE ATOMIC AGE' heralding, she feared, 'An unknown, ice-cold future.' She told Walter Strachan: 'We must all go and live in Wales. It's the only decent country left in Europe – outside they were talking about atom bombs, *inside* the only important thing in the world was whether Evan Evans had a purer top C than Dai Jones… I have become very Welsh since all this.' [32]

Interviewed for the *Guardian* in 1973 as one of a group of British 'exiles' living in France, Cecily stated that any nostalgia she felt was for the Wales of her childhood though she admitted that this Wales probably no longer existed.[33] Yet childhood had never connoted a happy family life for her and anyway the years that she would have remembered most clearly were spent in the West Country.

Spring's Green Shadow seems to have been a way for Cecily to explore in the mid-twentieth century her own identity and the stranglehold of the past at a time when she had opted to return to France for the foreseeable future. By her own admission, she spoke French with an unmistakable English accent in her adopted country but to her British friends she increasingly sounded French. She wrote for the press in both English and French, preferring French for abstract subjects. Walter Strachan wrote a poem for Cecily entitled 'Duality.' It refers to the 'two-fold tug' that she felt: 'Not always able to move or stay behind.'[34]

The *Guardian* interview was by Nesta Roberts, a North Walian who became the paper's Paris correspondent. She had the distinction of having been, in the 1960s, the first woman to run the news desk of a national newspaper when she worked for the *Guardian* in London. In the late 1960s and early 1970s Cecily and Nesta met quite often for dinner in Paris. Since the early 1960s Cecily had also been active in Cymdeithas Cymru Paris, the Paris Welsh Society, and sat for a while on its committee.

Cecily had declared in 1950 her determination to write novels in future. A second one, written early in 1952, was prompted by her travels in North Africa. A draft survives of this murder mystery set in Algiers. The body of a British wine-importer is discovered in the *casbah* and his murky past begins to be revealed. But this story was never published.

Cecily's only other published fiction was *Lucy's Nose*, forty years after *Spring's Green Shadow*. Yet, like a number of her books, it defies neat categorisation. The title nodded to the historical concept known as Cleopatra's Nose that advocates the importance of chance in determining historical outcomes. Whereas Freudian ideas had some influence on *Spring's Green Shadow*, *Lucy's Nose* went further.

Lucy was the 'Lucy R' from Sigmund Freud's *Five Studies in Hysteria*. Cecily visited Vienna to research the life of this young French governess who had arrived there in the 1880s and become the subject of one of Freud's case studies. Cecily found that all records had been destroyed. Her book therefore became in large part an imagining of Lucy's story, hence the tag of fiction. It was published in English in 1992 when Cecily was in her early eighties, and appeared in French translation in 1998. It provided an opportunity for the writer to analyse her younger self. She also considered the point at which fact drifts into fiction. Here was an issue relevant to how Cecily retold her own life story. She pondered too on the borderline between biography and fiction. The influence of experimental French writers such as her friend Nathalie Sarraute could be seen clearly in this work. *The Tablet* chose *Lucy's Nose* as its Book of the Year.

Cecily was far from idle during the decades between the publication of *Spring's Green Shadow* and *Lucy's Nose*. She was, for many years, the sole provider for herself and her daughter. Residing in Paris and paying boarding school fees for Pascale necessitated a regular income. Cecily wrote reviews for the *Manchester Guardian* in the 1950s, covering biographies of French literary figures such as Rabelais and Baudelaire. She became the Paris correspondent for the journal *Twentieth Century*. And she translated the journalist Renée Massip's second novel *La Régente* into English as *The Schoolmistress*. Set in provincial France, it explored a familiar subject: a small girl's reactions to a domineering mother. [35]

The strain of writing regularly for the press on both sides of the channel – rising at 6am daily to supply copy for one French newspaper – took a heavy toll on Cecily's health. She suffered a nervous breakdown, considered simplifying her life and returning to live full-time in England.

However, her fortunes changed dramatically as the result of a dinner party in Paris at Christmas 1955. Here the forty-four-year-old Cecily met a member of an old aristocratic French family: the Marquis Ebles Jean Dieudonné de Chabannes La Palice. One of his ancestors had been the companion of Joan of Arc. Born in 1900, he was divorced and, it seems from correspondence, actively seeking a new wife. According to Holden's diary, marriage was mentioned at Cecily's second meeting with him.[36] There were visits to his Normandy home early in 1956 before Cecily travelled to the Notting Hill flat that she had recently rented in anticipation of moving back to Britain.

During the next few months, she met Holden, Stevie Smith and Ivy Compton-Burnett, attended PEN meetings, and publishers' parties and visited her mother in Devon. However, she remained unwell with excruciating headaches and spent much of her time seeing her doctor. On 17 June she confided to Holden that, despite some reservations, she had decided to marry again. Holden's diary voiced concern but she recognised that her friend would gain a sense of security and 'with all her miseries and sorrows she cannot be alone.' She added: 'Cecily seems quite confident about it – even delighted.'

On 11 July 1956 Cecily recorded in her appointments'

diary: 'Married to Ebles.' The diary remained blank for the rest of the year. The couple were married in Kensington but Cecily then took French citizenship. Nevertheless, the journalist and television presenter Hedwige Chevrillon, resident in the same apartment block as Cecily in her later years, recalls that she always insisted that she was Welsh.

The Marquis's family home at Le Brévedent in the Calvados region of Normandy was a late eighteenth-century château (once a hunting lodge). Cecily didn't abandon her old friends – Stevie Smith and Holden were amongst those who stayed there – but her lifestyle inevitably changed. Her husband was eleven years older, with two children from his first marriage and he was essentially a countryman. From the 1960s he made his living by turning his land into an upmarket camping site.

All this was far removed from Cecily's intellectual milieu. She once overheard Ebles and a friend mention the word Rimbaud.[37] She rushed down to the terrace in excitement, hoping to discuss the poet's work, only to discover that a Rimbaud was an apple native to Normandy. Yet, as Holden noted in November 1956 when Cecily stayed with her in London, she was 'very happily married.' By all accounts, the Marquis was a gentle, tolerant and thoughtful man, who understood that his new wife needed to spend much of her time in Paris and to keep writing.

In 1961 Cecily produced an ambitious study of Guillaume Apollinaire, the flamboyant lyrical poet, art critic and champion of Cubism. It earned praise as a literary biography but was not so favourably received by art critics.[38] She was on surer ground with *English Interludes* (1974). It focused on four Anglophile French poets: Mallarmé, Verlaine, Valéry and

Larbaud. She was especially knowledgeable about Mallarmé, having contributed to the publication of *Les Lettres: Stéphane Mallarmé* (1948). The four poets spent time in England between 1862 and 1914. Cecily considered how they viewed and were influenced by English society and London in particular. Valery Larbaud, the least well known, was a novelist and translator as well as a poet. His travels also encompassed south-east Wales. *English Interludes* reflected Cecily's divided life. It was the subject of a BBC Radio 3 programme.[39] The *Guardian* called it 'a clever little book.'

Cecily long outlived Ebles. He developed pulmonary problems and died in January 1980. She stayed on in Paris. In her mid-seventies she produced *Ends of the World*, an episodic memoir of travels, transporting readers to remote locations such as the Sahara that seemed like the end of the world, so far were they in time and terrain from her familiar haunts. But she was also charting the end of worlds, as old orders changed, from Palestine to the last days of Franco's Spain. The travelogue ends in Morocco in 1960, reminding us too what these distant worlds shared with other societies. Hearing a Moroccan storyteller evokes for Cecily a competitor reciting Welsh poetry at the 1945 National Eisteddfod.

Cecily's last book, *Dreams and Poems*, a subscription edition of 150 copies, appeared in 1995. True to form, it was not just a poetry collection. It interspersed poems – most had already been published – with brief prose accounts of her dreams. It reflected her interest in Symbolism. She had, she explained, long kept a record of dreams, seeing them, like poetry, as part of the creative imagination. Cecily deliberately rejected being straitjacketed into one genre of writing.

Writer friends like Inez Holden and Nancy Cunard, gained

some notoriety for their literary lovers and friends (Holden's name, for example, was linked with George Orwell). Cecily too lived her life to the full but guarded her privacy in print. In the Preface to *Ends of the World* she claimed, not very convincingly, to be a mere spectator in its story, suggestively stating that details about 'my private life could only be irrelevant.' It included some carefully chosen journal extracts, breathlessly recounting fleeting impressions of places and people in times of crisis across the globe, and a section headed 'Remembering'. Ironically, *Spring's Green Shadow,* Cecily's sole book that is unequivocally in the form of a novel, seems to provide the most personal and revealing account of Cecily's perspectives – even if at times unwittingly – of all her published work.

In her nineties, the woman who had witnessed most of the twentieth century, was persuaded to write her autobiography. It is dated April 2006, just three months before she died. More than 300 pages survive in draft. It does not cover Cecily's entire life and the final pages are in note form. The fact that she changed some names (for example, that of her stepfather) and the corrections made to the typescript suggest that publication was intended.[40] It covers much of the same ground as *Ends of the World*, albeit providing more personal information.

Yet, even allowing for gaps in memory due to age, Cecily is guarded, even disingenuous, in the unfolding of her story. Well-practiced in dissimulation, she hides or camouflages knowingly, even as she appears to reveal. Aware of how memory can deceive, she shapes a narrative in which the contours of her life as a writer and traveller unfold but much remains conspicuous by its absence. The only mention of marriage, for example, is in a few words within brackets where she explains her European surname by pointing out that her late (first) husband had been Belgian. There is no reference to the fact that she had a daughter.

Cecily outlived most of her friends. According to those who knew her at this time, she maintained to the last, a zest for life. A very determined woman who had seen and survived many horrors, she did not let old age defeat her. She was seen as chic, even within the city that seems to embody this description. In her small but elegant apartment in a seventeenth-century building in the Marais, she continued to write for French journals into her early nineties, still enjoying café life, bookshops and attending lectures. She loved entertaining, got on well with young people and in her final weeks was anticipating the pleasure of a new project: learning Arabic. She died in Paris on 22 July 2006, a few weeks before her ninety-fifth birthday, and was buried with her husband in Normandy.[41]

In Raymond Williams' final novel, *People of the Black Mountains*, a young man climbs the mountain in search of his grandfather, so triggering the author's exploration of the long history of his land and landscape. Like Williams, a self-styled 'Welsh European', Cecily spent most of her life beyond Wales. She too saw climbing the Black Mountains as symbolic and recognised the ineluctable pull of her native landscape, though many of her personal memories were painful. A wartime visit prompted the observation that 'When the sun comes down over the Black Mountains, it has a very strange coppery glow – I've never seen it anywhere else. It is a warm glow that the sun sheds and grass takes.'

Landscape and memory are woven into *Spring's Green Shadow*. Cecily's powerful novel juxtaposes one of the world's best-known cities and her corner of Wales. This Welsh intellectual and creative writer, based in Paris, who witnessed and wrote extensively in a lifetime that spanned most of the twentieth century, deserves to be included as one of the cultural Euro-Welsh writers whose work has recently been explored.[42] It seems no coincidence that the title of Cecily Mackworth's draft autobiography, her final reflection on her long and turbulent life, takes us back to where it all started for this Welsh internationalist and free spirit, the spot where *Spring's Green Shadow* begins. It is called *Out of the Black Mountains*.

NOTES:

1   Christopher Hewett, ed., *The Living Curve. Letters to W. J. Strachan 1929-1979* (Taranman, 1984), p. 19. The Walter Strachan Papers, GB133 WJS/1 are in the University of Manchester Library.

2   Inez Holden (1903-74), socialite turned socialist, also reported on the Nuremburg Trials and was a screenwriter. Her *Blitz Writing: Night Shift and It Was Different At The Time* (Handheld Press, 2019) shows how she crafted fiction from both her war work and her diary. See too Kristin Bluemel, *George Orwell and the Radical Eccentrics* (Palgrave Macmillan, 2004), Chapter 3. Inez Holden Diary, 27 April 1945, private collection.

3   Hewett, *The Living Curve,* p. 19.

4   See too my entry: 'Mackworth, Cecily Joan' in https://biography.wales.

5   Pupil fee account books, Cheltenham Ladies College.

6   Angela V. John, *Turning the Tide: The Life of Lady Rhondda* (Parthian, 2013).

7   For Cecily's student file, see LSE Archives, 1/29/1002.

8   In her autobiography she calls him János to avoid identification though does mention that his father was a Budapest lawyer. He had lived in London since 1927 as an LSE student, graduating with a First in 1930.

9   Imperial War Museum Interview, 2003, Reel 1: www.iwm.org.uk/collections/item/object/80023832.

10 One chapter of Phillips' autobiography is entitled 'London, Paris and Cenarth', Eluned Phillips, *The Reluctant Redhead* (Gomer Press, 2007), p. 46. See too, Menna Elfyn, *Absolute Optimist: Remembering Eluned Phillips* (Honno Press, 2018).

11 The *London Mercury* had already published her first poem.

12 Cecily Mackworth (henceforth CM), 'Lawrence Durrell and the New Romanticism', *Twentieth Century*, clxvii (1960). See Gordon Bowker, *Through the Dark Labyrinth: A Biography of Lawrence Durrell* (Pimlico, 1988), pp. 99-100, 233, 416-7.

13 CM, *Ends of the World* (Carcanet, 1987), p. 3.

14 Unattributed quotes in this introduction come from Cecily's personal papers held by her family.

15 Routledge published five of her twelve books. The Labour Book Service also produced an edition of *I Came out of France.*

16 Irène Némirovsky, *Suite Française* (Vintage edition, 2007).

17 In Nancy Cunard, *Poems for France* (La France Libre, 1944).

18 Imperial War Museum Interview, Reel 3. Meffre was accused of forging letters to discredit the Chief of Naval Staff, Admiral Muselier, claiming that he was plotting against de Gaulle. Although not prosecuted, Meffre was interned for the rest of the war. Cecily did not acknowledge any MI5 connection in her published writings or her draft autobiography.

19 Started by William Emrys Williams in 1941, it provided an education for citizenship for men and women in the services though was soon extended to industrial workers.

20 CM, *Ends of The World*, p. 50.

21 Ibid, p.35.

22 CM, 'Dylan Thomas et la Double Vision', *Critique*, xix (June 1963), pp. 500-516.

23 He might possibly have been the Austro-Hungarian Abstract artist Géza Szóbel who had fled Prague and exhibited his 'Art from the Front' at the Czechoslovak Institute in 1942.

24 Inez Holden, 'Some Women Writers', *The Nineteenth Century and After*, xix (1949).

25 CM, *Spring's Green Shadow* (McGibbon & Kee, 1952), p. 118. The bracketed page number, and all subsequent page numbers in brackets, are to the Honno edition.

26 Hewett, *The Living Curve*, p. 73. Letter from Cecily to Walter Strachan dated 23 December 1946.

27 CM student file, 1/29/1002, LSE Archives.

28 Walter John Strachan (1903-94). Quoted in letter in Hewett, *The Living Curve*, p. 50.

29 Her father is mentioned but, unlike his brother Arthur, is not one of the main names on the memorial to the Fallen of the First World War at Abergavenny's Market Hall. The sandstone memorial in the churchyard of St Teilo's, Llantilio Pertholey where Cecily had been christened, names her uncle Ronald Lascelles.

30 Reviews include: *Daily Telegraph,* 21 March 1952; *Western Mail,* 26 March 1952; *Current Literature,* March 1952; *Manchester Guardian,* 25 April 1952; *Spectator,* 4 April 1952; *Time & Tide,* 26 April 1952; *New York Times,* 9 August 1953; *Paris Jour Après Nuit,* 6 February 1955.

[31] CM, *The Destiny of Isabelle Eberhardt* (The Ecco Press, New York, 1975 edition).

[32] Quoted in letter in Hewett, *The Living Curve*, p. 50.

[33] *Guardian,* 13 June 1973.

[34] W. J. Strachan, *Only Connect... Poets, Painters, Sculptors: Friendships and Shared Passions 1924-1994* (Jon Carpenter, 2006), pp.74-5.

[35] Published in 1954. Cecily knew Massip socially. She too lived a long life, from 1907 until 2002. In 1960 Cecily's translation of a book by Daniel Cordier was published as *The Drawings of Jean Dubuffet*.

[36] Holden Diary, 30 June 1956.

[37] She wrote an article about Rimbaud in *Horizon* IX, no.51 (March 1944).

[38] CM, *Apollinaire* (John Murray, 1961). For reviews see *The Times,* 2 March 1961; *Time & Tide,* 27 January 1961; *Observer,* 22 January, 19 February 1961.

[39] *Guardian,* 1 August 1974.

[40] She worked with the journalist Anthony Sheridan on this.

[41] Sheridan wrote her Obituaries in *Le Monde,* 17 August 2006 and *Guardian,* 7 August 2006. See too *Independent,* 2 August 2006. See also 'Women's Writing in the British Isles', http://orlando.cambridge.org. Cecily featured in the BBC's 'Last Word' on Radio 4, 11 August 2006, FB066332/7, BBC Archive, the British Library.

[42] See M. Wynn Thomas, *Eutopia: Studies in Cultural Euro-Welshness 1850-1980* (University of Wales Press, 2021), especially Chapter 7.

SPRING'S GREEN SHADOW

PART I

MY EARLIEST memories of my mother date back to my third or fourth year. At that time, she was a tall, athletic and even masculine-looking woman. She dressed in heavy hand-woven tweeds, had a passion for fox-hunting and was constantly accompanied by three or four noisy terriers. When her image recurs in my mind, I see her, for example, whistling to her dogs and setting off, gun in hand, to shoot rabbits in the orchard; or on horse-back (she was said to be the best rider in all Wales); or else returning triumphantly from one of those tennis tournaments from which she invariably brought back some massive silver pot, engraved with her victorious name, for she was strong and agile and gave herself up whole-heartedly to her craving for exercise and fresh air.

In spite of these preoccupations, she took time to supervise my education. This supervision consisted in luring timid governesses, chosen for their qualities of self-effacement so that their presence in the house should be as inconspicuous as possible. She herself undertook to teach me to jump hedges on a pony that was too big for me and frightened me to death. She was as authoritative as a sergeant-major. The submission and admiration of all around her was necessary to her as bread is necessary to others. She would have loved me if I had done her the homage of growing up in her own image.

Yet often, up to the time of my father's return, she would have sudden fits of tenderness. Then she hugged me until it hurt, stroked my hair and begged me to love her more than anything in the world. Since I was an impressionable child, I obeyed her implicitly. I loved her passionately. When she came to kiss me good-night, clothed in long dresses of silk or velvet, a pearl necklace encircling her brown and muscular throat, her beauty moved me to tears. I was jealous of the dogs and the horses on whom she lavished her caresses, jealous of every moment she spent away from me.

Sometimes she had fits of crying. She would tear at her handkerchief with her strong white teeth, sobbing so that her whole body heaved and shook, crying to me that my father would certainly be killed, that she would remain alone, and that I should be the only thing left in her life. I would stroke her hair, weeping harder than herself, agonized by my own helplessness to comfort her. Sometimes these scenes were so violent that I became ill for several days. Then she would visit me between two games of golf, sit by my bed and read me the adventures of Peter Rabbit.

When she was away from home, I enjoyed the comfortable, gossipy society of the servants. Especially I liked to visit Owen in the stables. He never talked to me and indeed, coming from one of the few old-fashioned Welsh-speaking families in the district, his English was slow and difficult. But he had taught me to ride, almost before I could remember, running tirelessly beside me, trotting the hairy pony and panting instructions:

"Bump the saddle, Miss Laura. Bump the saddle!"

I liked to sit on the oat-bin and watch him as he rubbed and polished at the tall, soft-eyed horses, hissing between his teeth, smoothing their silky coats till they shone like the glossy skins of the chestnuts that littered the floor of the woods in autumn.

Owen's society was more comfortable than that of my

mother, but less exhilarating. I loved him best after her, then came Winnie, then Dr. Johns from Llanglaslyn, then Nurse and Miss Morgan together.

I was seven years old when I saw my father for the first time. He had made his career in the Army and had gone abroad with his regiment at the outbreak of the war, shortly after my birth. Then, after the Armistice, he had remained for a long time in an English hospital, where he was being treated for wounds the nature of which I discovered many years later. I remember his return very clearly. The whole house seemed to shiver with expectation. From the kitchen rose the smell of roast beef, of crisp tarts overflowing with warm, golden jam, of Stilton cheese ripened with port wine. The maids hurried up and down the staircase with a rustling of starched dresses; the gardener drove his mower over the already close-cropped lawn. Upstairs they were preparing the dressing-room, moving furniture, polishing like mad at the heavy chests and the tallboy of veined nut-wood. Wherever I went, I seemed to be in the way of some hurrying, over-excited grown-up and my mother, whom emotion had rendered bad-tempered, soon exiled me to the nursery. Here nurse sat me down on a hard, narrow chair and forbade me to move for fear of creasing my clean frock. As she bustled about the room with piles of snowy linen in her arms, she scolded me automatically, but now and again she paused, watching me with a sort of avid light in her eyes, shaking her head and murmuring: "Dear Heavens! There's a shame!" until I was filled with a vague terror.

As far back as I could remember, my father s absent figure had held its place in the house. Morning and night, for years, I had asked for his safety in my prayers and I knew by heart the words in which, three times, he had been mentioned in despatches. There were photographs of him on the bureau in the drawing-room, in my mother's bedroom and on the wall above my own bed. I had a clear picture of him in my mind and I imagined him arriving in a cloud of dust, mounted on the back of a great white charger. He would be wearing a sort of shako, decorated with a great bunch of plumes, such as I had admired in the photograph taken on the day of his marriage, and his long, golden moustaches were to float in the wind of his galloping.

But when at last they called me into the drawing-room, I saw a man of the same height as my mother, skinny, red-haired, a scraggy neck emerging from the collar of a uniform that had grown too large. His face resembled that of a sickly bird, his eyes were the colour of dirty water and he had reddish, bristly eyebrows. The disappointment was too great. I burst into tears. My mother stamped her foot and shouted that I was a little idiot and I was despatched back to the nursery, sobbing and ashamed. Neither my father nor I ever quite recovered from that first, mutual bad impression.

Gradually I became used to this new presence which soon identified itself for me with the feeling of *absence.* The house was filled, hour by hour and day by day, by a creeping empti-ness which invaded its farthest corners. It was like a mounting tide that nothing can stop. The contagion undoubtedly emanated from my father. Everything around him became infected with a measure of his own unreality. Even the ser-vants became hollow and translucent like water. When I entered the kitchen, it was no longer the same place. Only the objects remained the same—the huge iron stove with its shelves for bread-raising, the kitchen table, massive and scarred with knife-marks, the blue and white jars labelled Salt, Tea, Flour.

The essential was missing. It was no longer enough to enter, to sniff that sugary, spicy smell, to be enveloped in that friendly heat, for me to feel immediately the sentiment of inner warmth and security which I had not yet translated consciously into the simple and lovely words: It will always be like this.

As for my mother, she existed above all as a memory, and a memory to which I clung desperately. It was as if she had gone away on a journey, leaving in her place a double who resembled her exactly in face and form. She seldom appeared to remember my existence, and no doubt found it natural that my life should be transformed according to the wishes of her husband. The intruder, whose health was far from reestablished and who considered all noise or untidiness as a personal insult, made no secret of the fact that my presence was disagreeable to him. When, by chance, his eyes fell on me, they became blank, as if veiled by a sort of film. A nervous tic contracted the corner of his mouth. Then my mother's face stiffened; it was as if she had been turned into a block of ice, and in a far-away voice, that impersonal voice which she used when speaking to unknown shopkeepers, she ordered me up to the nursery.

While I was still very young I learned that life has many facets and that nothing is quite what it seems, so I was not especially astonished when, a few years later, I made the discovery of the *second village*.

It happened in this way. I was in the habit of escaping from the supervision of my governesses, by taking refuge at the bottom of the garden, in a place where the grass grew wild and strong, scattered with the bleeding fruit of the mulberry tree, where the nut-trees joined their branches like cloister arches and the sun powdered the ground through their uncertain shadow. Close against the garden wall, rose up a huge oak-tree, half-hollow and several centuries old.

One autumn day, I realized that I had grown so much that it was now possible for me to scramble up on to the lowest branch of the oak. From there, since I was by now agile as a cat, it was easy to climb to the very top, and soon I was no longer in the garden, but rather suspended over the road, more or less on a level with the rooftops.

I understood at once that my life was about to undergo an irrevocable change. It was a matter of optics, of the angle of vision. The passers-by in the road were now mere rounded shapes, comically flattened at the top by the unaccustomed perspective. The grocer's cart, a couple of quarrelling dogs … they had no more significance than the insect life revealed by an overturned stone. Miss Morgan, trotting by with her shopping bag, was above all a purple hat. On the other hand, everything that went on in the attics or above the roof-tops had taken on a new and singular importance.

From that time on, I began to spy on the faces of people who believed themselves to be unobserved. Often, they were almost unrecognizable. I was able, for instance, to observe the desperate sadness that fell like a cloak over the face of old Colonel Musgrove who had never been seen otherwise than jovial and even clownish. I saw the cruel twist of Mrs. Williams' lips, when she had distributed the daily ration of good advice, of enquiries about the health of her husband's parishioners, of friendly pats on the cheeks of the young servant girls. I came to know the folly of Miss O'Gormon, the gentle old spinster whose only pleasure was to call the schoolchildren into her garden and stuff them with chocolates which they snatched from her, with hardly a word of thanks, and scurried away, since they were vaguely uneasy in her presence. When they were gone she hurried to her bedroom, where she locked the door but did not think of drawing the curtains. Her wheezy old poodle followed at her heels. Feverishly she began to rummage in her drawers, pulling out laces, ribbons, scraps of lovely, rich silks. When she had finished dressing the dog, tying bows and draping lace, she reddened his lips, sprayed him with scent, then, seizing her strange little partner by the fore-paws, danced like a mad thing—waltz and alternating polka—till he moaned and his hind legs dragged helplessly along the ground.

None of these things astonished me. Everything seemed natural to me because I had known these people all my life and the threads of our existence had been mingled since my birth.

On the other hand, everything about Mr. Howells and his daughter seemed strange to me, because they were foreigners, recently come from North Wales.

The very fact that he was master of the board school, seemed to wrap the father in mystery. This school had fascinated me for years and everything connected with it seemed to me at once irresistible and slightly diabolic. From my watch-tower in the oak, I could observe the children while they played in the courtyard. At eleven o'clock in the morning, this depressing square of asphalt, hidden from the road by a high brick wall, would be silent and deserted. At two minutes past eleven, a stream of children flowed from the school door, screaming, jostling, hopping, and leaping. Suddenly the grey surface became almost invisible beneath the shifting mass.

They played mysterious games, chalking on the ground signs which were meaningless to me, or throwing balls in a game which seemed to call for a certain, but always varying, number of bounces, and which I understood so little that I could never make up my mind who had won and who had lost. The big ones bullied the little children, so that I used to shiver with indignation on my branch and shout threats which no one heard. There were fights for obscure motives; tragedies in which the victims would howl unashamedly, rubbing their fists in their eyes; friendships which grew up and died with equal suddenness, betrayed by furtive kisses and the exchange of hair-ribbons between little girls.

Then, at exactly half-past eleven, a tin bell clanged out three times. The games stopped, fights were suspended in an instant, the weepers sniffed and blew their noses in their fingers. Each child straightened his back, took on suddenly a *different face.* Nesta Morgan, the assistant teacher, appeared on the doorstep, making gestures with her hands, like a conductor who signs to his orchestra: *piano, piano*! The children lined up docilely and marched through the door to be swallowed up in the gloomy building into which I should never enter.

After that, I could no longer imagine their existence. Nothing remained of them but the monotonous chanting which rose through the windows … *un, dau, tri, pedwar, pump*, counted the children, faceless now, and disembodied.

Mr. Howells lived in the ugly little red-brick villa next to the school and I could observe him as he made his way to and from his home. He was tall and thin, very stiff and severe-looking. He always walked in a way which gave the impression of a man who, although impatient or furious, forces himself to keep a measured pace. On the other hand, he never gave himself away to me, since, even when he believed himself to be alone, his features never relaxed. I disliked him for his excessive caution, feeling vaguely that he had locked the door of a house into which I had the right of entry, but he never allowed himself to fall into the trap of my curiosity.

I had to content myself with the acquaintance of his daughter, Mair.

She was a brown, shrivelled little person, whose excessively mobile face could screw itself into the most fantastic grimaces. As soon as she discovered that I learned my lessons at home instead of going to the board-school, she considered me as her intimate enemy and soon we were exchanging insults whenever we passed each other in the road. Here again, she showed a degree of imagination which moved me to unwilling admiration. Soon she discovered another weak spot and began to address me exclusively in Welsh, shrieking with ironic laughter whenever she saw that I had not understood her. In this way, she scored her first advantages over me.

My father had not been slow to make up his mind about the newcomers:

"There is something wrong with that man!" he announced solemnly, a few months after their arrival. "When a man is not liked by his own sort, there is always something wrong with him. Now, I was talking to Prys the Farm this morning and he does not at all care for this Howells."

"I am not surprised," said my mother.

"Prys is a sensible chap," said my father. "He knows what he is talking about."

"At any rate," said my mother, "the child is impossible. She has no idea of keeping her place and I forbid Laura to have anything to do with her."

Both of them turned to regard me keenly, with eyes that tacitly accused me of keeping bad company and I felt myself blushing violently.

My mother bent over me, her face stern and inquisitorial. "You don't play with her, do you Laura?"

I shook my head but dared not speak. I did not play with Mair but merely quarrelled with her, usually at a distance. Yet, under my mother's gaze, I felt myself guilty of disobedience, as if I knew already that the day would come when I should have much to do with Mair, when she would have great importance for me, and that to deny her in advance would be as good as a lie. Luckily my mother noticed nothing. She was watching my father anxiously, scrutinizing his face for the peevish irritation that swept over it whenever she paid attention to me for more than a few minutes at a time. Already I had ceased to exist for them. They were withdrawing, beneath my eyes, into that narrow chamber where their minds lived together, where no one could follow them and which was surely full of the stale odour of a love that is never nourished and which transforms itself imperceptibly into hatred. No one was allowed to disturb them there. They guarded the entry as fiercely as if it had really been a sacred place. They desired only to be alone together so that they might learn without interruption how to hate.

MY MOTHER had wished for a son—"a real boy", she used to say, and the very tone of her voice evoked a tall, fair young man with the shoulders of an athlete; a rowing Blue with an open, empty face and ears red with excessive health. As she had only a daughter, she had hoped at least that I might correspond in some way to this unfulfilled dream, but the games which she forced me to play either left me indifferent or else excited me to such an extent that I became ill and upset the household by being sick unexpectedly in incongruous places. She had to admit that I was not precisely a liar, as she considered all the Welsh to be (for she was of English origin and had a poor opinion of her husband's people), but I was incapable of distinguishing clearly between the real and the imaginary. In fact, I resembled her not at all and thus gave her little satisfaction. A weaker woman might have left it at that, but she had too much character to admit herself beaten because the Lord had made me according to His idea, and set to work to remake me according to her own.

The first and most obvious step was to send me to England to a good boarding school. My father made no objection and soon she had discovered an establishment where, according to the prospectus, there reigned an atmosphere of perfect moral and physical health. Tempting illustrations showed bouncing girls in gym-tunics playing hockey on a beautifully kept sports ground. All the right subjects were taught by highly qualified mistresses and folk-dancing was a feature of the curriculum. I was fitted out with a felt hat trimmed with the school colours, with white flannel blouses and black woollen stockings that tickled my legs insupportably.

Then the blow fell. A short written examination, which was supposed to decide the class which I was to join, revealed that I was almost totally ignorant. My docile governesses, understanding that my mother considered book learning as largely unnecessary, had taught me only what I wished to know, and that was little. At thirteen years old, I was hardly able to do the simplest sums; the principal dates of English history and the rivers of Europe were equally unknown to me and I did not yet suspect the existence of the Latin language. Politely but firmly, my mother was told that certain standards were maintained at all reputable schools and that I failed to satisfy them.

I do not know how the idea that I might take private lessons with Mr. Howells was first born. The rumour had gradually been growing in the village that he was no ordinary man, but a university graduate who had renounced for some unknown reason a brilliant career.

"He must have got into trouble," hinted Mrs. Williams darkly. She detested him because he was a Methodist and because he did not seem to understand that a board school teacher is not the equal of the wife of an Anglican vicar. At first, the village had been inclined to support her theory, which I had heard discussed at length among the servants. Little by little, however, the calm and decent demeanour of Mr. Howells, joined to a piety which approached fanaticism, disposed them to a more indulgent view:

"He is a godly man," said some, "who would rather give his life to the little children of his own land than seek worldly fame elsewhere."

These were the two extremes. In general, he was not greatly liked, but was respected for his learning, and also, perhaps, because he was so grave, so gentle and so entirely removed from the preoccupations of those around him. He had never been seen to joke familiarly with the villagers or to stop and gossip with one of them in the road, but he spoke to them kindly and gravely as if he had come from some far-off place to learn to know them, or perhaps to bring them some message which he would never state in words.

This mystery which surrounded the schoolmaster increased the interest I felt in him. It seemed to me that he must know the

answer to some of the many questions which were beginning
to take form in my brain. I was getting tired of having nothing
to do and was beginning to feel certain intellectual curiosities.
Since my failure to enter Claremont College, I felt humiliated
by my own ignorance. I wanted to learn, to become someone
remarkable, to force my parents to respect me. Since fate had
brought Mr. Howells to Pont-y-Gibby, I was ready to believe
that it had done so in order that he might be of use to me.

One day, early in the autumn, a message brought me down
to the drawing-room. I found my mother there, standing
beside the empty fireplace, with Mr. Howells, also standing,
several paces from her. Hostility was heavy in the air. She
signed to me to approach. Although she spoke amiably
enough, I realized at once that she had noticed that my
stockings were coming down and that there was a fresh ink-
spot on my blouse.

This is my daughter," she said, and with an evident effort she
added: "Yours must be about the same age but I expect she is
much farther on. It seems that Laura knows absolutely nothing."

She was smoking a cigarette and as she spoke she allowed
the smoke to drift slowly from her nostrils.

Mr. Howells made no reply, contenting himself with a stiff
little bow, but his eyes regarded me with courteous attention
and I understood at once that to him I was a human being,
worthy of his interest in spite or even because of the fact that
I was a child.

My mother was not even looking at him, her eyes were
fixed on space, somewhere above the mantelpiece. She said
to me: "I wanted Mr. Howells to see you for himself. It is
possible that he may give you some private lessons."

Her manner was vague and a little irritated and I should

have understood, if I had taken the trouble to reflect, that she was purposely avoiding a decision because Mr. Howells displeased her by his appearance and manner. I myself thought only of my desire for these lessons—less, perhaps for themselves, than because they would be a means for satisfying my curiosity. In my naïveté, I imagined that I should encourage her by showing my pleasure and I began to skip with joy and cry out that I should like to begin at once.

She regarded me coldly.

"This is not a question of your amusement but of learning to add fractions and knowing a little history and some irregular verbs. It seems that you know nothing of all that and, what is more, you have the writing of a child of six."

"When an intelligent child does not succeed at his studies," said Mr. Howells quietly, "it is often because he is not interested. We should blame ourselves rather than him if we cannot find the right door through which to enter his mind."

"I do not understand that sort of thing," said my mother sharply. "I simply want her to learn enough of certain subjects to be able to pass this ridiculous examination."

"Mair is preparing for her scholarship to the grammar school," said Mr. Howells. "The two children could study together if you wish it."

There was a moment's silence which Mr. Howells seemed to find natural but which evidently irritated my mother. I could see that she was searching for something to say and finally she asked:

"And what is your Mair expecting to take up later on?"

"My daughter will follow the path which the Lord has chosen for her," replied Mr. Howells with simplicity.

I knew immediately that all was lost. My mother had a

profound horror of the habit by which the old-fashioned Welsh Methodists invoked the name of God on the most unsuitable occasions. It seemed to her a mark of bad taste and insincerity, for she shared the tabu by which this name is pronounced only in church or on certain solemn occasions, such as those on which I had displeased her and must be stirred to a sense of my sinfulness.

Already her lips were opening to pronounce the words which I could foretell all too easily—"Well, Mr. Howells, I must think this over"—and that would put an end to the matter. At this precise moment, though, my father made his entrance. I saw at once that he was in a bad temper, for his eyes were more brackish than usual and the hand which he held out to the schoolmaster trembled slightly.

I never knew the explanation of the short scene that followed. My father may have been a little drunk, since it happened, although rarely, that he took more whisky than was good for him; or perhaps he had already had an argument with my mother and was in the clutches of one of those heavy, resentful moods which sometimes seized him without anyone understanding the exact reason. He may even, and quite simply, have wished to prove to himself that he was a man and the master in his own house. (He often used this expression and so did my mother. "Your father is the master here. He does as he thinks right!" she would exclaim and everyone, himself first of all, knew that this meant nothing at all. Perhaps he merely wished to give a meaning to these empty words.)

At any rate, he held out his hand and greeted the schoolmaster with the affability which he always used towards those whom he considered to be his social inferiors. My mother said a few words of explanation to which he hardly listened, but he must have realized vaguely that there was a question of taking some step which would hasten my departure.

"Give her lessons, did you say? An excellent idea. It seems she knows nothing."

My mother interrupted hastily: "Nothing is settled yet…"

He glanced at her with irritation. "Not settled? It's an excellent idea. Mr. Howells can tell us how much he wants and she can start next week."

At this point, Mr. Howells committed an irrevocable *faux pas*. Instead of treating my father's gesture of independence with apparent respect and taking his leave with the certainty that the whole affair had been called off, he accepted with simplicity the decision of the head of the household, named a modest figure and retired after declaring that he would expect me at five o'clock on the following Monday.

"Are you mad ?" cried my mother, as soon as the door had closed behind him. "I would not dream of trusting my child to a man like that."

"And why not, if you please?" asked my father calmly.

"Why not? Because he is quite unsuitable! He is one of these so-called intellectuals, full of revolutionary ideals. I wouldn't think of taking him on."

"Then why did you send for him?"

Her face reddened with annoyance: "I wanted to make sure… . You know that I only want the good of Laura and of everyone else in this house. Now that I have talked to him, I realize that he is impossible."

"Well, I don't," said my father. "I found him a lot better than I had thought and I insist that Laura start lessons with him next week."

My mother gazed at him with stupefaction. Ever since his

return, she had played the comedy of the good and submissive wife and it had always been tacitly understood that he would carry out the role allotted to him—that of showing a certain figure to the world, and for the rest, effacing himself spontaneously behind her personality. The rules of this game had become for her an unchangeable law and she had never imagined that he might fail to abide by it. Thus she found herself in an awkward dilemma, having either to impose her own will brutally and thereby modify the relationship which she had built up with him during their life together, or else to give in and admit her defeat before her husband, myself, and the unwitting Mr. Howells.

The rest of the discussion was lost to me, since at that moment she remembered my presence and sent me off to the nursery, but on the following Monday I was despatched, shivering with excitement, to the villa next the schoolhouse.

MR. HOWELLS opened the door himself and showed me into his parlour. The room smelt of must. The walls were papered in chocolate brown with a riotous design in prussian blue, and upon them hung many yellowing photographs of the Howells family, varied with poker-work texts announcing that the Eye of God never closes or calling on sinners to repent. Dust accumulated in the folds of the heavy red plush curtains; the mantelpiece was cluttered with china ornaments bearing inscriptions such as "A souvenir of Porthcawl" or *"Cymru am byth"*, as well as a heavy bronze reproduction of the Discobolus and a number of complicated vases containing dusty bouquets of everlastings. The table at which we were to work was covered with a red plush cloth, fringed with red bobbles, and little squares of crocheted cotton drooped over the back of every chair.

As for Mr. Howells himself, I hardly dared to look at him, so intimidating was his lean dark form and the sensation of strain and tenseness that emanated from his being. But when at last, in answer to some question, I lifted my eyes to his face, I received from him once more a smile so warm, so fraternal, so different from any smile yet offered me, that all apprehension disappeared. Even Mair, already installed at the table and busy with decimal fractions, appeared friendly and moderately subdued. A sensation of warmth swept over me. It seemed to me already that this stuffy and hideous parlour was more beautiful than the gracious rooms, furnished with tepid good taste, of my own home.

From that day on, I lived a double life. Each day, as I passed the threshold of the red-brick villa, I was seized with an inexplicable excitement. It was the ante-chamber to a new world, a world to which Mr. Howells alone possessed the key. Even now, across the expanse of years, I cannot analyse the magic. He spoke quietly, using only simple words, yet without making any concession to facility. If an idea was difficult, he refused to alter or reduce it but explained it with such clarity that its very difficulty became an added attraction. The driest facts took on a life of their own and became dynamic. It was thus that the detested arithmetic which I had successfully avoided until now, opened up for me the world of abstract ideas and the history of the Roman Empire gave me the sudden revelation of the million links in the chain of man's evolution. The study of bygone times, of ancient wars and long dead kings, seemed to liberate my imagination like a pent-up river. I passed from century to century, evoking the image of its splendour and misery. At the same time, these images evoked innumerable questions, since I began to suspect that there existed not one, but many conceptions of the world, that it might be possible to make a choice, to accept this, to refuse that, and to build up for oneself the house of one's own mind.

The result was that these lessons soon began to take on for me the flavour of sin. For the first time in my life, I was hiding something from my mother. Exactly what that thing was I could not have said and it was not till many years later that I could have named this strange new sensation as intellectual curiosity. I plunged into it as a child plunges into sexual experiments, knowing that they are wrong but neither understanding nor asking himself why. I only knew that, if my mother had overheard one of our lessons, she would have pronounced the definitive anathema, "unhealthy", and put a stop to them on the spot. Thus I was careful to hide from her the pleasure I took in them, pretending a decent boredom which would not prevent me from making serious progress. In this way I misled her six days out of seven and knew for the first time the equivocal joys of deception.

When my mother questioned me about Mair, I said that I did not like her. This was true. I found her selfish, conceited and disagreeable, a tremendous liar, without any of my own scruples. Yet none of these faults prevented her from exercising on me an irresistible attraction. Perhaps it was her air of always cherishing some important secret that intrigued me. I should have liked to gaze into her heart, to surprise her most intimate thoughts. I worried her constantly and she only laughed unkindly and put on a mysterious expression which perhaps hid nothing at all.

One day I arrived as usual at five o'clock with my books and the homework I had prepared during the day. Mair opened the door to me and, informing me briefly that her father was detained at the school-house, whisked upstairs, disdaining my company or busy at her own affairs. I remained alone in the parlour and was able for the first time to inspect the room in detail.

Immediately I turned my attention to the framed photographs on the wall. Here at least the Howells, father and daughter, were deprived by the camera of their evasive quality, here they were immobilized, pinned down, robbed of their defences. Mair, a wizened baby, clearly recognizable, peered from the arms of a thin young woman who was surely her mother. The same woman, a little older, a little thinner, was framed in mourning ebony above the piano. Tucked into the corner of the frame was a yellowed snapshot of a prim-looking grave.

Another photograph showed Mair at the age of six or seven, posing stiffly beside a thin, unhealthy-looking boy who stared sulkily into space, ignoring the photographer's plea for a smile. This, surely, was the elder brother of whose existence I was vaguely aware. He looked uninteresting and I turned from him to a group which showed an elderly man in clerical clothes, posing stiffly in the centre of a group of younger men arranged in ascending tiers, standing, sitting and squatting. They wore tight, dark clothes of old-fashioned cut and among them I thought I could recognize Mr. Howells, lean as a rake, with a look of fragile youthfulness and incertitude.

At that moment he entered, excusing himself, with the grave courtesy he always used towards me, for his unpunctuality. I started, feeling vaguely that he had caught me in the act of committing an indelicacy, and immediately, as if to soothe away my confusion, he said: "That picture was taken the day our choir up at Penmaenmawr won the male event at the North Wales Eisteddfod. My father was minister there for twenty years and he conducted the choir every year of his ministry."

His fingers caressed the glass.

"Miners. Their misery was terrible in those days. It was hard to believe that their state of life was in accordance with the will of the Lord."

"They were poor?"

"Such poverty as you could not dream of, Laura. At the mercy of one and all they were. The owners were Englishmen. A heavy weight they must have on their conscience today."

I pointed timidly to the fragile youth in the second row:

"Is that you, Mr. Howells?"

"Yes. I sang baritone then." His face contracted with the violence of a sudden memory:

"It was the day before I left for London. The last day of my ..."

He turned away sharply and began to flutter the pages of a Latin grammar. We could hear Mair banging about in the room over our heads, opening and shutting drawers, singing scales in the rich, true voice I so much envied her.

"You went to London?"

"Yes, yes, my dear. A scholarship."

I held out the exercise book, defaced by a large blot of ink on the cover. It contained the essay on Oliver Cromwell which I had written that morning.

Mr. Howells took the book, glanced at a few sentences and put it aside. Then he asked me, in his kind, grave voice:

'I hope, my dear Laura, that you enjoy your lessons here—that they do not appear to you merely as a disagreeable task?"

His question astonished me. It seemed to me that the joy I felt in the discovery of the new world opened up to me in his red-plush parlour must be visible, almost tangible, that its existence must at least be evident to all. Now that he had questioned me, I felt that I must express—although I had no idea in what manner—the love and gratitude I felt for him.

It was not necessary. The expression on my face must have been enough. Mr. Howells had understood.

He sat down at the table, folded his hands upon the Latin grammar. For the first time I saw in him a tired and elderly man. The deep lines on his face were furrows now, the eyes veiled, the taut skin had taken on a greyish hue, like that of a man wracked with physical suffering.

I stared at him, frightened by this sudden change, but he motioned to me to be seated and spoke in the low, controlled voice to which I was accustomed:

"I am glad, my dear," he said slowly, "that you are happy in your work, and indeed you show an aptitude for learning which makes my task both easy and pleasant. Yet I must warn you—it is my duty to warn you, that learning can be an evil, a pernicious guide, that it may lead you into many dangerous places. I have a great responsibility towards you Laura..."

He broke off. We could hear Mair running down the stairs and an instant later she slipped into her place at the table.

"We will go over the ablative case once more," said Mr. Howells. His head bent low over the book, his long dry fingers busied themselves among the pages.

I hardly listened to his explanations. I was thinking of the thin youth in the high collar and butterfly tie who had sung baritone in North Wales and taken a scholarship to London. I could imagine that village; it would resemble the familiar mining villages around Pontypool, with their sordid cottages, the men squatting on their heels the length of the single street, the heavy, dust-laden air and the mountain of slag towering up behind the chimneys. In the Methodist chapel, built of corrugated tin, the fine Welsh voices would rise up in "Cwm Rhondda" and "Aberystwyth" and Mr. Howells' father would preach those same immense sermons, full of exhortations to repent and terrifying images of hell, that were preached in our own Methodist chapel and commented on, with relish, by our servants on Sunday afternoons, over the kitchen fire. Mr. Howells would listen and nod and admire his father's eloquence and pray for protection against the perils of heathen London. Then one day he would pack his tin suitcase, place his Bible reverently on top of the folded shirts and socks, hoist it on his shoulder and make for the station. His father would accompany him, grave and heavy with misgiving. In the street the miners' wives would call out to Mr. Howells: "Good luck, David boy! *Pob dymuniad da, Dafydd bach!*" At the station the train would be waiting. Mr. Howells would hoist his luggage into the rack, his father would kiss him gravely on the cheek; the guard would blow his whistle and he would be off. After ... impossible to imagine. I had never seen London and could follow Mr. Howells no further on that journey, nor guess at the events which awaited him at its end.

"*Canis, canem* ... come Laura, you are dreaming, my child," said Mr. Howells.

I was supposed to come straight home as soon as our lessons were finished. Mair often accompanied me and we took as long as possible to cover the hundred yards or so that separated our homes. Today, when we left the schoolmaster's house, it was raining and the summits of the surrounding hills seemed to have drawn, yet nearer so that they reared up, huge green masses veiled in cloud, immediately behind the huddled roof tops of the village. The sky was so low, it seemed that one might touch it simply by rising on tiptoe and stretching up one's arm. Wisps of mist floated along the street and the water pattered monotonously down the gutter-pipes and formed parallel streams flowing along either side of the road.

Stepping out into this sad, grey and too-familiar landscape, I felt the desire for escape surge up in me. I too, like Mr. Howells, might win a scholarship. I too might board a train, hoist a suitcase into the luggage rack and wait for the whistle which would signal me away into a new and enchanted world, a radiant climate and an intoxicating liberty. Suddenly and quite without reflection, I said:

"When I am grown-up, I shall go to London and be a student."

Mair's face hardened, for it was insupportable to her that I should be the first to have a good idea.

"Oh, dreary old London!" she said airily. "Why London?"

"Your father went there … He was telling me."

"You would have to copy him. If you could see how silly you look when you drink in his words! As a matter of fact," she said, "London was only a bit of it. He went to Cambridge after that, then to Paris …"

"To Paris?" Unbelievable. "What to do?"

"Oh, he'll never talk. As a matter of fact, I shall go there myself as soon as I am eighteen."

She had just thought of this, but already the idea was stiff and rooted in her mind.

"I shall be an opera singer," she said.

I tried to sneer, but she realized that she had scored a point and threw me a look of triumph.

"The people will unharness my carriage," she said. "And

drag it themselves through the town. I shall wear diamonds in my hair—presents from my admirers—and the crowd will cheer me wherever I pass."

Her eyes glowed. She believed in the scene as completely as if it had already taken place. She stood there, and I knew that neither the mist, nor the rain, nor the familiar village, existed for her. She opened her arms in a dramatic gesture, her head poised high and proud as if before a vast audience, and sang into the wet air with all the force of her lungs.

"Worthy is the lamb that was slain," sang Mair, transfigured and wrapped in glory.

I listened to her with discouragement. It was not enough for her to be so much more advanced than myself in her studies that we could not even prepare the same homework, to be more witty, more vivacious and generally more sure of herself than me, beyond all this she had the promise of a very fine voice, while I could not even sing in tune. For an instant I had the bitter vision of a radiant Mair, standing in her carriage, bowing and throwing kisses from the tips of her fingers, while I mingled humbly with the worshipping throng. The prospect of going to London had already become less exciting.

"… And honour, and power …"

The voice, clear as crystal, was lapped up by the mist, beaten back into her throat by the rain. She stopped, furious: "Horrible, loathsome Pont-y-Gibby! What's the good of pretending? Father will never let me go. I'll be here all my life."

"If your voice is really good, he will let you study."

"Never, I couldn't even talk to him about it. He would rather I died than let me go away … go away to some place where I could really learn … London, Paris, Rome …"

"But he went himself…"

She threw me a glance of furious irritation:

"Idiot! That's just why. Once I found an old letter in a trunk up in the boxroom. It was from someone in a University, in Cambridge, I think. It said Father could have been a great something—I can't remember the word—and it said it was a sin and a waste for him to bury himself here. Father heard me up there. He came up and he saw me with the letter in my hand. He took it from me and when he saw what it was, he tore it up, he went on tearing and tearing until the shreds were as little as confetti, then he threw it down and ground it with his foot into the floor."

"And then?" I asked, breathless with interest.

"Then he turned round and went away without a word."

"How extraordinary!"

"Everything about him is extraordinary," she said bitterly. "It's all very well for you. You don't have to live with him. I want to be like other children. I want to play and amuse myself, not spend my life listening to his sermons."

Suddenly I realized that she was crying. The rain mingled with the large round tears that scurried down her cheeks.

At that moment, seeing her so helpless and desolate I was filled with love for her. I flung my arms around her, hugged her and begged her to come and play in our garden.

"Nobody will bother us if we keep out of the way. You can climb my tree with me and we can watch the whole village without anyone knowing, and I'll teach you to ride and there is a whole litter of new puppies."

If I expected gratitude, I was disappointed. That I should offer her my protection, however whole-heartedly, was almost an insult. A grating little laugh informed me that I had been injudicious:

"You know quite well they wouldn't let you. I'm not in your class (she caricatured successfully my mother's English accent). We're good enough to stuff you with history and geography, but we can't mix otherwise.

"As a matter of fact," she added, "my father wouldn't wish it either. We have nothing in common—that's what he says himself— and he just does what he is paid to do for you."

The cruelty of her words almost stunned me but by now we had reached the garden gate and I perceived my mother facing us, weeding the herbaceous border with three fox terriers at her heels. Mair gave her an insolent stare over the gate, then turned away with a nonchalant whisk of the skirt and a wave of the hand.

My mother's face was like thunder. She said to me, loudly enough for Mair to hear before she had strolled out of earshot:

"Having lessons with that child is one thing, Laura, as it seems the only solution, but playing with her in the road is another. I forbid you ..."

Ironically, in the distance, Mair hummed:

"Daisy, Daisy, give me your answer do ..."

"An appalling child!" said my mother. "This must be put a stop to."

"I can't tell her to go away," I said sulkily, betraying Mair. "She should know for herself what is suitable."

WHEN MAIR had spoken of her father's stay in Paris, I had been inclined to scoff at her story as an invention. Yet one day Mr. Howells astonished me by speaking himself of this experience.

We were having our weekly lesson in geography. The map of Western Europe lay open with its wriggly lines and darker splashes, that were rivers and mountains. We were tracing the course of the Loire but for once I was uninterested. My breasts, which had recently begun to swell in two uncomfortable hill-ocks on my chest, were hurting, and I had that curious feeling of flatness and unreality that occasionally took possession of me. I was in the room, yet a part of me seemed to have remained outside. I heard clearly all that Mr. Howells was saying, yet his voice seemed to remain in my ears instead of penetrating my brain. My head felt heavy, with a dull, leaden heaviness that ex-cluded all other sensation. It was a bad day, a day for trouble.

Mr. Howells himself appeared a little absent-minded, as if he was not convinced of the interest of his own words. Our lesson continued in this way for a certain time. Then suddenly he rose and crossed to the window. He opened it, leaned out, with his head in his hands. His body trembled in a sort of spasm. It was the gesture of a madman, a gesture springing from some mysterious necessity, inexplicable surely to himself as to others.

A moment later, he turned, closed the window and came to sit down quietly at the table. He said: "This river Loire you see marked on the map, is not really a black line drawn on paper, you know. It is an immensely wide, silver-coloured stretch of water that flows slowly through the most peaceful landscape you can imagine and reflects castles, as beautiful as those in your fairy-tales, built by the kings of France many hundreds of years ago. If you can imagine it like that, you will find it more interesting."

"So you really did … ?" The words broke out before I could check them.

He turned on me a look of grave amusement: "Really did what, my child?"

"Go to France. …" I was confused, for neither I nor anyone

in the village had yet dared to ask Mr. Howells a personal question. Mair shot me an offended glance. She had caught me in the act of doubting her word.

"To France? Certainly. I was there many years ago."

His finger hovered again over the map and the subject seemed to be closed, when he said:

"There is much to be learnt from travel in foreign countries, but, to my mind, it is not a thing to be undertaken lightly. It is likely to produce a change in the traveller himself and one which has nothing to do with the difference in customs or in the landscape. He will have reactions, thoughts and dreams which he would not have had at home. He will discover an unsuspected personality."

He hesitated and I noticed that his index finger oscillated, like the pendulum, above the spot on the map marked Paris, then he continued: "You should consider this before you decide to leave your own homes. A journey is a serious thing, it can bring good or evil, but it is sure to bring change. You will never return exactly as you were before your departure."

"Tell us," begged Mair. "Tell Laura about Paris!"

"Paris," said Mr. Howells solemnly, "is the city of ambition, where every man is tormented by the desire to surpass his fellows. I cannot explain this to you, but it is as if the city were an enlarging mirror that deforms everything one sees through it and above all one's own reflection."

Mr. Howells looked very sad as he said this and I realized, although I hardly understood his words, that he himself had gazed deeply into that fantastic mirror and that he had only torn himself away after a great struggle.

Mair, however, was practical and would not allow herself to be diverted by abstractions:

"But what was it *like*?" she insisted.

For an instant, Mr. Howells' expression became more sombre, and I guessed that he was irritated by her insistence. Then he said patiently:

"In Paris the streets are immensely wide—far wider than in Cardiff—and they are bordered by trees, especially by chestnut trees that are covered with flowers in springtime and scatter the pavements with chestnuts in autumn. There are very old churches and houses that are so old and crooked, they seem to stagger like drunken men. The Sacré Coeur is like a fairy tale castle from a distance, high above the city, with white towers and cupolas, that gleam in the sun.

"There are an immense number of cafés and they have terraces on the pavements, where people sit for hours, wasting their time and even taking strong drink, but it makes the streets very colourful and gay… ."

He paused and glanced at us almost mischievously:

"Is that enough?"

Of course it was not enough, but the course of the river Loire claimed our attention and there were no more digressions that day.

When the lesson was over and I was preparing to leave, Mr. Howells stopped me with a gesture. The moment of relaxation was over and he looked tired and old. He held out an envelope:

"Will you kindly give this to your mother, my child. It will explain to her that I cannot give you a lesson tomorrow. My son will be arriving late in the afternoon."

The weedy boy of the photograph … Idris … Idris Howells.

"Father is in a terrible state," said Mair, as the wicket gate closed behind us. "They quarrel all the time when Idris is here, yet Father is furious with him because he hardly ever comes."

"What does he do?"

"Oh, he's at the University in Liverpool, studying something or other. He's a black sheep," she said, then added unexpectedly:

"So am I, only people don't know it."

Something in her tone prevented me from scoffing. It seemed to me that I was on the point of penetrating into those hidden places of her mind that she defended so jealously. I waited, expectant, but she only said violently:

"I might do *anything.*"

"But your brother … ?"

"Idris? I don't think much of him really but he does as he likes. It's easy for a boy. He won't have anything to do with Father's ideas, he says Father is a hypocrite and he hates Pont-y-Gibby and he lives away in Cardiff."

"How extraordinary."

"I expect we think a lot of things extraordinary that would seem quite ordinary to other people. How can we know … ?"

She gestured towards the mountains as if to say: We are guarded against the world.

It was summer now. High in the ancient oak, astride the branch where my thighs had worn smooth the bark, I watched the village sucking life from the sun. In the street itself there was no one in sight, nothing moved, but the grey stone houses were tinged with a warm golden colour, a light dust powdered the street and a single bird rose singing, higher and higher, sprinkling the air with its light, sharp notes. The village slept in such deep quiet that I could hear the distant crash of the waterfall that, high in the mountains, near the very source of the stream, bounded in an explosion of foam and sun upon the rocks. A dog barked, somewhere up on the Sugar-loaf, then there came the faint call of a shepherd and, from yet farther, an answering cry. The leaves that caressed my cheek, moved by an instant's breeze, had a heady smell of sap. They were living and growing all around me. The sap sprang like a tide through the trunk, the branches, through every twig and the throbbing veins of every leaf, and it seemed to me that I too participated in this pulsing life and vigour, that I too was drawing sap from the vital flow of the tree.

Now from the church tower, broke five thunderous strokes, and a few moments later I heard the coughing of an engine. The bus from Llanglaslyn was approaching. The sound of its horn, distant at first, became clearer at every bend and presently the singing of birds, the crash of the waterfall and the cries of the shepherds were all swallowed up in the rumble and chugging of its arrival.

At this moment, I heard the sharp click of a gate to the right. Mr. Howells had emerged into the road, followed by Mair. The two lean, dark forms hurried along the pavement and took up their position outside the grocer's shop, just in front of the framed timetable of the bus service. Mr. Howells face was shut and expressionless, as if he had drawn a curtain over his mind. Mair looked cross and spiteful, as if she had been dragged unwillingly to this encounter.

Now the big red bus turned the corner and gasped to a standstill. Out got Gwilym the Post, then Mrs. Jones, then two foreign spinsters carrying baskets, rugs and sunshades. Then, at the moment when the bus was on the point of starting, a young man sprang from the running-board, suitcase in hand and advanced towards the waiting couple. It was Idris, the black sheep, a long, dark youth with untidy gestures, and a lean face built up all of jutting angles. He exchanged un-

enthusiastic kisses with his father and sister and the three
marched off with the stiff, jerking Howells walk.

That was all. I had hoped for drama, but the reunion could
hardly have been flatter, more banal. Once more the Howells
family had refused to play their part in the legend I had prepared for them.

The next day, when I arrived at the schoolmaster's villa,
Idris was not to be seen. Nor did I meet him on any of the
following days on which Mr. Howells, a little preoccupied,
gave me my lessons as usual but made no mention of his son.
Mair appeared to avoid my company and disappeared upstairs
as soon as we had closed our books. The only signs of Idris'
presence were a tweed jacket hanging in the hall and the
crumpled newspapers abandoned in armchairs. Our own
maids however, madly intrigued, informed me that the young
man usually left the house early in the morning, carrying
books and packets which probably contained sandwiches, and
marched off in the direction of the mountains.

When Sunday came, I welcomed this usually detested day
with eagerness. Even Idris would not dare to break the iron
tradition that governed the Methodist Sabbath.

My parents had visitors to lunch that day—Sir Thomas and
Lady Wynn-Evans, from Abergavenny, over the county
border. Sir Thomas was a master of foxhounds, a bluff, red-
faced man with a loud voice, to whom the whisky must not
be passed too often. Lady Wynn-Evans was frail and
dignified. She looked much older than my mother, although
they had first met as young brides, and my mother despised
her a little for her passive sweetness and lack of vigour.

I was present at lunch, since there was no longer a governess to preside at schoolroom meals, but it was understood that

I was to be seen and not heard. So I sat, quietly eating, watching the sunlight that splashed through the french window on to the mahogany dining table, feeling the terrier's rough hair rubbing in a warm, friendly way against my legs and wondering whether Idris would attend afternoon chapel. I was not aware that Lady Wynn-Evans had spoken to me until my mother's voice called me sharply to attention:

"Wake up, Laura, for goodness sake."

"Another dreamy one!" said Lady Wynn-Evans, with a kindly smile for me. She went on: "I was saying that you must come over for tennis one day. My boys will be home for the holidays soon."

"Laura's hopeless at tennis," said my mother. "She won't learn to keep her eye on the ball."

"Oh well, it will be just the children, you know," said Lady Wynn-Evans, but Sir Thomas laughed his big, baying laugh and said:

"Going to be a highbrow, eh, young lady? Not interested in all that sort of thing, eh?"

"Oh, Thomas, she rides beautifully," Lady Wynn-Evans enveloped me with kindness. She was the soul of tact, certain to find some good point in everyone. But my father was tapping nervously on the table. He averted his eyes from me and spoke gazing straight at the sporting print on the wall above my mother's head:

"Now Laura, I think we've heard enough from you. You've finished your fruit, haven't you? Suppose you run and play in the garden."

"But you must really come and see us, my dear," said Lady Wynn-Evans, taking my hand, while Sir Thomas, bellowed across the table:

"Nothing like playing with other children for waking a girl up. She'll take after you yet, Molly."

My mother shrugged her shoulders; "One never knows. School may do wonders for her."

It was barely half-past two, but I could think of nothing to pass the time until the hour for chapel, so I took a book and made for the bottom of the garden. I sat for a while in the swing, scuffing my toes against the worn earth and rocking gently, but I could not take my thoughts off the Howells. They were so near me, their intense, mysterious life was being lived out almost under my eyes and yet it was impossible to envisage their existence at this moment. Mr. Howells, surely, was reading the Bible, for what else could a godly man of the Methodist persuasion be doing on a Sunday afternoon? This assurance was not enough for me. It answered only a fragment of the question in my mind. Was he seeking at this moment a consolation in those ancient tales of the Children of Israel for the unkindness of his own children? Was he wrestling with the devil for the soul of erring Idris, as I had seen the wandering preacher wrestle, at the Spring Revival, for the souls of his audience? I remembered the gaunt face of the famous Llew Lewis, which indeed, now I thought of it, resembled in some way that of Mr. Howells. He had stood on a small hillock, a mere mound of earth that dominated the stretch of wasteland out behind the chapel, and beside him stood a great zinc tub that some men of the village had brought in a cart earlier in the day. He had prayed with his arms stretched above his head, as if to snatch God from the clouds. He had prayed as if he had power to bring great Moses thundering down from heaven in a chariot of fire, as if he had power to drive the devil himself back into hell, and after the

great voice had rolled for a while over the heads of the as-
sembled people, they began to shiver and to cry "Allelujah!"
and sob and confess their sins. And Llew Lewis stretched out
his long, thin arms to the sobbing people and called on them
to save their souls and wash themselves clean. One after
another people ran forward, climbed to the summit of the
mound where Llew stood and standing beside him, testified
to their conversion. Then Llew plunged them, one after
another, like sheep in the dipping pool, down into the tub.
Head and all, in they went, and emerged dripping and breathless, gasping, "Praise the Lord!" through streaming, undone
hair. Our own scullery maid, poor Bron, was one of the first
to go in, but for a moment I did not recognize her, so wild and
dishevelled did she seem, so unlike the timid Bron who
scurried to cook's order. I myself was caught up, transported
by Llew Lewis. I would have liked to be a child of some vil-
lager, a child who might run sobbing to Llew's arms and
disappear for a saving instant into that magic water. But I
knew that I had no right to be present at this place, I knew that
Llew Lewis was a charlatan and the people who pressed
around him were vulgar and hysterical. My mother had said
so, she had read in the local paper of the preacher's visit and
tossed the paper away with a snort of disgust. So I skulked,
furtive, on the edge of the crowd and envied, although she
filled me at the same time with distaste, little Glynis Roberts
who knelt weeping and ecstatic in the pool of water that
flowed from her own sodden clothes.

The scene was vivid in my mind as I swung slowly in the
heavy silence of the Sunday afternoon. What would Mr.
Howells have thought of Llew Lewis? Would he have taken
part in that frantic scene? I could not imagine it, yet I was dis-

turbed by the sudden realization of some indefinable likeness between the two men and it seemed to me that that likeness was intensified in Idris.

Voices, clear and assured, floating across the lawn, told me that my parents and their visitors were taking coffee on the lawn. I knew that there would soon be a ritual stroll round the garden and I should be better out of the way. I slipped out of the swing, ran across the unkempt patch of grass beyond the privet hedge and soon I was groping in the chilly, leafy darkness of the tree. A minute later, I was astride the bough, my eyes fixed on the Howells' window.

The blinds were drawn and the road, as far as I could see, was lined with those eyeless Sabbath houses. Windows were muffled, doors closed. In the orchard behind Robert's farm, I could see Nellie, the mad woman who lived in a hut in Glenmawr Woods, the only living creature abroad, with her ten idiot children, out picking mushrooms. She wandered vaguely, stooping and rising, searching for the little round white mushrooms and the children loped beside her, drooling, stumbling, half-blind and verminous. They were beyond the pressure of custom and opinion, untouched and untouchable.

In the schoolmaster's villa the blinds were closely drawn and there seemed to be no movement in the house. It might have been empty, so still it was, but I felt sure that Mr. Howells was there and that Idris and Mair were sulkily engaged in some occupation suitable to the day. At this moment a shadow crossed the blind, then a few notes tinkled out, half-stifled, from the lower floor. Mair was playing a hymn on the piano, thumping laboriously. She stopped in the middle of a phrase and I imagined that Idris had irritably shouted for silence.

After a long time, during which I read two chapters of the Scarlet Pimpernel and listened to the vivacious leave-takings of the Wynn-Evans, the chapel bell began to ring. As the first notes sounded, doors opened all along the double row of cottages and the people emerged, black-clad, with downcast, Sunday eyes. They carried large shiny black prayer books and began to walk primly down the street in the direction of the ugly, corrugated iron chapel.

The bell had clanged for a few minutes when the door of the schoolmaster's house opened in its turn and Mr. Howells appeared with Mair beside him, wearing a sailor hat with a blue bow. They walked side by side, unspeaking, down the path and out into the road. There was no sign of Idris. He was there in the empty house, defiant, barricaded behind his own refusal. He would have no part in the daily life of the Howells. He was manifesting his quality as a stranger.

I WAS SITTING beneath the magnolia tree, doing my home-work, the magnolia tree that had bloomed suddenly and unexpectedly that summer so that its boughs were smothered in great flowers that looked as if they had been moulded out of wax. Mr. Howells had set me an essay on the subject: What is justice? I had used the word during a discussion on the be-heading of Charles I and been unable to explain clearly what I meant by it. Mr. Howells had said with his grave, swift smile:

"You are in the same position, my dear child, as rather more than ninety-nine per cent of the people who employ that and other abstract words. It would please me very much and be useful to you in the future, if you would attempt to clarify your ideas."

My mother came out of the house and stood in the drive, shading her eyes from the sun. She caught sight of me and said:

"Are you doing your homework, Laura? You had better move to the bottom of the garden. Your father will be bringing the deck chairs out here and he won't like to be disturbed."

She picked up my exercise books, glanced absent-mindedly at the page and said:

"I must say, I think your writing has improved a little."

Then she frowned: "What an extraordinary ... what a ridiculous title. What is it all about?"

"An essay ..."

"An essay. But that Howells man must be mad. What does he mean?"

"I don't know," I said. "I am trying to think it out."

Her foot tapped on the grass. "A waste of time and a lot of unhealthy nonsense, too. I don't pay him for that sort of thing."

Beneath the title I had scribbled some notes. She glanced over them.

"King Charles and Cromwell ... oh, history." For a moment she was relieved, then: "Miners." She read out. "What on earth ... ?"

"I was trying to think about justice. Mr. Howells said something about the miners, how poor they are, how terrible the work is ...?"

I could see that I had annoyed her but she spoke patiently: "My dear Laura, all this shows that Mr. Howells is not a proper sort of person to teach you, just as I always thought. You are too young to understand what nonsense you are talking. The miners are poor because they have no sense of thrift. Do you know that during the war they were earning up to twelve pounds a week? And what do you think they did with it? They bought fur coats for their wives, green peas out of season, anything senseless and extravagant. I remember myself going into Williams in Pontypool and seeing those men, with their faces still black from the mine, buying boxes of chocolates, such as I would never have dreamed of buying myself. Then they were surprised when the war was over and the mines closed and they found themselves back on the dole, with nothing saved."

"But why should they be on the dole, and the children hungry?"

"You are talking about things you cannot understand," she said. "If Mr. Howells and all the cranks like him had their way, everything we have would be taken away and given to your wretched miners and we should probably be on the dole ourselves. How would you like that?"

While my mother was speaking, my father walked slowly across the lawn. He wore a deer-stalker hat and carried a long stick with a small prong at the end and with this prong he dug at the dandelions embedded among the grass.

By the time he reached us he had three of the offending plants, which he held by their roots, waving them accusingly under my mother's nose.

"I don't know why we keep a gardener—look at these!"

"Slack!" said my mother. "You can't get a decent man these days."

She still held my book in her hand and now she began to explain about the essay to my father, but I could see he was not listening. As she finished, he jerked his mind to attention.

"What's that? Howells again?"

"I knew it would be like this," she said with something like triumph in the tone. "He puts ideas in her head."

"The man's a bolshie," said my father absently. "I always told you so. He's not cared for in the village."

"I shall write him a little note to thank him for his help and say we think it is time Laura had a holiday."

She reflected and then added: "No, I think it would be only right to tell him what I really think. He's probably corrupting all the village children."

"Time someone took a stand," said my father.

"No wonder Laura is getting so self-opinionated and out of hand. These lessons must stop at once."

"Stop?" said my father.

"Of course. You don't want her head stuffed with all that nonsense, do you? *Worse* than nonsense."

"Tell him to stick to arithmetic or whatever he's supposed to teach her," said my father.

My mother did not betray her impatience except by the hardening of her eyes. She said, with a tolerant little laugh:

"You haven't been listening, have you, dear? I was saying that Laura must not go back. You can't trust that man an inch."

"Not go back? What'll we do with her till she goes to school then? Can't have her always under our feet, can we?"

My mother sighed and began to explain once more the impossibility of allowing me to fall under Mr. Howells' influence, but he interrupted her crossly.

"Nonsense! Howells is all right. A bit of a crank, that's all."

All through this discussion my mother had been strangely tense and I realized once more, as I had done on the day when the schoolmaster first visited us, that he was inexplicably important to her, and it seemed that whenever the question of Mr. Howells touched her, she was vulnerable. In all innocence he had become her implacable enemy with the power to scorch and wound.

Suddenly my mother lost her temper. A wave of purplish-red swept over her face. A vein in her forehead swelled and her mouth tightened thinly.

"Perhaps you don't care if Laura is turned into a bolshie, filled with immoral ideas! I wonder what would happen to her, to all of us, if I was not here. You can be thankful there is someone here to remember that decency exists, to prevent everything going to pieces."

He drew himself up. His thin cheek twitched nervously. The hand, still clutching the three dandelions, was trembling.

"If you mean that you are the master here, Molly, you have no need to remind me of it."

"So now I am to be insulted!" She seized a magnolia blossom, ripped it from the branch and began to tear it to shreds in her strong, brown fingers. "These are the thanks I get for all I have done, all I have put up with. I thought at least that no one—no one who has ever met me, who has met us— could ever suggest that I was selfish."

"You are admirable, my dear Molly," his voice was thin with sarcasm. "Admirable in an impossible situation, and none of us is ever allowed to forget it."

He turned his back and walked off, whistling in a trembling, indignant way. My mother was left standing, helpless and furious. Tears were coursing down her weather-beaten cheeks and her hands opened and shut spasmodically. Seeing her suddenly weak and defeated, my old love surged up and with it hatred for the foolish, intrusive creature whose mere presence made of me a stranger in my own home. For the first time I realized that a merciless drama was being played out all around me, in this peaceful house, between the couple apparently so united.

But she turned on me in fury: "You see what you have done. You bring nothing but trouble! Nothing! Everything is your fault."

She turned and ran towards the house, her shoulders shaking.

One idea only was in my mind by now. To run away— the eternal, hopeless dream of childhood. I wished I was a miner, I wished I was a slave, I wished I was dying of hunger. Anything would be better than this. To be in everyone's power …

I was out of the gate and down the street before I asked myself where I was going, but I knew the answer already. I was going up the Sugar-loaf, the curiously-shaped conical mountain, or rather tall hill, that rose steeply up from the pastures behind the war memorial. It was forbidden land to me, because of its great solitude and because the rocky summit, covered with sparse bushes and loose stones, was known to be dangerous. In summer I had sometimes picnicked with my governesses among the lush grass near the stream, or visited some of the farms scattered over the lower slopes, but I had never ventured into the mysterious and forbidding heights, known only to a few shepherds and to village boys in search of adventure.

I ran without drawing breath till I came to the war memorial that stood at the end of the road, high up, overlooking the village. It was a granite cross inscribed with the words: "Dulce et decorum est pro patria mori," and below them a list of "The men of our village who have lost their lives in the Great War." I could just remember the day when it had been unveiled, the attentive crowds, the quietly crying women, the droning voice of the Provost and the singing of God Save the King and Land of Our Fathers. My mother had explained to me that the motto meant that it was sweet and fitting to die for one's country and I had often imagined myself doing so, in some heroic way and my name graven beneath those of the Morgans, the Rhys' and the Roberts' who had thus entered into glory.

As soon as I had passed the war memorial I turned aside from the road and plunged into the odorous fields. The hay had already been cut and the short, stiff grass pricked my ankles, but in the ditches and close to the hedges it grew high and rich with juice, all entangled with those delicate white flowers, with their sugary perfume, that we called maidenhair. Then there was Jenkins' farm, then Rhys' farm, where cows and pigs waded in yards knee-deep in filth and troops of angry geese croaked at the gateways. From afar, I could hear the bellow of Jenkins' great bull, waiting, attached to a stake by a cord passed through a ring in his nose, for a farm-boy to fetch him for a nuptial visit to one of his hundred and fifty wives.

I skirted these farms, keeping as far as I could to avoid their stench, and soon found myself on the narrow path that wound upwards, gradually at first, then more and more steeply, till it lost itself in the blue heights. As I climbed, I remembered all the small, black figures I had watched from afar as they took this same upward path. From men with familiar faces, they had shrunk to moving toys, then to mice and finally to flies ascending without visible movement upon a wall of mist. I told myself that, at this moment, I myself was no more than a mouse for some spectator in the valley and the idea amused me so much that I almost forgot my misery.

"I am getting smaller and smaller," I said to myself. "Soon I shall be nothing but a black speck. Soon I shall stop existing."

I was surprised to see that the grass at this point was as

green and fresh as it had been in the valley, for, from below, it had appeared blue, grey or violet according to the season. There were no more hedges now, only the great stretch of pale green grass, scarred at certain spots by rows of white stones which probably marked the limits within which this or that shepherd might allow his flocks to pasture. The path had disappeared, melted away into the steep grassy slopes.

It was growing late now and my legs ached from climbing. Great boulders rose here and there and piles of stones which seemed to have been erected for some mysterious reason, perhaps by ancient peoples who had prayed to savage gods beneath boughs of mistletoe. I sat down beneath one of these boulders, leaning my back against the rock. The air was warm and soft and the reflection of the setting sun turned the grass to a shining copper colour. The air itself, indeed, seemed to be full of constantly changing colour and it seemed to me as if my skin had slid from me and these colours were penetrating me gently, creeping through muscles and nerves to the very core of my body.

My unhappiness had died quite away now and I felt only an extraordinary exaltation at the thought that, for the first time in my life, I was really alone. Down there, I thought, I am never safe from their voices. It is enough for them to call my name and at once I am a prisoner, obliged to come and to go, with the words they demand and the expression that they wish to see upon my face. But now they can shout themselves hoarse, they can burst their lungs, but their voices have no power over me. They are calling now perhaps, in every corner of the garden and out in the street, but the wind carries away their voices and I am as far as a ship alone in the middle of the sea.

I was so enchanted by this thought that I did not at once perceive that I was less alone than I had imagined. Gradually, however, I became conscious of a presence and, lifting my eyes, I saw Idris Howells standing at a little distance as if he had been descending the mountain and had stopped at sight of me. He was watching me, his head tilted a little to the side and blinking his eyes in the blinding evening sun.

For a moment I was afraid, because he seemed so tall, so lean and so dark standing there on the mountain side with his shadow, like a second giant figure flattened against the copper coloured grass. But he walked over and spoke to me so naturally that it seemed as if we were old friends and that he found it quite normal to meet me at sunset in this lonely spot.

"Do you come here often?" he asked, as if I had been a grown-up person free to wander as I pleased.

I replied that it was the first time.

"I come nearly every day," he said. "A little higher up there is a wonderful view. You can see across all the Beacons and the whole of Monmouthshire, right down to the Usk."

"I want to go up there, to the very top of the mountain," I said. But he put his hand lightly on my shoulder and said:

"It would be better to do that in the daytime. It is getting dark now."

We walked for a while in silence. I began for the first time to realize the gravity of my flight, to imagine the panic into which I must have thrown my mother and the reception I was likely to get on my return. Idris strode downward over the slippery slope, paying no attention to me and humming gently to himself. It was nothing to him that I should be scolded, that there would be a scene and that I should soon be convinced of my own wickedness and selfishness.

I stopped and called after Idris' striding figure: "I don't want to go back."

He looked back over his shoulder, unsurprised.

"One never wants to go back. The point is, quite simply, that it will be very cold and wet up here at night, and it is better to sleep in a comfortable bed than on the ground."

"I don't care about that," I said obstinately. "I don't want to go back to my parents."

"I don't wonder," said Idris calmly. "I have seen them and Mair has told me things. Your father is a fool and your mother is a shrew. What does it matter? The world is full of people like that and it is better to get used to the idea as soon as possible."

His words shook me profoundly. It seemed impossible that anyone should dare to say such things, and to say them calmly, without excitement, as if they were a matter of proved fact. Until this moment no one had ever criticized my mother before me and I myself had never seen her through eyes other than her own. I began to wonder what she would say if she could hear Idris' words at this moment. It was unimaginable, as it would be unimaginable to her that I should not spring instantly to her defence. Far from wishing to do so, I felt a curious pleasure in listening to such blasphemous phrases.

Idris must have guessed my thoughts in part for he cast me an ironic glance and said:

"I suppose I have shocked you?"

I was not going to confide in him and I remarked primly that I did not like to hear my parents spoken of in such a way.

He laughed sarcastically: "You have been well brought up, haven't you? If you only knew what I can say about my own father."

"Your father?" To my own surprise I felt the genuine indignation I had been unable to summon up on behalf of my own family. "How can you say anything against him. He is the best man, the cleverest man I ever met."

He regarded me with a mocking smile and said, without slowing his pace: "You are a good little lamb and people will always lead you wherever they wish. I'm a bad lot. I'm a bad lot because it is the only way to be free, the only way not to resemble my father."

Suddenly he caught me by the arm, swung me round to face him. In a deep strained voice, he said: "Look at me! Look at me carefully! Do you think I am like my father?"

Obediently I considered his face, illuminated by the last crimson rays of the sun. It did, indeed, almost uncannily resemble that of Mr. Howells, not only in structure, but in the unquiet expression of the deep-set eyes. Only in Idris' face there was something wild and cruel that was lacking in his father's.

As I hesitated, he said bitterly: "I need not really ask you. I can answer myself. As like as two peas in a pod."

His tone put me in a rage and I said furiously: "You would be very lucky if you could be like him. He is extraordinary."

Idris replied calmly: "I know that. He is wise, kind and virtuous. But he is also a coward and a hypocrite. He is intelligent enough to see all the filth around him. He knows where it comes from and he knows just what people like your parents and all the others of their kind are worth. He knows the world is a stinking drain, but rather than say it aloud he hides himself here, he does his little job and he keeps quiet. I know quite well that he is a great man and I shall never be worth half of him. That is why I hate him. Because he could cry out the truth and make the whole world listen to him if he would, and he does not do it."

He was speaking at the top of his voice, gesturing with his long, delicate hands. He seemed to have forgotten my presence for he walked so quickly that I was obliged to run, slipping and sliding on the steep hillside, to keep up with him.

"Everyone admires him because he has renounced a fine career to come and look after the children in this hole. They believe he has done it in a spirit of sacrifice, of love, all the grand sentiments. But I know that he is afraid of having to say out loud what he thinks, or even admitting to himself what he really thinks. Here, there's no danger. No one asks anything from him except to behave like everyone else. He and his fine brain are left to peace. There is only me to disturb him."

A cow lowed out of the dusk. The dark mass of Jenkins' farm loomed before us. We were nearly home and soon this encounter on the Sugar-loaf would slip into the past and grow vague like a remembered dream.

THE LESSONS with Mr. Howells continued, but at home his name was never mentioned and no one ever enquired after my progress. The hours I passed at the red-brick villa were, for my parents, holes in the passing days. They were not referred to because they did not exist.

Idris was once more invisible. Everything had slipped back to normal. Each day, at five o'clock, I rang at the white-painted door, Mair opened to me, sulky, aggressive or elated according to her mood of the moment, and we entered the parlour together, set out our books and compared the results of our problems in algebra or the parsing of a phrase. A minute later, Mr. Howells was there and immediately a feeling of warmth and security enveloped me. I felt myself urged on and protected; I could advance in safety; reassured and encouraged, I explored the country of the mind.

"I can't think why you get so excited about these old lessons," said Mair. "One would think you enjoy them better than anything else, yet you aren't even specially good at them."

It was quite true. In spite of my enthusiasm I was still less advanced than her in most subjects. I could not explain to her, though, that these hours of study meant to me something quite different from the storing of useful facts. Nor could I tell, since I was myself only half-aware, that it was only in contact with her father that I felt myself truly alive.

Often, though, I was surprised by the grave and troubled way in which Mr. Howells would regard me. Sometimes I thought that he was displeased with me, but, when I suggested this to Mair, she laughed her tinny laugh and said:

"Don't be silly, you know you're his pet lamb."

"Why does he look so worried then?"

"How should I know? No one can understand Father." She was practising her singing ardently, encouraged by the secret reading of a biography of Adelina Patti, lent by Miss O'Gorman. Often, when I passed the schoolmaster's house, I could hear her rippling up and down the scale, or repeating the complicated arpeggios prescribed by a correspondence course in voice-training which she had ordered from Cardiff.

"Four more years and I shall be in Paris," she would say, jigging from one foot to another in her excitement. When she was in a friendly mood she would take it for granted that I should accompany her.

"We will sit in one of those cafés on the pavement like

Father told us about and drink lemonade and no one who sees us there will guess all we are going to do."

"We shall only be eighteen," I objected.

"Just the right age. But Father mustn't know till the last minute. I tell him I am practising so that I can help with the choir."

One day I had been riding with my mother and, as we reached the house, we saw a child from the village school fumbling at the gate. My mother reined in her horse.

"Did you want something, Johnnie?"

"Teacher's sent a note for you, Ma'am."

He handed her the cheap, yellowish envelope, tugged politely at a lock of hair and skipped off.

My mother took a sheet of paper from the envelope, read it and handed me the letter, saying stiffly: "You had better read this for yourself."

The letter says:

"Dear Mrs. Gethryn,

As I have many preoccupations and a great deal of work at present, I fear it will be necessary to put an end to Laura's lessons. She has already made excellent progress and I think she will have no difficulty in passing the entrance examination for the school you have chosen.

Yours sincerely,

D. Howells."

At lunch she showed the letter to my father. He read it slowly and said:

"Unreliable sort of chap, eh?"

"You know what I feel about the whole thing," said my mother. "Luckily there is no need for any discussion!"

But she added: "He doesn't even say Miss Laura, and Yours sincerely! It might be the Prince of Wales writing."

"All this education," said my father. "These chaps get above themselves."

That afternoon my mother kept me at her side, obliging me to mark out the tennis court with a machine that dribbled lines of whitewash across the grass. She was in a good humour and talked encouragingly about my future at Claremont.

As soon as I could escape, I slipped through the gate and ran up the street to the schoolmaster's house. Mair answered the doorbell, and did not hide her surprise at my arrival.

"I thought you weren't coming any more?"

"I want to see Mr. Howells."

She asked hopefully: "Are you going to make a fuss?"

At this moment, Mr. Howells opened the door of the parlour and called out:

"Who is there?"

"It's Laura," said Mair.

"Laura?" Mr. Howells came into the hall. "Did your mother not get my note, my child?"

"Yes. But I want to know why."

He hesitated: "Did I not explain clearly?"

For once I felt no timidity, no instinct for polite words or deference.

"It wasn't true ... what you said."

His eyes avoided meeting my own as he said:

"Not true ? Why should you think ... ?"

He held open the parlour door: "Come in, my child." Then standing by the mantelpiece and nervously fingering the bronze Discobolus, he asked again: "Why should you think that my explanation to your mother was not true?"

"You would have said something to me before."

He spread out his hands helplessly. "What could I say? My poor child, why do you search so far, why do you not accept … ? This causes unnecessary unhappiness."

I could only stare obstinately and say: "I want to know."

"Let us sit down."

We sat opposite, staring at each other across the red plush table cover as we had done for so many months.

"You put me in a difficult position, Laura," said Mr. Howells. "There are things which cannot easily be explained to a child of your age. Will you not believe that, if I put a stop to your lessons, I am acting in your best interests?"

I could not speak now, but I shook my head. Mr. Howells' distress was evident on his face.

"It is worse than I had thought," he said. He sprang up and began to pace up and down the room.

"My dear Laura, I have been giving you a drug, a most dangerous and pernicious drug."

He had come to stand close beside me, gazing intently into my eyes as if forcing me to comprehend him.

"Try to understand, child. Imagine that a doctor gives a certain medicine—a harmless, useful medicine, to a great number of his patients. But to certain organisms, this medicine can act as a dangerous drug, create a habit, a craving, so that the patient must always have more and more. What can he do but to cut it off, even if he causes privation and suffering."

I was lost. I understood nothing of what he said. "Learning, knowledge, the questioning of God's ways," he said. "These can be the most dangerous of drugs. How can I take this responsibility, Laura? How can I set your feet upon a path which may lead to your undoing?"

He sat down beside me. Gently, almost shyly, his hand caressed for an instant my hair.

"Reflect a little, Laura. Education is necessary so that you may take your place in the world. You will go to school. When you return you will be a well-educated accomplished young woman. Believe me, that is enough. Ambition, the thirst for knowledge, the desire to find an answer to certain things which God intends should remain mysterious, all this can lead you into great danger. I know that for you, the harmless medicine I dispense may act as a terrible drug."

"I have had what the world would call the advantage of having a number of teachers who were among the most brilliant and subtle scholars of their time. Not only was their own knowledge immense, but they had the gift of inspiring in others the desire to emulate them, to go farther and still farther. I loved those men and believed that I owed everything to them, but today I curse them. What does it matter, we are told, if a man gain the whole world and lose his own soul."

He jumped up and began again to walk up and down the room with his furious, controlled stride. The little room, over-crowded with ugly, useless objects was a ridiculous cage for his tamed energy.

"I should have said this to you long ago, Laura. Or rather, I should never have allowed it to become necessary to say such things. Perhaps you too will curse me one day. Perhaps though, it is not too late. You have understood what I have been saying to you, have you not? It is not too late. You will be tranquil, you will not know remorse."

I got up. I knew now that I should never enter this room again. Even if Mr. Howells relented, even if he were ready to continue as before, our old relationship had become impossible. His words had evoked something which I could not understand but which would always hang between us like a curtain of anguish and heaviness.

Mr. Howells was once more the grave, gentle schoolmaster that Pont-y-Gibby had always known. He opened the door for me and walked with me to the front door, his hand on my shoulder. We said good-bye, standing on the top step.

"You will soon be off, Laura. School will be a new experience for you and a very interesting one."

"I expect so, Mr. Howells."

"I shall be most interested to hear how you get on. Perhaps you will write to Mair when you get time."

"Yes, I will, Mr. Howells."

"Good-bye, my dear child."

"Good-bye, Mr. Howells."

THE SUMMER was almost at an end. The leaves were fading; wasps burrowed in the fallen apples and pears that littered the orchard. Already the Virginia creeper flamed scarlet upon the walls and the great yellow chrysanthemums hung their massive heads in the borders on either side of the drive.

The school term would soon begin now and the house was seething with activity. Two solid trunks had been dragged down from the attic. In the schoolroom, Annie was busily marking my underwear with little tapes bearing my name embroidered in red cotton. A shiny hockey-stick had arrived from Cardiff and my mother had traced my initials on the wood with a red-hot knitting needle. Sponge bags, linen bags, shoe bags were being hastily run up on the sewing machine and tucks were being made in the sleeves of blouses bought to allow for growth.

One day we even made an excursion to Monmouth and there, seated in front of a counter which seemed enormous to my unaccustomed eyes, my mother, a printed list in her hand, ordered handkerchiefs, navy-blue serge knickers, flannel pyjamas and a host of other objects which Claremont College considered indispensable to the well-being of its pupils. When everything on the list had been ticked off, we went to the cutlery department to buy the knives, forks and napkin ring which I must take with me, and leave them to be engraved with my name. Then, exhausted, we took a lift that whisked us up to the restaurant on the fourth floor, where we restored our strength with coffee and meringues.

My parents were being unusually affable. My father assured me that my school-days would be the happiest time of my life and my mother spoke enthusiastically of sports and the benefits of the team spirit. I could see, however, that she was annoyed because I showed so little emotion at the idea of leaving home. She could not have imagined that I should go from her with so little grief and my pleasure in the preparations seemed to her indecent, yet another proof of my selfishness and lack of heart.

"I don't know what they will say to you at Claremont if you are so untidy (or so unpunctual, or so careless)," she would say sharply from time to time, to remind me that, after all, life at school would not be all roses.

But I was impatient to be gone. There was nothing now to retain me in Pont-y-Gibby and my imagination had been at work, creating adorable friends and astonishing successes at work and games. Sometimes, to render these dreams yet more enjoyable, I imagined that Mair accompanied me, witnessing my triumphs and grateful for the protection and kindness which

I should be careful to show her. Only occasionally a cold fear caught at me, late at night, before sleep came, and I remembered that I was going into a strange world, among strange people and that all my roots would remain behind, in the house and garden, the village and the stretch of land that ran on one side to the Beacons, on the other down to the silver ribbon of the Usk. Then I would feel a cramp just in the middle of the stomach and a sudden chill in feet and hands, and I would lie awake, listening to the clock on the landing ticking away the hours and the owls chasing each other, hooting, through the trees in the garden. But when morning came, my fears would have disappeared and I should be eager as ever for departure.

The board-school holidays were over already and all through the day the hum of recited lessons rose from the school-house, punctuated by the shrill uproar of recreation in the play-yard. I had caught sight of Mr. Howells, graver and more withdrawn than ever, it seemed to me, hurrying across the road with an armful of books. Mair I had met several times in the street, shopping with an important air, but she showed no desire for my company and contented herself with a patronizing little wave of the hand. There was no sign of Idris, who continued, no doubt, to spend his days wandering over the Sugar-loaf with a book and a packet of sandwiches to pass the time. I was glad there seemed no risk of meeting him, for our encounter had left me with a feeling of guilt. Yet, I should have liked to have put him out of my mind altogether but, to my annoyance, I had dreamed of him several times and, in my dreams, he harangued great crowds, urged them to revolt, and then his face aged and became thinner and more lined and it was the face of Mr. Howells.

And now it was the last Sunday of the holidays, a grey,

autumnal day, heavy with mist. At ten o'clock I had caught a glimpse of the Howells family, black-clad, on their way to chapel. Then I had accompanied my own family to church and sat beside my mother in the family pew while my father nervously read the lessons. The rough tweed of my mother's suit had caught the moisture of the air, so that tiny drops glistened on the hair and it smelt of peat and dogs. Then I remembered far-off Sundays, so distant that I could not exactly situate them, when I had sat close to her in this same pew, leaning my head against her arm, eyes closed and breathing in this same homely smell, which meant love and security, and unquestioning contentment.

On the steps, we exchanged greetings with Mrs. Williams, who observed sourly that school would do me a world of good; with Miss O'Gorman, who held my hand and begged me to call in for a little parcel she had prepared for me; with Colonel Musgrove, who buttonholed my father in a long, confused conversation about the cubbing season.

"Your last Sunday," said my mother, waiting impatiently for the Colonel to be done. She glanced at me quickly, expecting to arouse a decent sorrow, but I was imagining a sunlit lawn before a huge, rose-red building and a beautiful child who would ask me timidly: "Will you be my best friend?" Her lips tightened and she pointed out sharply that one of my stockings was coming down and that I should soon be in trouble at Claremont if I could not even dress myself properly.

After lunch, because there was nothing else to do, I climbed once more into the oak. In the grey light, the village seemed deader and drearier than ever. Miss O'Gorman, revealed through the only uncurtained window in sight, slept on her bed, the poodle pressed against her bosom. The schoolmaster's house was as white and blind as usual on that day. I should have liked to visit Mair and discuss my departure with her, but I knew that Sunday in Pont-y-Gibby was not a day for worldly visits. The occupants of the house might all have been dead or sleeping, for there was not even a shadow on the blinds to show that someone was stirring in the dim rooms.

I was about to climb down again, since there was nothing to be seen in the village, when I realized that something was happening in the upper room where Mr. Howells—so much I had learned—was in the habit of locking himself up on Sunday afternoons to meditate and read the Bible. Idris must have come into his father's shadowed room and switched on the light, for his long thin silhouette was now distinctly outlined against the curtains. He was gesticulating in an agitated way and, by straining my ears, I seemed to catch the echo of incoherent cries. Idris and his father were evidently engaged in a terrible quarrel and I crept toward the end of the branch till it cracked dangerously, leaning out as far as I could over the road to get a better view of the villa.

Several minutes passed. Idris must have moved away from the window, for his shadow was no longer visible and I began to think that all must be calm again, when a great cry rose from the house.

This time there could be no mistake. It was a long, hoarse cry, a howl of rage and despair that resembled the cry of some tracked-down animal rather than that of a man. It was so loud and so strange that all along the street doors and windows were thrown open and alarmed and curious people came running to their thresholds. The village seemed to be holding its breath, waiting for something that was about to happen.

At that moment I was seized with a sort of sacred terror, a

fear such as is felt before no known danger. I knew that the thing which was about to happen would change the course of my life.

Yet, when the door of the little red brick villa opened at last, the spectacle it revealed was grotesque rather than terrifying. Idris stood on the threshold, his face livid and his clothes disarranged. For a moment I believed that he had gone mad, because of his convulsed features and because he appeared to be struggling with frantic, disordered gestures against some shadow adversary. Then I saw that he was dragging behind him a thing that defended itself weakly, with groans and little breathless cries, that made a futile resistance, hanging back with all its weight and was finally pushed and dragged from the house and out into the road.

It was hard to recognize Mr. Howells in that congested face, those drooling lips, those protruding eyes. His hair hung dankly over his forehead, his tie was pulled sideways. His arms hung limply at his sides, while he dug his heels into the ground, and, shaking his head in foolish obstinacy, weakly opposed the efforts of his son.

I had seen enough drunkards in this country where misery was so commonly forgotten in alcohol, to recognize the condition of the schoolmaster and my first reaction was to burst into a sort of terrified laughter. To see the austere Mr. Howells, always so dignified in his gentle reserve, transformed into this moaning, dislocated puppet, into this hideous piece of wreckage, was at once horrible and comic. I had already learned how fragile can be an apparent reality, but never had the wall of appearance crashed so brutally to pieces. With the disintegration of Mr. Howells, the world itself crumbled suddenly and irreparably into the grotesqueness of disorder.

When the struggling couple reached the pavement, Idris let go his hold on his father's shoulders and the schoolmaster stumbled forward, attempted to regain his balance, then sat down suddenly on the pavement, burying his head in his hands. Even from where I watched, I could hear the sound of his painful sobbing.

It seemed now that the whole village was astir and agog to profit from this unprecedented sensation. The people came running, the road in front of the house was flocked by the crowd, they pushed their way forward with excited cries, stood on tiptoe for a better view. Only the children seemed embarrassed and unhappy. Their laughter was strained, as if they only laughed because it was demanded of them by public opinion, and some of the little ones were crying noisily.

No one paid any attention to Idris at this moment, and I saw that he wore a surprised look as if he was astonished to find himself at that spot and in that situation. I understood instinctively that he had imagined and accomplished an isolated gesture, without understanding that none of the instants of life, not even those which seem the most laden with significance, can be detached from the chain of which each is a link. There would always be a moment before and a moment after. I did not, of course, understand this truth in any precise and certain way, but I knew that Idris had not realized that, after he had accomplished his gesture, he would have to continue his existence, and live out the minutes which would follow that accomplishment. Now, hesitating and uncertain, he realized that he must explain, even before anything was asked of him he must speak.

When at last he made up his mind and the gaze of all those eyes were turned upon him, he appeared with his tall figure towering above the broken form of his father, to be making the funeral oration of his victim. I could not distinguish the words that came stumbling from his mouth but I could see that he was already emptied of his anger. It was no longer the inspired executioner that spoke, but the ashamed son, seeking to justify himself.

He said something. A few words drifted up to me:

"He has done it for years, and for years he has been taking you all in."

He was about to turn away, to retreat into the house, but now a low growl of protest rose from the crowd. Already its mood had changed. The fine bass voice of Rhys the Farm rang out: "Thou shalt honour thy father and thy mother. Undutiful son, breaker of God's commandment!"

Other voices approved him.

"Let him who is without sin throw the first stone," proclaims someone. But: "Woe to him through whom scandal arrives," cried Maggie the Milk. "To think that we have trusted our little ones to that!"

The voices grew sharper. They took this or that side, disputed angrily, and Mr. Howells moaned gently and made vain efforts to rise.

At last two men elbowed their way through the crowd, took him by the shoulders and hoisted him to his feet. Then, half pushing, half dragging him, they helped him along the path and up to the door. As they reached the steps, the door opened and I saw Mair, her face hard and grey as if cut in stone, waiting in the doorway to receive her father.

When, much later, I returned to the garden, I found my mother raking the path. By the tone in which she asked where I had come from, I understood that she knew what had happened. She had no need to question me. My face told her that I had been a witness of the scene.

"Perhaps you will believe me next time I tell you that certain people are not suitable friends for you," she said triumphantly. "I have rather more experience than you, I suppose, and I knew from the start that there was something wrong with that family."

The curtains in the Howells' villa remained drawn, as if there had been a corpse in the house. No one was seen to come in or out. Nesta Morgan hurried back and forth to the school building, haggard and exhausted, with all the weight of school upon her shoulders. In the village the notables met together, argued and discussed. Clans were formed and intrigues were born. On the evening before my departure for Claremont, Mrs. Williams brought a petition addressed to the Ministry of Education, demanding the removal of Mr. Howells. My mother signed it without a word but her eyes glowed as they did on the days when she brought home some silver trophy won at a tournament.

FOUR YEARS of school passed away. Cold, dull years of uniformity, of sleeping in draught-swept dormitories, of meaningless lessons and yet more meaningless games. Four years blotted out of the book of life, without relation to the past or the future.

Each year my mother's face became more strained, more weather-beaten. The lines at the corner of her mouth deepened, her splendid green eyes, flecked with gold, glowed with a sombre fury. She was more energetic than ever, hurrying from the golf-links to the stables, from the stables to the garden, always followed by her band of well-trained dogs.

My father was a fragile ornament; she cosseted him, watched over him, held him constantly imprisoned within her sharp, protective gaze. She was devouring him very slowly, but already almost nothing remained.

Soon I understood that it was unbearable for her to watch me grow to a woman. My figure, my clothes, everything about me that proved I was no longer a child, seemed to her repulsive. Was it on my father's account or on her own? I could not understand. The first time she saw me use powder on my face, her anger was so great that she appeared to me suddenly like an old woman, seamy and bitter. When, in response to Lady Wynn-Evans' repeated invitations, we motored to Abergavenny for tennis with her tall, adolescent sons, she watched me with uneasy concentration, apologizing for my bad play and constantly sending me to retrieve stray balls. On the way home she complained crossly of a headache and said that she should not visit them again for a long time.

"It really isn't fair to expect those great boys to waste their time playing with a child. They were obviously longing for a single between themselves. Lena has no idea how to treat her sons…"

Mr. Howells' name was never mentioned, had indeed never been mentioned in my hearing since that strange and terrible Sunday which reoccurred so often for me, at night, in the deep, tangled world of my dreams. The red-brick villa was occupied by an elderly, grey-faced man from Swansea who was soon to die from duodenal ulcer. Nesta Morgan married and her place was taken by a wizened little woman of uncertain temper. The children who had recited their lessons within the mysterious school-house and played hopscotch in its forlorn yard, had become farm-hands or servant-girls, passing into the remote, adult life into which I, their contemporary, might not be admitted.

The last term was over and I arrived, laden with accumulated belongings, at Llanglaslyn. My new life was there, open, prepared to receive me and I had only to slip into it and be, as my mother so ardently begged me, a nuisance to no one. There was tennis and riding, even a hunt ball or so for pleasure and Infant Welfare so that I might feel myself useful. If I wished to write, certainly no one would prevent me. It was as harmless a way of passing the time as any other, but when I suggested going to the University, my mother fell into a rage.

"You are quite difficult and eccentric enough as it is," she said. "And the people you would meet there would make you worse." Then she asked if I thought that she was made of money, and ended up by saying:

"I know quite well how you got all these foolish pretentious ideas into your head."

The conversation took place in the saddle-room, where I was helping her to polish harness.... . The place smelt of soap and leather and chaff. The light filtered down through the skylight on to the great bins containing oats for the horses and shiny yellow maize for the hens, and through the thin partition we could hear the bay cob grinding his teeth against his manger.

My mother stopped her angry words to bang against the partition.

"Stop it, Starlight!"

The grinding ceased for an instant, then began again.

"A horrible habit!" she said crossly. "I had a mare who did it. Dahlia, she was called. You wouldn't remember ..."

"I remember her," I said. "She had a white star on her forehead."

She looked up in astonishment, forgetting for a moment her anger with me, seeing me again as a little child, docile to her will, and in my own mind I saw her upraised face, still smooth and bright with youth and felt her hand against my thigh, steadying me upon the back of the tall, grey horse.

"Good gracious! You can't have been more than three. It was when your father ..." She broke off biting her lip.

"It was in spring," I said.

"Yes. The first time you were on a horse. Owen was leading you and you were not afraid in the least."

But we could not live together for more than a minute in this happy past.

"You were different then," she said.

"How could I not be? I am grown-up now. I want to live."

"You have your home, your parents, everything you need. Hundreds of girls would envy you."

"You are killing me slowly, at the very moment when I should be beginning to live."

"I think you are mad !" she said violently. "Every word you say shows me how unfit you are to live on your own. You are hysterical, unbalanced. It is my duty to watch over you."

She turned her back and stamped out of the room, leaving me to hook the bridles back on the walls and screw the lid on the tin of saddle-soap. Already I imagined myself slowly turning into the village spinster, catalogued as a little queer, with my memories and no hopes.

With autumn came the rain. The circle of the hills seemed to draw in around the village, their summits wreathed in clouds like grey muslin. Water meandered in muddy rivulets down the street and the little stream that ran beneath a tangle of over-hanging bushes, down by the Methodist chapel, flooded and spread like a shining cloth over the fields.

The garden was full of the dripping of water. My footsteps left water-filled prints on the boggy lawn; the leaves lay rotting in sodden heaps at the foot of the trees and the petals of the last rambler-roses were strewn like wet tissue paper over the grass.

My father sat in the smoking-room, nodding over *The Times* beside an unwilling fire. Twice a day he went for a walk, clad in an ancient deer-stalking hat and an army mackintosh. My mother accompanied him, and indeed, it was rare that she allowed him to leave the house without her. She herself hardly noticed the rain. She bustled from stables to garden, from the garden to the headquarters of the Conservative Union and then to the Vicar's bridge parties.

"What ghastly creatures they are!" she would exclaim, rushing in from the village, tossing off her damp felt hat, her cheeks, where the little red veins showed like crackling on china, aflame with health. And she would add:

"But they count on me so, poor dears. I can't let them down."

When it was fine, she rode or played golf with my father.

"Why don't you learn to play?" she asked me impatiently "You complain of being bored yet you won't do any of the things the girls round here do."

Golf filled me with a passion of boredom. My favourite occupation was to take Starlight and ride, cutting through fog and cloud, up into the hills. One day a sudden impulse led me in the direction of the Sugar-loaf and soon I found myself upon the narrow path that I had followed four years earlier. It seemed less steep and far now and I was astonished to find myself so soon at the summit. The mist eddied and drifted like smoke over the soaked grass and the sheep huddled under roughly-built shelters, bleating protestingly as I passed, as if they imagined that I had the power to make them dry and comfortable. I seemed suddenly to hear Idris' voice saying with conviction:

"One never wants to go back."

I was late for lunch that day. Over the boiled mutton I recounted my expedition. My father, stung to sudden energy, banged down his glass and shouted:

"That path's nothing but flint and Starlight's only soft-shod. You've probably cut her feet to ribbons!"

"You've no more sense than a child," said my mother. "When you want to do something, you just go ahead and do it, without ever thinking of the trouble you cause to others."

"Can't you find something for her to do?" asked my father, spooning his pudding aside with a sulky gesture, demonstrating that I had taken away his appetite.

It was thus that my mother decided that I must find some more useful way of occupying myself and, after consulting Mrs. Williams, she handed me over to the Guide Captain at Llanglaslyn. The captain tried to look pleased and allowed me to stand about, a clumsy and embarrassed assistant, while her girls indulged in various healthy but meaningless pursuits, tracking each other through the sparse woodland of the valley, tying knots in string and unsuccessfully imitating the cries of various wild beasts.

Here I made the acquaintance of Miss Pugh. She was the music teacher at Llanglaslyn and she also taught folk-dancing to the girl-guides. She was a thin little woman with a rat's face, enlivened by shiny, intelligent black eyes. She played the piano energetically, thumping the chords with her eyes on the dancers, calling out instructions while her agile dry-looking fingers scampered uninterruptedly over the keys.

"Down the middle ... (lift your knees, Glenis Hughes). *Up* again ... and *into* the chain ..."

At the end of the second lesson, when the guides had rushed giggling from the hall and I was piling chairs under the scornful eyes of the captain, Miss Pugh invited me to tea at the Tylwyth Teg Tea Shop.

We sat at an orange-painted table, beneath a false rafter, artificially blackened, and drank tea from dainty china cups.

"I admire your dear mother so much," sighed Miss Pugh.

Everyone admired my dear mother, only I was not so sure and I was ready to suppose that only my evil nature stirred in me these doubts and this revolt.

"An inspiration to all of us," said Miss Pugh, helping herself to a muffin. "Always jolly, always on the go, never a thought for herself. I often think some of the younger women round here must feel ashamed of themselves when they see her."

Her bright eyes fixed me. She expected some comment. I nodded, murmured agreement. She lowered her voice, leaned forward confidentially.

"Now you are quite different dear. A more sensitive type, I should think, and perhaps your dear mother does not always quite realize your hopes and longings. Two strong person-alities—yes, dear, you have a strong personality though it may not be quite developed yet, you are so young—it is always difficult! Of course, I know how you adore your mother, but it seems to me that you might care for a friend who shares some of your private interests …?"

The offer was tempting and the fact that Miss Pugh was more than twice my age only made it more seductive. She had read widely and lent me books at the rate of six a week. ("*Not* on Sundays. Promise me, won't you dear?") She had attended lectures at the National Gallery in London and possessed a large collection of reproductions from the Italian Primitives and the Pre-Raphaelites, believing at the bottom of her heart that the latter were slightly superior to the former. On her tinny piano she played Chopin and Mozart, attempted to train my defective musical memory.

Miss Pugh loved everyone and thought everything beautiful. The Botticelli Venus above her mantelpiece was beautiful, so was the calendar, representing a litter of fluffy puppies, offered by the postman in return for his New Year tip. Anything that was too obviously not beautiful was simply not mentioned. When the Times Book Club sent her some novel dealing too crudely with the facts of life, she would tuck it away at the back of the linen cupboard until the time came to return the parcel, and reply to my questions with a firm "Let us not speak of it, dear."

In the same way, all her neighbours were fine and good, the more unpleasant points in their characters being ignored or referred to as their "little ways". Only notoriously evil conduct could remove a man or woman from Miss Pugh's list of fine, good people, but once removed he or she became a "poor thing" and disappeared from her conversation.

When my mother learned that I visited Miss Pugh, she said in her amused voice:

"Poor old girl! She thinks I'm the most marvellous thing on earth!"

Her tone was carefully ironic, but she encouraged our friendship.

Nationalism was in the air. *Cymru am Byth* had founded a branch at Llanglaslyn and Miss Pugh belonged to numberless committees for the encouragement of Welsh music, Welsh poetry, Welsh painting. In spite of my interest she would not allow me to attend these meetings since she knew that my mother did not approve of her new enthusiasms.

"Your dear mother has confidence in me," she would say proudly. "And we must do nothing with which she would not be in complete agreement."

But when it was announced that the National Eisteddfod was to be held at Carmarthen, not fifty miles from Llanglaslyn, Miss Pugh could no longer restrain herself.

"The greatest choirs in the land ... Aberystwyth male choir, the choirs from the Rhondda, from Pontypool. Dai Jenkins will be singing in the tenor event. He has sung in the Scala in Milan, my dear ... One of the great voices of our time. Evan Rhys Evans is Chief Bard, you know. I once heard him preach in Cardiff... such eloquence.... This is a great cultural event, dear."

It was not easy to obtain permission, for my mother disapproved of all interests which she did not share. They were avenues of escape, signals of revolt, reminding her this child she had conceived was no faithful reproduction of herself. So the excursion must be presented to her in the form of a picnic ... a trip to Carmarthen, a good walk over the hills, a concert in the evening and a night at the Temperance Hotel under Miss Pugh's most respectable chaperonage. She consented and so I found myself one morning, with liberty like strong wine in my head, sitting in a grimy railway carriage, opposite Miss Pugh, equally radiant and terribly loquacious.

THIS WAS one of the days of my life, one of the staring, flaring days that not all the passing years would dim in memory. The train was crowded with travellers bound for the Eisteddfod. At every stop more and more people pushed in—peasants and farmers in their Sunday clothes, speaking Welsh or a Welsh-English dialect. They spoke of music, gravely and with erudition, discussing the chances of rival choirs, the force and weakness of each, illustrating their points with sudden bursts of song. Miss Pugh was caught up in the discussion. Two of the Pontypool choir were natives of Llanglaslyn and she was thus its ardent supporter.

"And where will you find such altos as has Pontypool?" she cried triumphantly, but a stocky farmer with the profile of a Spanish grandee protested.

"Ah, but have they a conductor like Mr. Lewis, Treforest? I say nothing against Mr. Parry, but can he hold them like Dai Lewis? He cannot."

"The Treforest tenors were a splinter late in the Pilgrim's Chorus when I heard them at Swansea, Mr. Lewis or no Mr. Lewis," said Miss Pugh pugnaciously.

The farmer hummed a few bars: "The allegro passage? Ah, there's a teaser."

"They say there's a choir down from Flintshire has a great chance," said a stout woman in the corner.

People nodded wisely: "Ah, the North's a dark horse. They say that Anglesey man's a sure for the Bardic Chair."

And so it went on. At the junction we changed on to the main line and the train was so full we had to stand in the corridor. Miss Pugh's hat was pushed to one side, her white gloves were grey, but her face beamed with excited happiness. We ate hard-boiled eggs from the picnic basket, but it was hopeless to try for a drink of tea from the thermos, with all the jogging and jostling in the crowded corridors.

"There were ten thousand people come in yesterday and there'll be more today," said Miss Pugh.

Surely there were more. The little slate-grey town buzzed like a hive. Groups of miners strolled with linked arms down the street, singing ancient hymns that sounded like war-songs. Their faces were shining-clean, but the ingrained coal-dust made deep marks like bruises under their eyes and this gave them a look of strain and suffering in spite of their singing and happy smiles.

Children whirled about in twos and threes, practising their songs, their high bird-voices floating above the chatter. Some journalists took notes; families discussed in tight clusters the chances of such and such a one or gazed into the shop windows. Bright green and red charabancs, coming from every corner of Wales, kept driving into the main square, and out of them tumbled more and more people— rough-looking men from the mountains, trimly-dressed townsfolk, groups from the mining villages of the Rhondda or the factories of Cardiff, Newport, or Swansea. Everyone was speaking Welsh and it was a point of honour that not an English word should be heard.

They had set up the pavilion a little way from the town in a wide valley where grass sprang green as emeralds and fat with juice. Inside, a crowd of people were listening quietly while a little man with black side-whiskers played a composition for the piano. At the end the three white-haired men on the platform, the judges, consulted together for a moment, while in the hall heated argument arose on every side, faces reddened in a fury of contradiction and this or that passage, challengingly hummed, provoked bursts of counter-humming or furious denunciation.

"What will it be when we get to the mixed choirs?" said Miss Pugh with satisfaction.

When the event was over and the difficult *penillion* competition was in full swing, I left the pavilion and went to wander in the valley. There were tents where one might buy tea and buns and I hurried to refresh myself, knowing that Miss Pugh's mind would remain fixed above such mundane matters for a long time to come. Then there were tents where local handwork or vegetables or flowers were spread out on trestles and others where firms from industrial towns in the south were exhibiting agricultural machinery. People wandered about, smoking and drinking tea. A group of little girls was practising for the children's dance team event, weaving in and out of a moving, changing pattern, leaping to the centre with high, prancing steps and clapping their hands with little cries of exaltation. And the clear notes of a harp drifted out from the pavilion and seemed to hang for a moment in the still, sunny afternoon air.

When I slipped back to my place, the contralto solos were hard at it. I had counted on missing them and arriving in time for the male choirs but there had been many entries, it seemed and the event had not long started. A full-bosomed blonde sang an air from Tosca, then came a red-head with a song by some Welsh composer, sung in a voice so sweet and pure that I was suddenly glad to have returned too soon. Then a little dark, thin girl strode pugnaciously to the centre of the stage, signed imperiously with a skinny hand to the accompanist and broke into "O thou that tellest good tidings." Some one said "hush" and pulled at my elbow for I had half risen in my chair in my astonishment. The little dark girl up there was Mair Howells and she stood unperturbed by the gaze of thousands of eyes and sung with the finest contralto that Carmarthen had heard for many a long year.

"Oh, very nice indeed!" said Miss Pugh beside me, clapping hard. "There's a lovely voice. She'll get the prize, no doubt at all."

Then, "Why, Laura dear, where are you off to?" she called, but I was off, treading on people's toes in my haste to reach the aisle.

At the back of the pavilion there was a tent marked: "Competitors only". A steward wearing a red badge stood on guard outside.

"Mair Howells? I don't know the name. She may still be in the pavilion."

He shook his finger at me playfully. "You should learn Welsh, young lady! Forcing me to speak English on a day like this … !"

At this moment Mair herself appeared, holding a music case and patting at her hair with her free hand. She recognized me at once and for a moment it seemed to me that a sort of anguish puckered her face. Then, in an instant, she became a successful young singer, sure of herself, patronizingly pleased to encounter a childhood friend.

"You still live in that stuffy old village? How can you bear it, Laura? I am studying singing in Cardiff and next year I am going abroad. But come (she tugged at my arm, nervous and restive as an oat-fed horse) I want to hear the judging. Stay with me."

She pulled me along, feverish, her mind fixed on one thing only.

"Do you think I shall win?"

"I am sure you will," I said sincerely.

She flashed me a grateful smile and I thought—She is not so sure as she pretends to be.

"It's very important for me," she said. "If I win, I shall *force* them to give me a travelling scholarship next year."

We squeezed through the crowd at the main entrance and stood by one of the pillars. The judging had just begun and a venerable old person with a long white beard was going minutely into the points of the first singer's voice. I turned to whisper to Mair, too impatient to listen to this half-understood rigmarole, but she jabbed her elbow into my ribs and hissed savagely between her teeth. All her nerves were strained towards the moment when she would hear her own name spoken. Till this moment was safely past nothing else would exist for her.

I resigned myself, waiting impatiently while the incomprehensible voice droned on. I could see Miss Pugh screwing her head round, peering to left and to right, anxious at my sudden disappearance. At last I heard Mair's name. White-beard was speaking impressively, his hand uplifted as if in blessing. There came a storm of applause as he announced the marks awarded.

Mair clutched my hand, but I was not there for her. She would have clutched at a chair or anything else. Her eyes shone like lamps, but she signed to me not to speak.

"Wait a bit. There are more to come."

But there was no doubt about it, Mair had won. Her name was announced again at the end of the judging and there was another crackle of applause and people craned their necks to look at the little, dark contralto standing so modestly at the back of the hall, blushing with downcast eyes, a picture of modest confusion.

"And now the male voice choir ..."

"Come outside," said Mair.

At the fringe of the valley we found an oak tree, whose knotted roots formed comfortable niches for backs and elbows. The spot was relatively deserted; only a young couple were kissing and eating sandwiches at a little distance, absorbed in their own affairs and a few people strolled across the grass, talking or singing.

"Ants!" said Mair, flicking with her handkerchief.

We settled ourselves comfortably.

"Now tell."

I could think of nothing to tell. Nothing had happened, nothing ever would happen. There were a few incidents and I made the best of them for Mair's benefit, but as I spoke, there in the shade of the big tree, watching the people moving about in the soft late-afternoon sun, I thought to myself— I am alive today and I was alive for a little time, back in those old days when Mair and I were children, but between, really there has been nothing and I might have been dead or asleep all this long while.

Mair was leaning back, dreamily squashing the ants that scurried over her legs. She, too, was filling in the gap, but my mind, wandering among my own affairs, had let her words escape and with them a couple of years of her history.

"It was chapel, chapel, chapel," she was saying, "And reading the Bible and singing hymns to a piano half a tone out. I couldn't stand it, so I made her glad to get rid of me. She passed me on to another aunt in Cardiff. That's the one I'm with now. She's not bad, she lets me do as I like. I got

Cecily Mackworth

Professor Vaughan-Jones to listen to my voice and he's been giving me lessons for nothing ever since."

"You always knew what you wanted, didn't you?"

"Of course, I'd be a fool if I didn't. Do you remember I told you once I was going to be a great singer in Paris. It was raining and you were trying to be grand about your parents. Well, I haven't changed. That is just what I'm going to be."

I said, "I thought Germany or Italy were the places for singers. Why Paris?"

"An idea."

She lowered her eyelids and the thick lashes painted a fringe of shadow across her cheekbones. I knew where that idea had been born and for a moment I seemed to feel the rough red plush of the tablecloth beneath my hand and the low, controlled voice of Mr. Howells sounded in my ears.

Without stopping to reflect, I asked: "And your father?"

The long, soft lashes lifted. Her eyes were two oblong shapes of black glass, her mouth was a straight line gashed across her face.

"He killed himself. Don't speak of him."

Now that she had spoken, I realized that I had expected no other answer, that this death was already an ancient and familiar sorrow. There was a moment of constrained silence and I knew that the same image was passing through both our minds. Both of us were remembering the village street, the whispering, scandalized crowds, Idris' face, where hate for his father struggled with horror for himself, and the impotent figure huddled upon the ground. But this image must never be evoked between us. The past was dangerous ground if I wished to preserve our friendship.

I asked myself, glancing sideways at Mair, who stared

sulkily before her, black eyebrows drawn in a knot above the saddle of her sharp little nose, whether I did so wish. I had never really liked her and time had not increased our mutual sympathy. Yet for some reason liking had nothing to do with this friendship. Mair was, with, perhaps, the exception of Owen, who was inarticulate, the only person in whose mind I existed as a complete human being. For the rest of the world I was the daughter of the wonderful Mrs. Gethryn, entirely overshadowed by her. For Mair, wonderful Mrs. Gethryn was a slightly ridiculous figure, wasting a lot of energy over nothing in particular and I was Laura, a person in my own right. I knew, too, that in some obscure way Mair was jealous of me and for this jealousy I felt passionately grateful.

A westerly breeze brought the deep singing of the male choirs drifting to the edge of the valley. I became conscious of the sound when it ceased and the air felt empty with the absence of music. The sunlight had grown paler now and the shadow of the oak tree had spread out like a great black carpet over grass that the approach of evening had drained of colour.

"What will Miss Pugh be thinking?"

"Who's that?" Before I could answer she laughed and said: "Oh, I suppose you have a dragon to guard you. They wouldn't let you come alone, would they?"

She herself had come with a chapel party from Cardiff, as well chaperoned as I, but she managed to make me feel like a little girl out with her governess.

As we approached the pavilion, she turned suddenly and caught my hand in hers.

"Laura! Do you remember, you said you would come to Paris too? Will you? We could live together?"

Her face was gentle and appealing. She really wanted me.

"How could I do it? They won't even let me go to the university."

"Speak to them."

"I have. It's no good."

"Will you stay all your life there, in that hole?"

"All my life … It sounds so long."

"No. It's short, terribly short. Just one life for all one wants to do… ."

The crowd was emptying out of the pavilion. The day's competitions were over and people would be returning to town for supper and a rest before the Bach concert in the evening. I caught sight of Miss Pugh, pince-nez askew, worried to death, darting about in search of me.

"Look," said Mair, "I'll write to you when I know for certain. Does she open your letters?"

"Of course not." But I knew that I was expected to open my rare letters at the breakfast table and to mention the name of the sender.

Mair must have caught the doubt in my tone, for she said: "She'll make a fuss if she knows I write to you. She always disapproved of me. I shall sign Marjorie. It's a nice reliable name and you can say it was one of your school friends."

Miss Pugh caught sight of me before I could answer and skipped up, panting and reproachful.

"Where did you get to, dear? I've been quite anxious."

I introduced Mair hastily but Miss Pugh was too flustered to give her much attention. Later, as we bolted our sausages in the gothic dining-room of the Temperance Hotel, one eye on the clock, she said:

"That girl you were with, dear? Isn't she the one who won the contralto event?"

"Yes, she used to live in our village." I folded my napkin resolutely. "Time to be going."

"How strange! A lovely voice! Perhaps we shall have the chance of a chat tomorrow."

"She is with friends," I said. "I didn't know her very well."

The evening passed without a sight of Mair. Next day I caught a glimpse of her squashed between two severe looking chapel members, watching the chairing of the Bard. In the evening I returned home.

IT WAS autumn, it was winter, it was spring.

One morning there was a letter in a strange handwriting waiting beside my plate when I came to breakfast. For a moment the signature puzzled me, for I knew no one named Marjorie. Then I remembered Mair.

My mother looked at me enquiringly.

"A girl I knew at school… Marjorie Hardwicke."

Mair's letter said:

"Everything goes so slowly. People promise you this and that and nothing ever gets done. I know I shall get to Paris, but life is going by and perhaps by the time I am famous I shall be too old to enjoy it.

"A man from the Royal College of Music in London was here last week and Professor Vaughan-Jones made me sing in front of him. He said he thought I had a future and that means a lot for an Englishman.

"This is just to let you know that it is *serious* (The word was underlined so hard that the pen had torn through the paper) that I shall be in Paris soon and I shall expect you to come and join me. I am learning French. You speak it awfully well, don't you? So that will be one up to you.

"How are those awful parents of yours. Tell them Marjorie was a hockey captain or something and had a healthy influence on you."

I could feel myself blushing. It seemed that the words must be reflected in gigantic characters on the wall, clear for all to see. But my mother was absorbed in a discussion about the sale of one of the horses and took no interest in my correspondence.

And then, astonishingly soon, there came a post card from Paris, a post card showing a view of Notre-Dame and bearing the message: "I am here. Expect you soon."

My mother had not noticed the card. She was looking out of the window, intent on the weather.

"I think it's going to clear up soon. We might drive up to the links."

My father nodded: "Time to get some exercise."

"Yes, I think we'll risk it," she said. "Laura can carry my clubs. If she got more fresh air she wouldn't always be catching those awful colds."

We motored up to the links and by the time we arrived the sun had pierced through and was shining uncertainly. Now and again puffs of light cloud drifted across its face and brought a spatter of fine rain. A very pale rainbow appeared for a few moments, looking as though its colour had been almost soaked away. Our feet squelched over the rough grass and the little holes that held the flag at the centre of each green were full of water. The balls fell into the holes with a plop like the drawing of a cork and a tiny water-spout shot up into the air, trembled and collapsed.

As we walked slowly along at my father's pace, I thought of Mair. She was in Paris. She walked by the banks of a shining river that cut the city in two. A marble thread of a bridge spanned the water. She crossed it, her feet skimming on its surface, her eyes shining like diamonds. On the other side there was a wide avenue edged with chestnut trees that formed a roof of pink blossom over her head. Nearby there was the great, twin-spired church of the postcard, terrible and lovely, with gargoyles leaning out, ready to snap at her hair as she ran beneath them. But she paid no attention to this great cathedral, nor to the plain-chant that drifted from its open doors, but ran on, snapping her fingers at the gargoyles and then there was a place where the pavement was as wide as a field and people in gay dresses sat in the sun, holding glasses of brightly-coloured liquids and the sun sparkled in the glasses and shone on the pale hair of the women.… .

When the game was finished we went to the clubhouse. The rain had started again and the damp cold seemed to explore with clammy fingers beneath my clothes, but a cheerful fire was burning in the deserted lounge. My father went to the bar and fetched whisky for my mother and himself and a glass of lemonade for me. My mother took a copy of the *Tatler* from the table and began to study the portraits of cool débutantes with their fiancés inset in the right-hand corner.

"Ethel Bellenger's girl… . What a fright she looks! Here's one of the Altringhams engaged to a boy in the Navy…"

My father rose, glass in hand, and wandered again to the bar. Then he sank down once more in the leather-covered armchair and absorbed himself in *Country Life*. My mother looked anxious.

"Edward! That's a double whisky!"

"That's right, my dear," mumbled my father. "Ward off my rheumatism…"

"But Edward …"

"You don't want me to go lame again, do you?" he asked, squirting soda.

"It's not good for you," said my mother, doubtful and irritated as she was whenever a direct difference of opinion opposed her to her husband. He paid no attention, tossed off the whisky in a few gulps. His hands began to tremble a little, he went over to the window, stared out.

"Raining like billy-o again. We'd better wait till it clears a bit."

"Look at this," said my mother, "Bob Lanchester at the Dublin Cup. I haven't seen him for ages."

My father was out of the door. We could hear the barman say:

"Nothing like a spot of this stuff to keep out the rain, eh, Colonel Gethryn?"

"Quite right, Jones. Quite right."

He returned.

"It's all right, Molly. A single one this time."

"I can't stop you, I suppose," she said stiffly.

Bored to death, I had absent-mindedly taken Mair's card from my pocket to gaze again at the glossy photograph of Notre-Dame. Suddenly my father made a playful and rather unsteady grab at it.

"Aha, Paris!"

He turned it over and read, frowning.

"Who's this woman who expects you soon? She must be mad. Does she think you're going gadding out there?"

He sat there, the glass held loosely in his hand, a few drops shining on the ends of his straggly moustache, in his eyes was a look of sullen ill-temper, the look of an animal made savage by pain it cannot understand. "Paris!" he said again, giving a sort of snort that puffed a gust of whisky-laden breath in my direction. He was ready for aggression and I, who hardly noticed this really harmless and inconspicuous creature when he was in his normal state, responded at once, was ready at once to give battle.

But my mother intervened: "What nonsense! Of course Laura isn't going to Paris." She gathered up her gloves and suède jacket. "I can't say I am enjoying this very much. We had better be going."

But my father paid no attention. He sat there staring stupidly at the card, turning it over and over in his hand and saying furiously: "Paris!" as though he was speaking the name of some intimate enemy.

"Of course she isn't going to Paris," said my mother again with angry patience. "Why must you always cause trouble?" she said to me bitterly.

Suddenly I felt a hatred for my parents that astonished me. It was no longer the dull resentment, mingled with unwilling nostalgia, that I had known for so many years, but a fine fury, a liberating burst of rage.

"I shall go wherever I like," I screamed at them. "Anywhere away from you. I hate you …"

Out in the rain, on the steep hillside road, this outburst began to seem a little childish and indeed the whole scene ridiculous, but I was trembling and crying so much that it seemed impossible I should ever stop. I walked on, glad of the rain that was soaking swiftly through my clothes and the cold and discomfort that fitted my mood so well, not caring at all where I went so long as it was not in the direction of home. Quite soon I began to realize with pleasure that this would mean yet another attack of bronchitis and for a time I enjoyed the vengeful prospect of dying in a ditch. But it was not to be for here was a car drawing up beside me and Lady Wynn-Evans' kind voice saying:

"My dear Laura! What on earth are you doing here without a mackintosh?"

The comfort of her leather cushions seemed after all preferable to a ditch. We sped along the Abergavenny road.

"I am taking you back to lunch," she said. "We will telephone your mother."

The great house seemed strange and empty in the absence of Sir Thomas, with his baying voice, and of Mervyn and Robert, who were one in the Army and the other at Cambridge. Lady Wynn-Evans and I lunched alone in her little sitting-room, where a folding table had been opened and set in front of the blazing log fire. I had always considered the Wynn-Evans as rather grand people who were much richer and lived in a more ceremonious way than my own parents and this simplicity seemed to me a mark of special friendship. The room smelt of verbena and hot-house roses; flames sent their shadows chasing across the pale silver-green walls; my chilled feet, thawing at last in my hostess's furry bedroom slippers, sank into a soft, pale carpet. I felt warm and happy, yet somehow unreal, as though I had slipped unexpectedly into another world and as though a great gap of time already separated me from the scene in the clubhouse. It was imposs- ible, in this harmonious atmosphere, not to grow confidential. Lady Wynn-Evans' questions were so tactful that they were mere suggestions, a hand held out, that one might grasp or not as one wished. Soon we were talking as I had never talked to anyone. I told her everything about my life, not clearly, for I could not yet see it myself in any recognizable pattern, but with disconnected anecdotes, unthreaded memories, and through it all I was telling her of my desire to be gone.

When I had finished she asked me what I should like to do with my life if I were free to choose.

"How can I tell?" I said. "I think I should like to be a writer, but first I want to know what life really is and how other people live. Until I know that I cannot tell whether I am able to write or what I should do with the years to come."

"If you went away from your home, would you not think of it all the time and want to come back to it?" she asked.

"I should never think of it except with hatred," I said.

We sat silent for a long time, holding out our hands to the dancing flames.

"I have known your mother for many years," she said at last. "She is a fine woman, a woman I have always admired, but she has had a hard life and she has become hard and rigid to meet it. If she had not made herself hard her troubles would have been too great for her."

"Why do you say she has troubles," I asked. "She does as she likes in every way."

"She appears to do so," said Lady Wynn-Evans. "But is it only in appearance. Your father is also a good and fine man whom everyone must respect, but he received terrible wounds during the war. You are so young," she said. "It is difficult to explain certain things to you, but he was wounded in such a way that he has come to resent everyone and everything. He feels that the world has been cruel to him. He longed for a son, so did your mother. They have only you and they love you dearly but both of them, I think, formed too clear a picture of what they wanted and they cannot understand how you have grown up to be so different to the image in their minds.

Your mother has a very strong, violent nature. She was very much spoilt as a girl and grew up to think that her life would be always just as she wished it to be. She has had terrible disappointments that she still refuses to accept. She still believes, for instance, that she can mould all those she loves into a form of her own choosing. That is impossible of course, people are as they are, they cannot be changed."

This was a new and strange view of my mother and I felt at once that Lady Wynn-Evans was partly, though not wholly right. Her words smoothed away my anger. If I thought of my mother as being unhappy, I could at once love her again.

"I have thought for a long time that it would be better for everyone if you were away from your parents for a time," she went on. Then, after a moment, she asked:

"Would you like me to speak to your mother?"

"I have asked her so often," I said.

"I expect you are not very tactful, Laura dear. Your mother does not like opposition."

"It is so terrible to have to use tact, which is really only cunning, between people who love each other. Surely mother and daughter should be too close for ruse and feinting to be necessary ?"

"You are like your mother," she said. "You want the world to be just as you like to imagine it and you refuse any concessions to reality."

The idea that I was like my mother made me laugh and she, too, smiled gaily and asked:

"What am I to say to Molly?"

"Do you think she would let me go to Paris, for instance ?"

"Many girls do. It is quite a usual thing, after all. I know your mother worries a great deal about your health, and I think she would agree that a change from this damp climate would do you good. One of my own nieces studied art in Paris and lived in a student's hostel where she was very well looked after."

"I cannot believe this could come true."

"Why not? Many things come true when one is young."

We sat a little longer, then Lady Wynn-Evans said:

"Ellis will drive you home now. I will come to see your mother very soon and have a talk with her. I shall be taking a great responsibility but I know that you are sensible as well as clever and if I do succeed in persuading her you will know how to make the best of your opportunities and will avoid doing anything foolish that would make me regret my intervention."

She accompanied me to the front door where the car was waiting.

"My boys often ask after you," she said. "You must come over when you are home for the holidays."

She was sure of her power to help, this gentle, yielding woman. She spoke already as though she had won her cause. I should live in a strange land, among unknown people, live a life which I could not yet imagine. I should come home for the holidays and tell of all the exciting things I had seen and learnt. My mother and I would find each other again. She would understand. She would listen and make plans with me.

"What are you studying, Laura? Who are your friends? Who are your teachers ?" The life I should describe to her would seem to her strange and fascinating. One day she would visit me out there. I should show her every thing, introduce her to my closest friends. Surely she would be taken for my sister, she looked so young and vigorous when she was in a good mood. Life was going to change. Everything would come right.

foolish ideas.
She turns her back & walks out.

          x   x

Yet I got my way, unexpectedly.
An attack of bronchitis brought a specialist
from Cardiff & the specialist looked grave,
tapping my chest with a chilly stethoscope
& explained to my mother that the
damp climate of Wales was undermining
my health.

"Send her away," he said. "She needs
sun & the company of young people."
And suddenly her resistance
crumbled away. She seemed tired
Tired of my presence, of the tension
it brought to her home, of the continual
watchfulness it imposed on her, of
the constant necessity of shielding my
tension it imposed between herself
& my father from annoyance. Almost
overnight, the decision was taken. I must
go to Paris, live

This page from an earlier draft of the novel attributes Mrs Gethryn's change of mind to Laura's ill-health rather than Lady Wynn-Evans' advice (see p. 89). Cecily Mackworth Papers.

PART II

THE INTERNATIONAL Home for Female Students was situated near the Boulevard St. Michel and the tumult of the Latin Quarter seemed to sweep through it like wind through a heap of ruins. The noise of the streets, with their raging traffic and babel of voices echoed in the corridors and staircases, eddied in cloak-rooms and common-room and grew to hysterical pitch in the refectory where the simultaneous clanging of a hundred tin trays evoked the cymbals of some diabolic orchestra.

The walls of the entrance hall were plastered with notices; the music club, the language club, lecture time-tables, con-certs, offers and requests for private tuition. The letter rack was in the same hall, so that in order to penetrate into the living quarter one had to elbow one's way desperately through a seedling mob of girls, who craned on tiptoe to peer over each other's shoulders at the notices or forced a passage to and from their private pigeon-holes in the letter-rack. Beyond the hall there was a common room, with the newspapers and magazines and a battered ping-pong table, and beyond that another room, around the wall of which were hung notices written in chinese ink, enjoining silence. Here there were a number of little tables with inkwells containing a deposit of fluff and sediment and a row of shelves, referred to as "the library", with dictionaries, atlases and a Larousse encyclo-paedia. There was also the study of the directress and a slimy-floored cloakroom. The whole of this floor smelt of cooking from the refectory in the basement.

Upstairs, some municipal architect had adapted the great rooms, dating from the Second Empire, to their present use by dividing them into a series of smaller rooms by means of plywood partitions. As a result, they were oblong-shaped, reminiscent of coffins. My room was on the second floor. It contained a brass bedstead, with a plump red eiderdown and a crocheted bedspread; a wash-basin surmounted by a mirror and a shelf for my toilet things; a wicker armchair; a table with a brass inkstand representing the Eiffel Tower, and a bookshelf. When I had piled my notebooks on the table and installed the Oxford Book of English Verse, an anthology of modern verse and two novels by D. H. Lawrence in the bookshelf, I felt suddenly at home. The hole in the carpet, the feeble, naked glare of the electric light, the clamour of the streets that kept me awake at nights, were of no importance. For the first time in my life I was free of continual constraint. Yet liberty was so strange to me that I hardly dared to taste it. I moved in this new climate as gingerly as a swimmer adventuring into a sea of clearest azure that may be peopled by ravening sharks and terrible, poisonous sea-plants.

Because the great city frightened and bewildered me, it was some weeks before I began to venture out of the Latin Quarter. At first my horizon was bounded by the University and the Luxembourg Gardens, each of them a bare five minutes walk from the hostel.

The Luxembourg Gardens flamed in this late autumn season with red and yellow dahlias and the fountain catapulted a hail of diamonds into the sun. The Pantheon was veiled in blue mist. Students walked arm in arm, eating chestnuts from paper bags, repeating their lessons to each other, stopping sometimes to kiss, brushing their lips for an instant together, then bending their heads again over the open book, murmuring: "The consequence of Fournier's theorem"; "François de Guise at the Battle of Metz ..." Children scurried in a medley of balls and skipping ropes, deaf to the shrill cries of nursemaids, and young priests passed three by three, the tips of their cassocks brushing the crimson and gold of fallen leaves.

This was not the world as I had known it. It might have been a different planet, infinitely beautiful, gay and troubling. I, bringing with me the world of my childhood like a chrysalis covering that I could not shed, was as solitary in the flaming garden as if I had lived like an unusual shell-fish within a little portable glass house that isolated me from my surroundings without obscuring my vision.

I liked to imagine that one day I, too, would walk beside some tousled young man, feeling the ridge of his arm along my waist, that I would repeat: "The negotiations between Turenne and Christian of Denmark", and hear him say impatiently: "No, no ... Condé!" and feel his lips brush for an instant, as casually as the wing of a bird, against my own.

Meanwhile it would sometimes happen that from some group of students, one would hail me with a wave of the hand, a swift *"bonjour!"* or *"comment ça va?"* so that a crack marred for an instant the smooth glass, then closed again and left it as inviolate as if no one had passed. Children charged into me, dogs leapt in sudden friendship against my skirts, old men followed me, smiling rosily and passing the tips of their tongues over their lips. But I was enfolded by the Welsh hills and the passing of nineteen years and it seemed to me that all this was happening thousands of miles away and that I myself had somehow moved backward or forward in time, and might return at any moment, without movement or apparent transition, to my normal state of being.

Then, in occasional moments of terror, I felt that this normal state had disappeared, it was no longer there to return to and that I had taken an irrevocable leave of my own world without having had the prudence to make sure that another existed.

In the lecture halls of the Sorbonne I listened to elderly men speaking of the French Renaissance and the poetry of the troubadours, and these seemed less distant than the lunch of rissoles, vegetables and jam which I should presently consume in the refectory or than the conversation that morning with my neighbour, Mademoiselle Huguette Rodier, while waiting in the queue for the bathroom.

"Mademoiselle Gethryn has a sense of history," said Professor Demarest, handing back my essay and little realizing that the Duc de Joyeuse appeared to me no more distant and unreal than his own substantial figure.

Mair had written from Cardiff that she would be returning to Paris in the autumn, but I had no news of her. Every morning I joined the crowd of girls who scrambled and jostled before the letter-rack, in the hope that there would be a letter either from her or my mother. From her there was never a sign, but once a week, regularly, there was a square blue envelope containing a single page from my mother. She wrote stiffly, giving brief news of the village and enquiring after my health, but she never mentioned the news which I sent her in my own weekly letters. This reticence, I knew, was a mark of disapproval. It conveyed, as clearly as any words: You are living your own life against my judgment, therefore that life does not exist so far as I am concerned. Presently I began to retaliate in the same manner, detailing my own activities in a dutiful way but taking no account of her news, so that, to any third party reading our correspondence, it would appear as though neither of us ever received the letters of the other.

One day, in early December, returning from a lecture on philology, I found an envelope addressed to me in Mair's huge, curly writing. Without explanation or apology she gave an address in the rue Jacob and invited me to call on her on the following day.

I had been waiting for this letter so long and with such impatience that it seemed indeed a pity it should arrive on the one day when it must come almost as an anti-climax. The previous evening I had had an experience which was none the less exciting because it would have been taken as a matter of course by most of the students of various nationalities who lived at the hostel. I had been taken out by a young man. For the first time in my life I had been deliberately singled out from among other girls. I had been almost, if not quite, kissed. Although it was hard to believe that the pleasant excitement I had felt at the time was the love about which I had heard so much, it was at least a new and stimulating sensation.

The young man's name was Jean-Pierre Carré. Twice he had sat beside me at lectures and filled his fountain pen from ink dribbled out of my own. He was young, fresh-faced, with a sort of shy resoluteness in his manner. We had sat side by side in the dark little cinema watching the passionate caresses of Marlene Dietrich and her partner. Jean-Pierre's arm lay close to my arm, inert but warm and living. Sometimes his thigh touched my own. Afterwards we had gone to a café where we drank beer and discussed our professors. Presently Jean-Pierre had taken my hand in his own.

"Such pretty hair you have," he had said. "So soft." And he had leaned towards me so that his face touched my cheek. The contact had been enough to melt some precarious armour of indifference which was perhaps only that of inexperience. I had felt my face stiffen and freeze in the effort to hide the alarming fact that I suspected myself at that moment to be capable of what my mother referred to with tight and bitter lips as "disgusting behaviour".

Jean-Pierre had dropped my hand, but he remained pleasant and comradely. When we arrived at the pension the last couples were parting reluctantly and the porter was waiting, key in hand, to bolt and bar the door between one hundred and fifty young women and the temptations of the flesh.

So the next morning Mair's letter was less of an event than it might have been. I looked forward above all to discussing Jean-Pierre with her, but experience made me doubtful whether she would give me the chance. I found her in a sort of studio on the sixth floor of one of those ancient, decaying houses where every apartment, if one may believe local gossip, has been inhabited by the mistress of a king. There was a large hired piano, an iron bedstead and very little else, but Mair was radiant. Her black eyes shone like polished boot buttons, she was never still for an instant, skipping to the piano to play a series of chords, pulling me to the cupboard to inspect her clothes, pushing me down on an upturned packing case while she made tea over a spirit stove. She was immensely proud of living on her own and made no secret of the fact that she had been in Paris for the last ten days, too busy "moving in" to write to me.

Mair was a Parisian now. She had taken on local colouring as foxes in polar regions take on white coats with the approach of winter. Her sing-song Welsh accent had almost disappeared and now she rolled her r's throatily and sharpened her vowels till one would have sworn that French was her native language. Her sharp little face was skilfully painted and even the ill-cut, schoolgirlish clothes, bought in Cardiff, had taken on a careless chic, conveying the impression that they belonged to the lowest rank of a well-stocked and expensive wardrobe and were only worn because they suited an informal occasion.

We sat on the packing cases and drank tea from china pudding-bowls.

"Isn't this *extraordinary*!" said Mair.

"Extraordinary!"

We lapped in silence and before the eyes of each of us stretched a grey village street, bordered with houses where all the blinds were drawn in celebration of the Sabbath.

"I am glad you are here," I said presently. "I was lonely."

She stared. "How can one feel lonely in Paris! My trouble is, I have too many friends, it's all I can do to find time to work. I won't let anything interfere with my work."

"I haven't many friends yet," I said humbly.

She waved her hand carelessly. "Oh, I'll introduce you. Of course, most of mine are musicians. You may not fit."

My heart sank. I felt sure I should not fit. Mair had changed less than I imagined at Carmarthen. The price of her friendship was still the right to patronize.

"I've only been here a few weeks," I said. "I shall get to know people in time."

She pursed her lips. "Other foreigners, yes. It takes ages to get into a French set if one isn't properly introduced."

"Were you ?"

"Oh, there's an old boy who was professor in father's day. Monsieur Sougny. He's about eighty now. He used to invite me to his house and I met a lot of people there and that started it. He has a sort of regular day once a week when everyone goes there. He's quite famous in his way."

I waited for her offer of an introduction, but she remained silent, with that obstinate look in her eyes which meant that she had no intention of doing what was expected of her.

"I haven't been there for ages," she said suddenly. "It was rather a bore really."

She began to tell me about her work at the Conservatoire, her successes, her chance of obtaining a *premier prix* at the end of the year. It occurred to me to wonder whether she had ever had a lover. I hoped not. It would increase the distance that was widening between us, as if, of two runners in a race, one should draw steadily ahead. Yet a certain reticence of manner, a skidding away from certain subjects, warned me that the weight of her innocence was less crushing than that of my own. The episode of Jean-Pierre seemed now too tenuous to crystallize in words and offer up to her probable mockery. Indeed, during this short hour that I had spent with her, my interest in this gay and charming student had strangely declined. I could hardly remember the ordinary but pleasant cast of his features. My desire, I understood now, was for landmarks, to assure me that, even in the tumultuous strangeness of this city, I was still Laura, the very Laura who for nineteen years had moved among the Welsh mists and heard the pounding cataract in the mountain as a distant background to all other sound. And it was not the name of Jean-Pierre that rose to my lips, but that of Idris.

Mair turned on me the eyes of a frustrated witch.

"Never say that name to me. I'll have nothing to do with him. I have told him so."

"I understand. Yet you are both alone now."

"I would sooner be alone all my life than speak to him."

Instead of turning away in a fury, as I half expected, she turned to me as if for help.

"Oh, Laura! He should never have been born …"

"He did a terrible thing," I said. (But why must we speak of it; Why were we again on this treacherous, slippery ground that would lead our friendship to destruction?)

"The scandal!" she said. "The staring and the whispering! Our name dragged in the mud!"

That was the picture that had remained with her. We should never understand each other. In all this foreign place, no one was more foreign to me than Mair.

She glanced at her watch. Coldly she said she had an appointment for dinner. I left her with the thought that we should not meet again.

But Mair was more faithful than I believed. Before the end of the week there was another letter waiting in my pigeon-hole. We met in a dimly-lit café that smelt of ancient dust. She took me to concerts given by students at the Conservatoire. We ate together in restaurants where impoverished students devoured doubtful food. We spoke always of the future now. We strained towards it like dogs on a leash. Life could not go quickly enough for us. We were waiting constantly for something that was always just about to happen.

A FEW WEEKS later, the great frost set in. Paris became a city of diamond and crystal, like the home of a king's daughter of fairy tales. Ice crackled beneath my feet when I walked in the streets. Little tongues of ice hung from doorways and window ledges. Mair broke them off and sucked them with an air of wistful greed. The trees were like lace, chiselled in ivory against a sky of intense blue.

The hostel was badly heated and Mair, whose scholarship barely covered the cost of food and lodging, could seldom afford coal. I had got into the habit of coming frequently to work in her studio and there we shivered, crouched under blankets, warming our hands on bowls of steaming tea. When Mair had managed to thaw her fingers a little in this way, she would run to the piano, strike a few chords, begin the interminable vocal exercises which her professor imposed on her. The breath rose from her mouth like steam from a kettle. Soon her fingers stiffened again. Then she would huddle back into her blanket, warm her fingers and start to practice once more. She had astonishing courage and determination.

I had made a sort of tent out of my blanket and I squatted inside it, with my books and note-books, breathing hard in the hope of creating a zone of hot air. Sometimes my reading interested me so much that I forgot to feel cold but I was less obstinate than Mair and when my fingers began to grow numb, I would leave her and take refuge in some café where I could read for hours for the price of a *crême*.

In the evening, there was nothing warmer than a cinema, but it was often beyond our means. Sometimes Jean-Pierre would call for me at the hostel after dinner and take me to cafés in Montparnasse or the Latin Quarter, where the students from the Sorbonne liked to spend their evenings, or to lectures on the political situation or to discussion meetings at various clubs. I had introduced him to Mair, who found him ordinary and considered that he wasted my time. But when we were alone, he would sometimes take my hand, and then his face would change and become full of life and meaning and his eyes soft and tender. These moments were filled with expectancy. They seemed to promise something, although I was not sure what it would be, or even what I wished it to be. Mostly, though, we were with other people, students on the edge of manhood, who sometimes wrestled and played like children. Then Jean-Pierre would be as noisy as any of them, teasing me, imitating my English accent and playing practical jokes.

One day I was just leaving Mair's house to go to a lecture, when I noticed a man who, at the moment when I reached the road, stepped from an entrance gate opposite. After a few minutes I realized that he was following me and I hurried on, feeling his gaze like a physical touch between my shoulder blades. I found it hard not to turn round and meet his eyes. It had always seemed to me that the fact that someone should take in me an interest, from whatever motive, sufficient to turn him from his route, to make him go where I went, created between us a sort of inavowable understanding. The very fact of following me seemed to give the unknown man a mysterious right over me, so that it was as if the passive, involuntary state of being followed constituted a subtle and inexplicable sin.

The man's steps rang heavy against the frozen stone. He seemed decided to catch up with me, but I quickened my pace, feeling my cheeks stiffen in the bite of the wind. Now the steps were close behind me. A man's tall figure loomed at my side.

"Laura …"

I turned sharply. A young man, very tall, very thin, very dark, stood by my side. He wore a long, loose overcoat and a red scarf. His ears, jutting above the folds of the scarf, were scarlet with cold.

In a tone of reproach he said: "I've been waiting for you for nearly two hours. I saw you go up with Mair and I hoped you might come down alone."

He did not doubt for an instant that I should recognize him.

I could hardly speak, I was so surprised, but I stammered: "How did you get here?"

"Didn't Mair tell you I was in Paris? What a little bitch she is!"

He took my arm: "Let's go to a café. I'm frozen. What on earth were you doing up there all that time?"

This was as unreal as a dream. He was speaking to me with the same tone of affectionate irony that he had used some six years ago, at the time of our first and only encounter. To hear him, one would have thought we had remained in contact all these years and that it was quite natural that we should stand shivering together in the crowded rue de Seine, in the bitter cold of a Parisian winter.

Soon we were seated before boiling hot cups of coffee. Two workmen in blue overalls leaned against the counter, gossiping with a blonde barmaid. A stall-keeper had left her stand to warm herself up with three glasses of alcohol, tossed off one after the other. No one paid any attention to us. We were cut off alone with our common past.

A gentle warmth invaded my body. My limbs seemed to melt with comfort. Idris unwound his scarf, swallowed his coffee at a gulp.

"Two calvas! Come on, it'll do you good!"

"I don't understand," I said as the barmaid moved majestically over the sanded floor, bearing the two little glasses and the tall bottle. "What are you doing here ?"

"It would take a long time to tell. Let's say I came to see my sister and she said a lot of unpleasant things to me and slammed the door in my face."

"You knew I was here?"

"My aunt in Cardiff told me so. Or rather, she wrote that Mair had met a friend from Pont-y-Gibby and I supposed it was you. Mair wouldn't give me your address but I thought you would come to sec her. I often came through the street and this time I caught you."

He stared at me thoughtfully, head cocked to one side.

"You haven't changed at all."

"I'm sorry to hear it."

"Oh," he said. "You've grown, of course. But you have not changed essentially. All the worse for you, no doubt. Do you still want to be free?"

"That's why I'm here."

"I wonder," he said, sceptical. Then he added:

"I don't know where you live, but I bet, wherever it is, you keep your parent's photos on the mantelpiece."

"There isn't a mantelpiece."

"On the chest-of-drawers, then."

I could not deny it. The first thing I saw as I awoke each morning was the twin portraits, framed in leather, of my mother (enlargement of a snap-shot taken on the golf-links) and my father (a photographer's study, showing him at the age of thirty, in the uniform of the Welsh Guards). These photographs had always worried me a little, especially that of my mother, who, because she had the sun in her eyes, seemed to glare at me ferociously. But I had never thought of putting them out of sight.

"You see," said Idris. "You only half want to be free. How did you manage to get here?"

I told him of Lady Wynn-Evans' intervention, of the unexpected support of Dr. Johns, who did not like the sound of my bronchial tubes, and my father's undisguised desire to be rid of me.

"She didn't make much fuss in the end. I think she was glad in a way."

"Everything's all right, then. Throw the photos in the waste-paper basket and stay up on the Sugar-loaf as long as you like."

"It's not so easy.

He stared at me in silence for so long that I began to feel uncomfortable. Then he said suddenly in a voice that seemed heavy with pain.

"I know …"

We sat on without speaking, side by side on the worn, leather-covered bench.

As the moments passed, my astonishment grew. This man was almost unknown to me. I had spoken to him only once in my life. On that occasion, it is true, he had been kind and understanding to an unhappy child, but later, I had seen him do a thing that was horrible in itself and that, by its con-sequences, had deprived me of the most essential support in my life. It would have been normal for that vision— which repeated itself still, and so persistently, in my dreams —to have superseded the earlier one and to have left only an im-pression of horror and disgust. Turning my head a little, I watched Idris' face out of the corner of my eye. It had not changed much. He still looked very young, in spite of the jutting cheek-bones and the long hollow line of the cheeks. The eyes were as black as Mair's, but less brilliant, half-veiled by heavy eyelids. He had lost the spots which used to disfigure his forehead and his movements were less jerky, less uncoor-dinated, as though he had learned at last to control his nerves.

While I thus detailed his features, I tried to imagine them twisted in the horrid grimace of hatred which they had worn on that summer day, six years ago. I desired to imagine them thus because I was beginning to realize that the extraordinary impression of comfort and happiness which I felt at present, was not entirely due to the pleasant warmth radiating from the stove, but also to the presence of Idris and I had no wish to give myself up to this false comfort.

"You haven't asked me what I was doing all this time?"

He was taking our intimacy for granted. He spoke as though we had been close friends over a long period. For a moment I wondered: "Did I know him better than I remembered now? I was little; I may have forgotten." But I knew this could not be true.

He did not wait for my answer. Already he was telling his story.

"That summer I decided not to go back to Cardiff to take my degree. I was sick of Wales, sick of the provinces, with all their cowardice, their hypocrisy, all those eyes that never cease watching.

"Do you remember the poker-work text that used to hang on the parlour wall at home? 'The eye of God is upon you'. I often used to think the eye of God wasn't half such a nuisance as the eye of the pastor, and the postman, and the grocer and all the other people who have nothing to do but learn every minute detail of their neighbour's doings.

"In Cardiff, it was no better than it had been up north, or in Pont-y-Gibby. One imagines it is a great town because there are wide streets, thousands of shops and houses, traffic, the great docks. Then one soon realizes it is just another hole, a sort of expanded Pont-y-Gibby. I used to go off by myself, wander about in the lowest kind of streets, those down by the docks, or in the Arab quarter. I used to drink with the sailors and do a lot of other things that I wouldn't tell to a little lamb like you, just to prove to myself that I was free at last. Yet through it all I always had the feeling that I was being watched. Imagination, of course. Plenty of people go to the bad in Cardiff as well as anywhere else. Only in the end everyone knows everything, and what they don't know, they make up. It would have been impossible to go back." (Was he alluding, I wondered, to his father's death?) "I went to London. No money, of course. It was the old story of the poor but clever young man who makes his way in the big city. I was washer-up in a filthy café, then I worked as a docker. I had a stroke of luck then. There was a lot of bad feeling between the labourers and foreign sailors and one day a brawl on a really grand scale broke out just as I was going off. I tele-phoned the story through to a big daily. The news editor sent for me and by another stroke of luck he was a Welshman, with an accent you could cut with a knife. He gave me odd jobs of reporting occasionally. Accidents, minor police cases, any-thing no one else fancied. Then, after a bit, I got a regular job on the staff."

He interrupted himself.

"Mademoiselle! Two more calvas!"

"Not for me," I said. "I'm not used to it."

He patted my hand absent-mindedly.

"It won't hurt you. Personally, I am thirsty."

"I'm not surprised," I said.

"Are you being sarcastic? Dear me, it's like a canary trying to roar like a lion! I suppose I have been talking a lot, but I've been telling you all the things I wanted to tell Mair and she wouldn't listen to."

I asked: "Did you come to Paris to see her?"

"I suppose I did. My paper has an office here and I managed

to get sent out for a time. I suppose you think it queer that I should take so much trouble to see my sister when she won't have anything to do with me?"

"It does seem strange. You hardly ever came to Pont-y-Gibby."

"I know. And I can't at all understand why I want to see her now. I never cared for her much."

"I know how it is," I said. "I should like to tell all sorts of things to my mother, and yet I cannot believe I really love her. I often imagine the words I should use to tell her about Paris, words that would make her see the river, and the trees all sparkling with frost, and the people. Yet I know if I did try to tell her these things she would not trouble to listen, or perhaps she would tell me I was selfish and talked only about myself."

"That's splendid! We both seem to suffer from an ingrowing family spirit. So I shall pretend you are a Mair who will never make scenes and you can pretend I am a mother who will enjoy listening to your stories."

This seemed very funny and I was surprised to hear myself laugh loudly and to see that the workmen at the counter had turned to stare at me.

Idris looked at his watch. "I must go now. When shall we meet again?"

He went with me as far as the Boulevard St. Michel and when he had left me, I ran all the way to the hostel and raced upstairs to lock myself into my little room. A tepid radiator left the place only a little warmer than the street, but for once I hardly noticed the discomfort. I was in a state of extraordinary confusion. Now that Idris was no longer there, it seemed inconceivable that I should have had such an intimate conversation with him and above all that I should have taken such pleasure in it. I hated myself for this pleasure. I told myself that Idris was certainly unaware that I knew of the part he had played in his father's death. Even more certainly, he could not know that I had witnessed the whole scene which had led to it. If he had known the truth, he would never have dared to seek me out. To have received him as a friend seemed to make me in some way his accomplice. In some way I had ranged myself, by my complacency, among the men and women who had crowded to witness the humiliation of Mr. Howells and to triumph over him with evil joy. I was more guilty than they. Almost all, even those who had hated the schoolmaster, had ended by taking his part and reproving the act of his son. And I, who owed so much to him, who loved him as none of them could have done, I had tacitly made myself the assassin's ally.

I could not understand myself. Lying on my bed, my limbs gradually deadening in the cold, I sobbed with shame to know that I should keep the appointment Idris had made with me.

ONE MORNING, I awoke very early. It was still dark and I lay there in my narrow bed, listening to the sounds of the awakening city.

The carts and lorries, laden with fruit and vegetables for the Halles, were already lumbering down the street, so ponderously that the window panes rattled at their passage. Then the church bells began to ring out the first Angelus; the bells of St. Barbe, of St. Severin, the more-distant bells of Notre Dame, of St. Sulpice, of St. Julien-le-Pauvre and others that sounded softly from far away across the river. The notes fell heavy and muffled into the still, cold air, from quarter to quarter they answered each other, chiming a sort of rhythmic conversation above the roofs.

Now the window was a grey square in the black frame of the wall. Wheels ground to a stop, close beneath it. I could hear the trample of hooves then the noise of heavy iron dust bins being dragged across the pavement. A little later, sleepy footsteps scuffed through the corridor, a broom grated across the stiff pile of a carpet, from the basement rose the clatter of crockery. The day had begun.

This rattle of china brought a picture of the café-au-lait and slabs of buttered bread which would soon be served for breakfast. I was hungry already, but the refectory bell would not ring for nearly an hour. On the other side of the partition, I could hear Mademoiselle Paillot, law student, moving about her heavy volumes of jurisprudence and rustling sheaves of paper. She—no time-waster like myself—was putting in a little study before breakfast. She must have been cold, for the tip of my nose, freezing all alone outside the blankets, warned me that the thermometer was well below zero again.

Ever since my awakening, I had been conscious of the feeling of happiness that never ceased to astonish me because it was so new and unaccustomed. I lay there, savouring it, while the furniture in the little room gradually took on its accustomed form and colour. This elation, this feeling that I had become integrated into life, after hovering for so long on its boundaries, was no doubt partly due to the fact that I had an appointment with Idris and I was forced to admit unwillingly to myself that the mere prospect of seeing him for an hour or so in the afternoon was enough to give a special meaning to the whole day.

Idris, indeed, was part of my life now. We saw each other frequently and together we undertook the exploration of Paris. By preference we chose the most eccentric quarters for our wanderings. One day it was the rue des Rosiers, where we watched long-haired Jews, wearing flat felt hats and frock coats, dreamily drifting along the pavements, with the unseeing, inward-turned look in their eyes that marks a people who live in a world apart, a world formed of tradition and imagination, that ignores or despises reality. We entered a tiny restaurant, where we were served with cold cabbage soup accompanied by steaming hot potatoes. The owner spoke to us in Yiddish, deceived perhaps by Idris' darkness, and Idris, replying in faulty German, drew from him astonishing and half-understood stories of Polish ghettoes, of pogroms, of miracle-working rabbis.

Another day, we followed the quais of the Seine, farther and farther, leaving bridge after bridge behind us, till we were no longer in Paris, but in a strange landscape that was neither town nor country, with great patches of waste land sweeping down to the water, warehouses and riverside cafés from which floated over-sweet, nostalgic music. We stood on the sloping bank, watching the water swirl at our feet and the barges that drifted slowly down towards the locks while blonde Flemish women hung washing upon the decks.

Sometimes we found ourselves in ancient quarters, among crumbling houses that seemed to smell of crime, and behind those crevassed walls we divined hallucinating cruelties. Sometimes, too, we wandered in populous side-streets, among the tumult of street-markets and the ritual cries of vendors:

"Oh … é… . See what fine lettuces I sell!"

"Look at this, *petites menagères*! Buy and you'll never regret!"

"What are they saying? Can't you explain?" worried Idris, who spoke little French, and it was one of my chief pleasures to interpret and translate for him.

Now, counting each of these scenes, like a precious possession in the store-house of my mind, I asked myself whether
I loved him. I could give no answer, but already I could not
imagine my life without him.

As I turned to look at the time, my eyes fell on the twin portraits of my parents, now entirely visible in the morning light.
They made no secret of their opinion of me.

"So this is how you behave now that you have got your own
way! Running around Paris with a young man whom you
would never dare to bring to your own home—a young man
who is not even a gentleman and who has a thoroughly bad
reputation. I suppose you know what he wants of you ..."
Their eyes were fixed on me, insistent, inquisitorial.

In a second I was out of bed. The two photographs were
whisked out of sight, buried well at the back of my drawer,
under a pile of handkerchiefs and stockings. Then I felt the
relief of a criminal who has accomplished an act that has been
long and fearfully pre-meditated.

A few hours later, I was in the Café d'Harcourt, looking
around for Idris, who was lurking somewhere in this labyrinth
of mirror and shiny red leather. Presently I caught sight of
him, seated in a corner, isolated from the groups of noisy
students, pipe in mouth, pen in hand, scribbling away in a
black note-book. He greeted me absent-mindedly, told me not
to disturb him and set to work again.

I liked to sit beside him, immobile and attentive, while he
fidgeted, scribbled wildly, muttered to himself, crossed out
and blew clouds of smoke. I liked to feel that my presence
soothed him and that, simply by remaining quiet, I could help
him in his work. But when he had finished at last, he lifted his
head and I saw that he looked more ill and harassed than usual.

His cheeks were more sunken than ever, the dark shadows under the eyes met the sharp line of the cheek-bones and it seemed to me that the hand that was cramming papers back into the leather brief-case, trembled a little. Then he sat back, staring at me, morose and hoping for distraction, like a child that expects to be coaxed out of its ill-humour. This lowering face, heavy with unreasoning sadness, filled me with discouragement. When I myself was feeling sad or anxious, Idris' presence was an unfailing comfort to me, but when I was happy, his own constant disquiet weighed on me until his mood often became my own. Today, however, I had a plan which I was determined to carry out and enjoy. So I said quickly, before he could speak:

"I want to buy a picture."

He looked at me with surprise, already distracted from his dark thoughts.

"A picture! Why! And what sort of picture?"

I had no idea really: "A picture to hang in my room at the hostel."

"A reproduction, then. Unless you have plenty of money."

"I have very little," I said. A vision of my picture was forming in my mind now. "What I want is a good reproduction of some painting with bright, light colours and a feeling of space in it."

He laughed: "I see. An anti-Pont-y-Gibby picture! Let's go and look for it."

We went out into the tumult of the boulevard and walked slowly, jostled by the crowd, in the direction of the Seine.

Neither of us knew where pictures were to be bought but presently, loitering through the huddle of narrow streets between the river and the Boulevard St. Germain, we came on a shop window that was splashed with the colours of great, square sheets of paper on which were reproduced, so well that from a distance they seemed like originals, paintings from the great masters of the French School. We stopped and stood, arm in arm, gazing at the lovely images that glowed in the grey, wintry street.

"Impressionists!" said Idris. "They're the thing for you."

We went inside. Green cardboard folders were stacked against the wall. Idris began to hunt through them, rapidly and nervously turning over the thick, glossy sheets of paper. He knew exactly what I should have and the choosing of this picture that was to adorn the hygienic-looking walls of my room at the pension, seemed to be strangely important to him. I watched him as he squatted before the stack of folders, his black brows drawn in a frown of energetic concentration, his long hands flying among the brightly-coloured paper, and I understood that he was seeking for a symbol.

But here, suddenly, I caught sight of a painting that seemed to me the most beautiful I had ever seen. It showed a king with a sad and cruel face, who gazed with an expression of noble and intense sorrow at a rose held in his hand. A king of Babylon, I thought, alone at the edge of the world. I snatched it quickly from Idris' hand and said:

"I'll have this one!"

"A Rouault?" said Idris. "It isn't at all what you wanted. This picture is dark, there is a feeling of fear in it, almost an imprisoned feeling."

"It is beautiful," I said, because I had no desire to explain the emotions the picture roused in me.

"Beautiful!" said Idris. He was suddenly furious. "Beautiful!" he repeated scornfully. "That is all you ask for.

Beauty … picturesque places, poetry, sunsets. Anything that tickles agreeably your eyes or your ears. Anything that sings you prettily to sleep."

His face was suddenly strained and heavy with anger. Surely, this melancholy king could only be a pretext, for how could my taste for him really rouse such anger? In vain I searched my memory for some phrase, some attitude, which might have provoked him during the afternoon.

Furiously he scuffled among the folders till he pounced on a picture that he held before me like a banner.

"Look at that! This man has grouped certain objects—or a human form, perhaps—then he has thrown a bomb in the middle. This is the result. It isn't beautiful, perhaps, but it is true. I'll make you a present of it."

The shop keeper tied up the parcel.

"You evidently admire modern art, Sir …"

"Not at all," said Idris. "I detest it."

He took the parcel and walked out without a look for me and I could only follow. Away he strode at a great pace, while I trotted behind him, wondering how I ought to behave. I was cold, but dared not risk an explosion of this contained fury I felt in him by proposing to take shelter in a café. However, when we had walked the whole length of the road in stony silence, I began to get angry in my turn. I touched his arm.

"Give me my parcel. I'm going home."

He stopped and stood looking down at me. Suddenly his expression grew more gentle.

"Don't do that! Let's go and sit down somewhere."

We entered the first café on our way—a sad-looking *tabac* with a back room that smelt of dust, where half a dozen smeary tables awaited absent clients. A solitary negro pulled at the handle of a pin-table and succession of orange-coloured lights twinkled for a moment across its surface. A sleepy waitress brought coffee. Idris asked for a pernod and said to me:

"It's a drink I've just discovered—strong, yellow and wonderful for putting one in a good temper."

"I'm glad to hear it," I said crossly.

He laid his hand on mine.

"You mustn't be angry with me. There are certain things I can't stand, and above all a sort of drawing-room revolutionism that isn't even meant to get anywhere. I want people to be really free and they never will be because they only half desire it. You especially. It isn't your fault. All your instincts bind you to your past."

I realized, now that he was speaking to me again in his normal voice, how much I had feared to lose him and now I was annoyed to think that I had taken a mere outburst of ill-humour so seriously. Yet there remained a tightness at my heart, a chill that seemed to foretell emptiness and absence. It worried me like the muffled pain that brings a threat of approaching illness.

I said to him: "Perhaps I shall be able to kill those instincts, since I hate them and they often prevent my happiness."

He laughed contemptuously: "Never! Besides, those instincts are what I like best in you, as well as what holds me back from you. I'll even admit to you that I share them, so far as a man can have anything in common with a woman."

He took my hand. His long, dry fingers pressed nervously around my own.

"You know I hated my father. Not only because he did all he could to make my life as narrow and limited as his own, but because he represented hypocrisy and cowardice for me. Spiritual avarice, too. It's a sin the theologians have forgotten to mention, that consists of shutting one's talents, one's knowledge, one's experience of life, away in a mental safe and letting them rot there. Not forgetting, of course, to go and stick one's nose in it constantly, to breathe up the stink of corruption, to go into orgasms of pride at its possession. I said something about that to you once before, but I don't suppose you understood."

"I remember quite well," I said. "I understood perfectly and even then I knew that you were wrong."

He regarded me suspiciously. "You have a very good memory, my dear. Perhaps you know the sequel?"

"Yes, I saw everything."

He dropped my hand. "Ah! I should have guessed it."

We sat on, in a silence that grew heavier and heavier. The waitress had disappeared. The proprietor dozed at the cash-desk. The negro had spent all his loose change and slouched off, so that even the click of balls falling into the little holes was stilled. Through the window I could see that it had begun to snow. The soft, white curtain of snow fell gently and implacably, abolishing the outer world.

Idris said suddenly: "You see, we are bound together."

He rose and I followed him out into the road, where the snow deadened the sound of our footsteps and we passed as silently as ghosts.

"Where are we going?"

"To my place.

Suddenly, the gaping mouth of a metro station opened before us and we plunged into it, sucked downward into the reek of soot, sweat and garlic. The train was so crowded with homeward-bound workers that we could hardly force our way past the doors. The mass of people, with their pale, drawn faces, brutish at this hour from fatigue, crowded in on us from every side. I was crushed close against Idris, my shoulder pressed into his chest, my thighs moulded against his own, and I knew that this contact was unwelcome to him, and that he would have suffered this enforced intimacy from any anonymous man or woman more easily than from myself.

He lived in Montmartre, and we left the metro at the Place Blanche and climbed the steep rue Lepic, where stall-owners were stretching tarpaulin covers to protect their wares and Algerians with scarred cheeks huddled under the doorways, shivering in their thread-bare overcoats and muttering to themselves in their grunting dialect. Then we turned off into a quiet side-street, such as might be found in any country town, where children scuffled in the soiled snow, concierges, in their shawls, shrieked pleasantries from door to door, and a whole tribe of cats and dogs snarled and gambolled at our feet. The houses were narrow and somewhat dilapidated, but they retained a certain dignity, reminiscent of the days when they had been inhabited by a comfortable middle-class.

Idris lived in furnished rooms—a bed-sitting room and wash-room giving out over an unswept courtyard. As soon as he opened the door, I noticed the smell of cold tobacco, mixed with that—less easily to be defined—of a male who lives and works in a little space. It seemed to me that Idris was there already, waiting for me, that he had never left this room and that in a moment I should surprise him in an unfamiliar aspect, that aspect which people take on in their own homes, among their books, their clothes, in the shadow of their sleep and of their most intimate existence.

He pushed me before him and closed the door. I looked

around me and saw, by the carelessly-made bed and the pile of plates that had been washed but not dried, that he did his own housework. Several pairs of shoes lay scattered over the floor and a sheet of paper, fixed in the typewriter, bore an unfinished phrase:

"The economic situation in the agricultural regions…"

Idris was prodding a poker into the stove. "It'll burn up in a moment. Come nearer. You're cold."

Then he said in a sarcastic tone: "But perhaps you are shivering because you are afraid."

"I am not afraid," I said, although this was by no means true.

He put his hands on my shoulders and, holding me thus at a little distance before him, gazed at me with a sort of grave and concerned scrutiny and said:

"You are not speaking the truth, of course. I know quite well that you are afraid and so, as a matter of fact, am I to some extent, though not for the same reasons. Anything that happens between you and me is bound to create a link stronger than any I feel prepared to accept in my life. We know too much about each other, my dear. If we had any sense, we should put seas and mountains between ourselves. Yet we are here together and you are trembling with fright and I …"

This was like nothing I had ever imagined or read about love. Idris' hard, grave voice held no tenderness. It seemed that whatever existed between us was too frail to support the weight of his distrust, that it must be crushed then and there and leave only a man and a woman staring coldly at each other in the impersonal décor of a hired room. Yet through the chilly disappointment and through all the distrust, I felt the desire to be held in his arms, to feel him press my head against his breast and to hear his voice soften to say: I love you. My imagination went no further and I could only feel that this would be the beginning of happiness.

But he continued to hold me at some distance, and I could see that he, too, was troubled and hesitant. At last he said:

"I know that I am hurting you. I want to be honest with you but I am beginning to realize that it is not so easy as I had thought. I do not want to say that I love you for fear of telling you a lie, but I am just beginning to realize how immensely I want to hold you in my arms and that I have never wanted this so much with any other woman. So perhaps I do love you."

It seemed to me that I was struggling in a sea of ice. I knew that he was trying to reassure himself as well as me. I knew, too, that in some way nothing he had said was really addressed to me, but rather to some phantom whom we both half perceived. Yet I could not make the least movement to free myself.

He said: "Go if you want to. I shall not be angry." But I shook my head knowing that it was impossible and that whatever was about to happen was inevitable.

IT IS no easy thing to organize a communal life between two people who live at opposite ends of a great city, have little money and less leisure. I would have been ready enough to cut my lectures, but Idris would not permit it. He himself worked sometimes by day and sometimes by night. It often happened that I made the long journey to Montmartre only to find a notice pinned to the door: "At work. Wait for me." Then I would take the key from under the doormat and go into the room. I would begin to tidy up, to wash the crockery, hang clothes in the cupboard and dust. When everything was in order, I would lie down on the divan and read the magazines that Idris always left scattered over the floor, or simply let my imagination float over the doings of the day.

Half an hour or so might pass in pleasant reverie, but soon a moment would come when I felt a tightening of the nerves, a prickling sensation of disquiet. Then I would begin to fear that Idris might not come at all, that I should have to go home alone and unconsoled, undress and lie on my hard bed, where I should remain sleepless, feeling an infinite emptiness. Then a really physical anguish would seize hold of me, that anguish, I suppose, that starving men feel when they can no longer hope for food. I could no longer read or even think. My whole mind strained to evoke the sound of footsteps ringing upon the flagstones of the courtyard.

Sometimes he came so late that I barely had time to hold him in my arms for a few minutes before we must rise and hurry to the metro. Idris would accompany me, irritated and taciturn, while I took surreptitious glances at my wrist-watch. We would arrive at last, breathless, hardly daring to exchange a last kiss beneath the peevish regard of the concierge who signified by the impatient rattling of his keys that this was no time for sentiment. When I fell asleep at last it would be to dream of the other Idris, the pitiless executioner with his mask of hatred.

There were other evenings, however, when it was he who had waited long and impatiently for my arrival. He would have done the shopping already and laid the table. I had only the vaguest notions of cookery, but a series of experiments had taught me how to make passable omelettes. We ate ravenously, washing them down with draughts of strong red wine, a single glass of which was enough to make my head spin. Then there was pungent-smelling, creamy, blue- veined cheese and fine fruits, rich-coloured and smooth to the touch. When the meal was over I would make coffee. Idris drank it sitting on the divan, but I liked to sit on the floor, resting my head against his knee. We would remain thus for a long time without speaking, and from time to time I would feel his lips brush against my hair. Then it seemed to me that I was returning to that amorphous state which, it seems, was the original manifestation of female life. I was heavy, gelatinous, immobile, created with the sole aim of completing the male element. I felt nothing but a deep, unreasoning contentment, and the little room enfolded me, warmly and safely, and nothing outside its walls had any real significance.

Nous fermerons partout portières et volets
Pour bâtir la nuit nos féeriques palais… .

The words drifted through my brain as lightly and lazily as words written by an aeroplane in smoke across the sky.

We continued to take long walks together whenever Idris had a free afternoon. On a certain Sunday we roamed even farther than usual so that presently, almost without noticing how far we had come, we had passed the ancient toll-gate of Paris and were out in the southern suburb of Montrouge. We found ourselves after a while in a long avenue, in the midst of a strange décor built of factories that had been burnt out in some long-forgotten fire. Their gaunt black silhouettes were profiled like a row of gigantic scarecrows against the pale winter sky. The road was lined on either side with wooden huts, roughly constructed of rotting planks. From them rose an acrid and persistent odour of stale urine and a sluggish liquid seeped beneath the doorways and spread in pools over the broken pavement. One of the huts bore a sign: "Permanent wave, 50 francs", and the open door revealed a rickety chair, a bench on which stood a tin basin, and, looming from a corner, a vast, rusted machine from which curlers dangled like corpses from some miniature gibbet.

A yellow dog circled uneasily, seeking a propitious spot; two women were waiting apathetically, disinterested in their fate, gazing into space and tracing circles in the mud with the point of their shoes. A mulatto lurked nearby, but failed to make up his mind. The road was under repair, full of water-filled ruts and holes and a naked drain pipe surged up between the loosened paving.

"Come along," said Idris. "This is only the ante-chamber to hell. We must see what it will be like farther on."

But farther on the district became more reassuring. There were small houses, white-washed bistros, their terraces decorated with neat, potted evergreens. The place had a provincial air. Comfortable housewives, children romping on the pavement in front of the Infants school, a squat little granite church displaying a parochial notice-board … nothing remained of that strange land through which we had come but a few of its strayed inhabitants, dilapidated prostitutes or equivocal young men with shiny little moustaches, who swayed at the hips as they walked. They wandered, nonchalant and provocative among the peaceful suburban dwellers, disquieting by their very presence … foreigners come from *over the frontier.*

A square opened on our right, surrounded on three sides by high brick buildings. A morning market had been held there for the place was still encumbered with trestles and light scaffolding which must have supported the awnings of the stalls. Whisps of straw and a few trampled vegetables scattered the ground and a faint smell of fish and oranges still hung in the air. At the back of the square there was a little garden, neatly kept behind an enclosure of grilled iron-work, and women sat there, knitting, beneath the frail, bare trees, while children played ball or dabbled in the sand-pit.

"Let's go in. I'm tired."

We seated ourselves on a rather damp bench. A single bird sang obstinately in the branches just above our heads. Children stumbled against our legs, steadied themselves, clasping our knees with hands sticky from tea-time jam.

"This place makes me think of soiled nappies," said Idris. "There are too many children in Paris."

"Don't you like children?"

He wrinkled his nose: "Not much. I like to be left in peace and that's not possible wherever there are children around."

"We can go if you like."

He stretched: "There's plenty of time. I grumble, but on the whole I like this place. It's tremendously French—by which I mean that it is homely and frivolous at the same time. Worthiness doesn't weigh as heavy as it does at home, there is always a breath of fantasy to lighten it."

"Perhaps that is because we are foreigners," I said. "I suppose other people's virtues always appear less dull than one's own."

"I daresay you are right. The glamour of the half-under-stood …"

I asked: "Would you like to live here always?"

"Here as well as anywhere else. Only I have no intention of living anywhere for ever. I should get sick of anywhere in the world after a bit."

I rose. My head ached a little and I had a vague sensation of anxiety.

"Actually, this place seems almost outside the world," said Idris, following me along the sand-strewn path that led to the gate. "You saw the Zone we came through just now. Like a landscape from Dante ... Really there was nothing human about it. It seems there is another strip of zone-land a little further on from here that is just the same. Here, you see, we are on a sort of island. Desolation before us, desolation behind us, but here it positively smells of comfort and security."

"The people here must live in fear of an invasion."

"Surely! I expect the others sometimes mass along the frontiers like packs of wolves, ready to attack. Then the alarm sounds, the housewives arm themselves with their saucepans and rolling-pins; the banners are unfurled, the trumpets blown and they prepare to defend themselves."

"And the Others ... ?"

"Well, they are soon frightened off. One can see their eyes gleaming in the dark and hear them panting with concupiscence, then they disappear and when morning comes, there is not an enemy to be seen. They know there is nothing more ferocious on earth than a human being defending his peace of mind."

We went out, laughing, from the little garden. Opposite us rose a tall, narrow building, resembling all the others that surrounded the square. It seemed to consist of a number of studios, since on each floor there was one immensely large window with another much smaller window opening onto a narrow balcony with an ironwork balustrade. Over the main door there was a notice: "Studio to let".

"Let's have a look at it," said Idris. "You might like to enrol in the local battalion."

The concierge was a massive Italian, whose face was ornamented with an ample black moustache and an incipient beard. She cuffed away the three or four children who clung to her apron, took her heavy breasts, one in each hand and, holding them like two fine melons carried before her, she preceded us up the stairs.

The studio was square-shaped, with a high ceiling and a stone floor. The huge window looked over a sort of work-yard situated behind the house, strewn with rusty iron stakes and wooden beams. A small staircase led to a half floor with a second room and a washroom, while below it there was a kitchen hardly larger than a cupboard.

We inspected the premises with the serious air of a couple who intend to settle down and found a family.

"How do you like it?" asked the concierge and went on before we could reply: "If you're a sculptor, Monsieur, it's exactly what you want. The one on the next floor has made a fine statue—six foot five inches, from tip to toe, it is—in a studio exactly like this one. He gave me a ticket for his exhibition and there it was, right in the middle of the room. Quite a turn it gave me. It was a young man, without a stitch on, the way they do them nowadays, and I said to myself: 'As for you, my boy, I knew you when you were just a block of stone!'"

She stood there, in the very middle of the big, empty studio, holding up her breasts with her hands and, seen thus, she herself resembled a statue carved in some brownish-grey, flaccid matter. I could see that Idris was impressed.

"You are foreigners, aren't you?" she went on. "So am I, though I married a Frenchman. We get all sorts here ... Poles,

Russians, Germans, a Spaniard, a Swede. You'll feel quite at home here."

We trailed down the stairs. In the lodge, the children were howling noisily.

"Here you are! Here's the agent's address. It's quite cheap, you know, for what it is. I'm pushing it a bit with you because I like having English and Americans. They're not mean like some are. Those Slavs, for instance! Don't talk to me about them … !"

Idris slipped a note into her hand and took the paper, which he folded and placed in his wallet. We went out into the square, which was already enveloped in the falling dusk.

"I suppose there are buses that pass by here. Let's look for a stop."

Under a lamp-post he unfolded the morsel of paper, gazed reflectively at the laboriously written words.

"As a matter of fact, it isn't a bad idea. Would you like us to have a place of our own? You must have had enough of that damn hostel."

I supposed at first that he was joking, but his face, obscured by the twilight, appeared immobile and attentive.

"How could we? My parents would never let me."

"You could tell them you are going to share a flat with a friend. They aren't likely to come and see for themselves, are they?"

A bus drew up beside us. It was nearly empty and we settled ourselves in the front seat, just behind the glass partition that separated us from the broad, leather-coated back of the driver. Idris took tickets. I should have liked him to give me some sign of affection, since he was asking me, in effect, to deliver myself over to him irrevocably and I knew that, whatever the outcome of this strange afternoon, I should have need of all my courage. But he sat quietly beside me, without making a gesture. It seemed as if he wished to leave me entirely free to decide as I pleased, and suddenly I suspected that he hoped thus to protect himself from any responsibility in my decision.

We sat in silence, while the bus jolted over the uneven road. Presently Idris said, half-unwillingly :

"You must be astonished at what I have just suggested to you?"

"Why should I be astonished? It would be more practical for both of us."

The word "practical" I brought out like a sword for my defence. I did not dare, for so many things still remained unexpressed between us, to tell him that I desired nothing more than to remain always near him and that I was afraid and apprehensive of the very violence of this desire, as if I knew it in advance to be leading me to disaster. Then I felt ashamed, for it seemed to me that, when one loved, one should lay down all arms, set aside all ruse and give oneself up completely.

He did not take up the phrase and perhaps had hardly noticed it. A few minutes later, as we passed through the Avenue d'Orléans, we were discussing the details of our moving in.

IT WAS early spring when we moved into the studio in Montrouge. The whole world was sprouting, budding, springing to life. It seemed to me that the earth itself was moving and labouring beneath the asphalt paving. It was the first spring I had ever spent in a town.

The little garden in the square wore the successive colours that told of the passing weeks—white of snowdrop, yellow of crocus, blue of iris. I used to pass through it each morning on my way to fetch milk, and each morning I saw that the earth had brought forth new flowers. The pale morning sun would be shining through the young foliage and peppering the grass with gold. The children would be coming out of the houses, the big ones flying off to school, satchels flapping against their backs, the little ones in their gay pinafores, scrambling in groups, shepherded by maids or mothers, towards the sand-pit.

All around rose up the noise of the market. The stall holders would be dragging from their lorries great wooden crates filled with onions, carrots, cheese, fruit or household goods. Men in bloodstained overalls advanced, staggering, bent double beneath the heavy carcasses of sheep or pigs they carried on their backs. Women were arriving from the country-side with baskets of eggs and butter. And everyone would be shouting, gesticulating, quarrelling, in the shadow of the flowering chestnut trees, among the hammering, the throbbing of engines, the cries of children, the cursing of workmen and, distinctly heard above the tumult, the indomitable singing of hundreds of starlings.

Sometimes these impressions crowded so strongly upon me that I would stop and stand there, quite still, in the very middle of the garden, with the milk-pot dangling from my finger, and simply feel myself living. It seemed to me at such moments that I was participating so completely in this life that throbbed around me that I really *became* a tree, a flower, a child, a bird, a market-man. The spring sap ran then in my veins with such violence that I almost expected to see my whole body burst into leaf and flower. I was crammed full of sun and music, old songs heard in my childhood chased through my brain and mingled with the surrounding clamour. I began to run, for the joy of movement, but in two bounds I was already at the barrier. Then my pleasure fell a little, for the finest town in the world must be a prison in springtime. At such moments I had the sudden vision of the high hills and deserted valleys of my home, I seemed to feel the springy grass beneath my feet and to see the great stretches of country sweeping away before me, where I could run or gallop my horse for hours without meeting a living soul or any barrier to check my flight.

Then I would shake myself and remember my sur-roundings. I would go through the turnstile gate, cross the road, where women in bedroom slippers, mackintoshes thrown over their night-clothes, busied themselves with the morning's shopping. I would hurry to the dairy, then to the bakery, concentrating on my immediate business, a pre-occupied young wife, frowning over the price of sugar. In a little while, I knew, the coffee would be filling the studio with its delicious fragrance; I should be eating croissants still hot from the oven so that the butter melted and rippled over their golden crust; and Idris, who was never hungry in the morning, would be smoking cigarettes and taking his coffee black. He would still be in bed and I should sit on the edge, with my cup in my hand and my plate balanced on my knee, and I should see the hollow that showed where my body had rested all night beside him.

It had not taken me long to get used to my new life and indeed the old one now seemed distant and a little unreal. I felt myself now unusually solid, securely anchored for the first time in my existence. So long as Idris was beside me, this feeling of *safeness* persisted, but when he was absent— for he was sent frequently by his paper to report events in the provinces—I would feel lonely and vaguely apprehensive.

These days were like cracks in the foundations of my happiness and through them seeped the insidious doubt, instantly dispelled by his return; perhaps the time will come when I shall be alone like this for ever.

These brilliant and transitory patches of happiness, alternating with a disquiet that had so little apparent motive, stimulated my new avidity for life. I could hardly bear to think that the *today* which I was living with such intensity would slip in next to no time into *yesterday* and from thence, progressively losing its colours and contours, slide away into the past. So, attempting to fix these terribly illusive hours, I wrote endless poems, short stories and the opening chapters of novels which read, on later reflection, like faithful copies of my changing literary fancies. The core of truth seemed to slip and vanish as soon as I tried to touch it. Yet I persisted, encouraged perhaps by the very fact that Idris refused to take any interest in my writing, as if some instinct warned me of the necessity of guarding a fragment of myself inviolate.

During this early spring I thought often of Mair, and always with a certain uneasiness. Since my first meeting with Idris, I had gradually seen less and less of her and since we had taken the studio I had avoided her altogether, fearing that I should be moved to some confidence that I should regret later. I feared, too, the sharp, inquisitorial glance that told me all too clearly that she sensed a mystery, and the sudden and terribly pertinent questions that were so hard to elude. It had seemed safer to avoid her company altogether but I often reflected uneasily that Mair offended—and, worse still, Mair faced with a mystery—was redoubtable. I could not believe that she would accept so easily a disappearance that she certainly considered as an affront, yet the weeks went by without news of her, Idris never mentioned her name and, for my part, I was careful never to recall the past. It was almost as if she had never existed.

I might almost have succeeded in forgetting her if it had not been for my visit to Professor Sougny.

It was during one of Idris' short absences from home that Jean-Pierre Carré took me to meet this ancient and famous man, who had retired long since from his Chair of Philosophy but whose influence still extended far beyond the Sorbonne. The name seemed familiar, but it was not until I was on my way to keep the appointment that I remembered that Mair had once spoken of "an old boy who was a professor in father's time".

Jean-Pierre was waiting for me at the corner of the rue du Val-de-Grace. It was pleasant to look at him, to see that young, open face, those clear eyes that had never been clouded by any anxiety worse than an unlearned lesson or a deficit at the end of the month. Even his body—a little short, but solid and supple—gave an impression of calm assurance. I remembered my emotion on that first evening when he had taken my hand in his own, tried to recall the sensation, but today the pressure of his fingers on my arm as he guided me across the street, left me unmoved. He was a comrade, the first I had ever known, and I found this relationship as delightful as I could wish.

As we walked, Jean-Pierre talked of Professor Sougny and of the people who frequented his Saturday receptions. Meanwhile, I was asking myself what could have been the relationship between this old philosopher and Mr. Howells. Had he been his teacher? I had always had the impression, though for no special reason, that Mr. Howells had studied history. Yet there must have been some close connection, closer surely than that which ordinarily links professor and student, for M. Sougny to have remembered his pupil for thirty years and to have welcomed his daughter on her arrival in Paris. I tried to imagine Mr. Howells as a student of philosophy. Although I knew little of the great ethical systems, it seemed to me impossible that he could have reconciled his rigorous and austere religion with the determinist principles I had heard discussed among my contemporaries and of which the Professor had for long been one of the foremost exponents in France. And suddenly a voice seemed to sound in my ears: "Learning can be an evil, a pernicious guide." How could he, this stern man, have listened to the words of Comte and Hegel without rising to denounce the ungodly, to call down a judgment of fire on those who taught such impious doctrines. Then I remembered that Idris had called his father hypocrite, I remembered that fallen figure that I always tried to forget... .

"You aren't listening," said Jean-Pierre. "You're always in the clouds nowadays."

Professor Sougny lived in a flat on the first floor of a very old house in the rue St. Jacques. We found him seated in a rocking-chair, holding a marmalade cat on his knees. He was a little old man, bald save for a coronet of fluffy white hair that neatly ringed his pink skull. He had lively blue eyes in a face like a ball of crumpled paper.

Jean-Pierre introduced me: "An English student who is hoping to become a writer: Laura Gethryn."

Professor Sougny smiled kindly and said:

"I am glad you brought her along."

I sat down timidly. There were six or seven people present, all of whom were gazing attentively and expectantly at their host as if waiting for him to finish some explanation that our entrance had interrupted. I felt at once the deep and almost religious respect in which these younger men and women held their host.

Madame Sougny, who looked astonishingly like her husband, with the addition of steel-rimmed spectacles, brought us coffee and biscuits. Then the conversation became general again. These people discussed ideas, those ideas that exist in themselves and for themselves in an abstract and perfectly disinterested world. The language they spoke was still unknown to me. Nothing had prepared me to receive that which was offered to me. So I sat sadly, excluded, not daring to move, while precious words that I would have given much to understand, faded into the air.

Madame Sougny must have realized my embarrassment, for she drew her chair near to mine and began to talk kindly to me. First she questioned me on my impressions of Paris and I guessed that she had pronounced the same phrases, hundreds of times, through half a century, to intimidated foreign students. But suddenly she said:

"There is another English girl who comes to see us sometimes. She is from Wales and her father was a pupil of my husband. I should like you to meet her. She would be a companion for you."

"But I think I know her already," I said. "Surely you are speaking of Mair Howells."

"Well, how strange!"

She raised her voice to attract her husband's attention: "My dear! This young lady knows that little English girl, Howells' daughter."

The professor turned his head to smile at me politely. "Well,

well! You must tell her to come and see us again. Her father was a remarkable man—one of the most remarkable I have ever known."

"I know," I said: "I knew him very well, too."

Again he said: "Well, well!" but this time his voice was alert with interest.

"Please come nearer, Mademoiselle. Tell me what you know of my old friend. He is dead, his daughter tells me."

"He died about six years ago."

"The girl told me nothing else. I saw that she did not wish to speak of him. I fear his end was … tragic."

I nodded my head and he sighed deeply.

"It does not surprise me. I never managed to understand him though he became my intimate friend towards the end of his time in Paris. I felt that something in him was … torn apart."

Presently he asked me in what circumstances I knew Mr. Howells. When I told him, he reflected a little while in silence, while he gently gnawed at the ends of his long white moustache.

"He wrote to me for three years, then he never gave a sign of life again. Why the devil did he do it? Why did he go and bury himself alive in this lost village you speak of, where he can only have taught the rudiments of education to children destined to become farm hands. All that must have been a living death to him. Why, then … ?"

He seemed to put the question to himself rather than to me.

I asked timidly: "He was very intelligent, was he not?"

"More than that… . Brilliant. He was born to handle the great abstractions. And he became a teacher in a primary school…"

Suddenly he put his tiny, dried-up hand upon mine and whispered so low that I could hardly catch his words.

"He committed suicide?"

"Yes."

"I guessed it. We often spoke together of the right of man to dispose of his own life. At first, he denied this right, but his studies and specially the reading of Schopenhauer gradually led his mind in another direction. Finally he arrived at conclusions which were entirely nihilistic, although his personal life always remained exemplary."

Was he really speaking of Mr. Howells? Everything he said seemed to be impossible, so monstrously unlike the man I knew, that I could hardly believe we were speaking of the same person.

In my astonishment I murmured the first thing that came into my mind.

"He was so religious."

"Religious!" He regarded me intently and surprise lent a sudden gleam of youth to his eyes. "I have never known a man so free of prejudice! He had really annihilated the very idea of God, which persists, in spite of everything, in almost all of us who are the products of a Christian civilization. He had shed, not only every vestige of religion but the very notion of good and evil. He had really made a clean sweep of every preconceived notion, of all superstition, of everything that could not be proved by scientific examination."

The guests were taking their leave. I rose and offered him my hand.

"No, no! Please stay a little. I should like to talk with you of all this. If you are free, will you take supper with us?"

When Jean-Pierre had gone with the last of the guests the

little room seemed very silent to me. Madame Sougny had left us to help the maid. The professor softly padded round the room, showing me books and ornaments and questioning me about my studies and my plans.

"You say you want to be a writer, Mademoiselle? That is a profession which demands terrible sacrifices. You will continually be obliged to *make a choice*—that is, to reject a thousand things and accept only a few. You will have to concentrate your energy continually, not merely at certain working hours. Yet instinct drives man and especially the artist, to taste everything that comes his way, to disperse himself in many directions. It gives him the impression that he is in some way prolonging his life, playing a trick on time. Writers are seldom happy people."

I replied that it was not precisely for happiness that I was seeking and that I believed moments of happiness to be precious in proportion to their rarity.

He looked amused and in his amusement, it seemed to me, pity was mingled (for this wise man understood, no doubt, that youth is the time for suffering and that pain makes the fiercest assaults on those who have not yet had time to forge themselves arms against it). Then he asked me why I believed this and added:

"Perhaps you ask too much of life?"

"Oh no! I really ask very little." I knew that what I did ask for was love, but I would not have admitted this for the world to a distinguished man who must certainly detest all that was banal. He seemed to notice my embarrassment, for he refrained from asking of what that little consisted and a few minutes later, Mme. Sougny called us to supper.

It was not till the end of the meal that we spoke again of

Mr. Howells. Then the old professor pushed aside his coffee cup, took the marmalade cat on his knee and, stroking it gently till its purr rose and fell in an uneven throbbing, begged me to talk to him of Pont-y-Gibby.

I told him everything. The school with its unkempt, noisy children, the little red-brick villa, the lessons with Mair in the musty parlour, all that I knew of her father's youth in North Wales. I evoked all this for myself as much as for him, but I said not a word of those Sundays passed behind close-drawn shutters, nor did I speak of Idris.

The professor listened attentively, blinking his eyes and nodding with little clicks of the tongue. When I had finished, he sighed and said:

"In fact, Howells returned to his original state."

He leaned towards his wife.

"How far we were, my dear, from suspecting our friend of having such a background—pious, more than conformist. It had really left not a trace on him at the time when we knew him."

"Absolutely none! He came to us from Cambridge, I think. He had a degree in physics, if I remember rightly. One might have taken him for a typical young English scholar if it had not been for this almost frenetic desire to penetrate the farthest possible distance into the domain of pure thought."

She said this in her quavering, old woman's voice … a voice that seemed made for counting stitches.

The professor regarded her tenderly. "It was exactly that. I never met a more audacious mind. There was something inhuman in him, a sort of 'thinking machine' quality, yet at the same time he seemed to be torn by some interior struggle. Now, after all this time, I am beginning to understand the origin of that struggle."

He reflected, mechanically caressing the cat, whose purr wavered and swelled beneath his fingers.

"Yet I fail to understand this renunciation, this return to ideas which he *could* not, in view of his intellectual development, consider seriously. I have sometimes seen a sudden religious revival in men as remarkable as him. I understood them. Certain natures have a tendency to mysticism which cannot be denied without danger to the whole mental structure. The very fact of continually asking questions to which the answer, in spite of all the philosophic systems, must necessarily remain incomplete, sometimes arouses the desire for a divinity—that is for a definitive and absolute answer, arrived at by instinct rather than reason. For my own part I refuse to admit irrational solutions, just as I refuse to admit any frontier to human intelligence, but I can conceive that a man of superior intellect may be carried away by this idea of God that has obsessed so many great minds. Yet, if I have properly understood you, there was nothing metaphysical about the religion of my friend Howells. It consisted, you say, in a blind belief in the whole teaching of the Bible. The creation of the world in seven days, Noah's Ark… . And all that mixed up with an ethical system that consisted principally in tabus. …"

He made a gesture of impotence. "A brain cannot go back in its tracks to such an extent. Unless, indeed, it has become entirely debilitated."

"That was certainly not the case with Mr. Howells."

"What, then?" He seemed irritated at my incapacity to satisfy him.

I remembered what Idris once said to me, a long time ago: "Perhaps he was afraid."

"Afraid? That is not impossible. A man formed by this

puritan education, its very product in fact.... . The innate fear of damnation. ...."

I had not meant this, but suddenly I understood that he was right. Idris had reduced his father's fear to the scale of the struggle between man and man. He had seen him as fearing his fellow-men, and himself. Now I understood that he had feared only God.

"Unquiet natures are always looking for their childhood," said Mme. Sougny. "They never escape. I think our friend Howells had such a nature."

I seemed to see him at this moment. The image in my brain had almost the solidity of vision. He is seated at a little table in a bedroom with a green-shuttered window through which filter a few rays of uncertain light. He wears black as usual and sits, although he is alone, straight and rigid on his hard chair. The Bible, bound in black moroccan leather, is open before him. He is reading. He reads avidly, indiscriminately, devouring page after page, hypnotizing himself with the incantatory words. "Believe! Believe!" But he cannot believe any more, the power is gone from him. Then, to still the reason which is leading him to damnation, he stretches out his hand towards the bottle that stands nearby. There is a tooth glass beside it. He has foreseen everything, known in advance that he will be defeated. He pours the golden-coloured liquid, swallows, pours again. Already the words fill with meaning. Clumsily he turns the gold-edged pages. "The Lord is my shepherd, I shall not want ..." His eyes are fixed on the page but his hand gropes, closes on the cool roundness of the bottle.

A FEW DAYS after my visit to Professor Sougny, I happened to stop on my way home from the University at the crossing of the Boulevard Raspail and the Boulevard Montparnasse. There was shopping to do and it amused me to visit the big grocery stores on the boulevard, to buy foodstuffs which were still only half-familiar to me and to plan meals which Idris might be persuaded to praise. When all my purchases were stowed away in a string bag and I had counted out my francs at the cash-desk, I wandered out into the square and stood for a moment, enjoying the bright sunlight and the sight of the great cafés where people from all the corners of the earth were drinking and gossiping gaily. Their shirts and dresses made a multitude of bright splashes of colour, like those that fill the canvases of the Pointillist painters. Street vendors threaded their way between the tables offering slices of crystallized orange, peanuts or little dolls with movable limbs which they jerked into action by means of threads attached to their fingers. Newspaper sellers passed up and down, crying out the latest sensations:

"Another trunk murder!"

"Vote of confidence to-night!"

Their shrill voices rose above the clatter of glasses and the clamour of a hundred exotic accents. Everyone looked happy, or perhaps I imagined they did because I felt happy myself. At the corner of the street, near the spot where I stood, was a stall piled with purple and white lilac and its fragrance was so strong that it almost drowned the odour from the nearby vespasian. These smells mingled with those of new-baked bread and printer's ink and formed together a heady, violent summer-smell and the sun shone so bright and steady that my bare arms prickled and stung beneath its rays...

But I had no time to linger, for Idris was back from the north and would be lunching at home. I remembered that I was no longer a care-free student, at liberty to loiter in cafés to my heart's content, but a woman with family cares, her arms weighed down by a string bag full to bursting with the week's provisions. So I turned away, half regretful and half proud of my responsibilities and prepared to cross the road. It was at this moment that I caught sight of a young girl who, standing just around the bend of the street, turned her head sharply as if seeking to avoid my gaze and disappeared into the shadowy entrance to a courtyard.

This brief vision was enough for me to recognize Mair and the sight of her filled me with a vague anxiety. It was hard to believe that she was here, lurking in my passage, with the sole aim of spying on me, yet I could find no other explanation for her behaviour. She must, I thought, have caught sight of me by chance—in the Latin Quarter, perhaps —and have followed me here to discover where I should go and what I should do.

At this moment the bus drew up beside me. The queue surged forward; the conductor barked out the numbers, impatient to be gone.

"Eighty-five, eighty-six, eighty-seven ... and we're full up!"

He pulled the dangling chain. "Ping!" went the little bell, and off we went, crowded like sardines on the platform, jamming our elbows into each other's stomachs as we fumbled for our tickets, bumping gaily along, sniffing the sun and the dust, while the chestnut-lined boulevards, the tall buildings of the Cité Universitaire and the sordid huts and burnt-out factories of the Zone flashed past us on either side. I was going home. I repeated the words like a charm and presently they began to work—for it was impossible to worry on such a radiant day as this—and I began to believe that her presence had been a mere chance. She must have caught sight of me at the same moment that I saw her and turned away, offended by my abandon, to avoid greeting me.

Yet, when I arrived at the studio, I became uneasy again. The room, with the north-facing window designed for artists, appeared chill and gloomy after the gay sunlight of the square. Our primitive furniture looked small and lost on the great expanse of stone floor. From below the window resounded the blows of hammer upon iron. A couple of workmen were engaged, as usual in the daytime, in making lift shafts. Then the blows ceased and I knew that they were settling down for lunch, sitting straddled on a wooden beam and taking long, slow, alternate drafts from a bottle of red wine.

Idris arrived soon after. I had resolved to say nothing of the morning's encounter but somehow, almost as soon as we had sat down to lunch, I allowed myself the incautious luxury of confiding in him.

At once he was furious.

"That little pest! I'll wring her neck if I catch her sticking her nose into my affairs!"

Already I was regretting my words, knowing that Mair, obscurely, had made him suffer. "Like a tap that is never properly turned off!" I said to myself disgusted and remembering how often, during my childhood in Pont-y-Gibby, I might have saved myself by silence.

Idris was chewing his beefsteak, his face thunderous. He must have been chewing over black memories at the same time. He grumbled:

"I wish she'd do her damn singing somewhere else." But there was a note of sadness in his voice.

We spoke no more of it, but all day I saw him silent and tormented.

Nearly three weeks passed before I saw Mair again. This time there could be no mistake. She had carried her reconnoitre as far as Montrouge itself and was standing near the entrance to the square, just beside a deserted stall. When she saw me, she made no attempt to hide but fixed me with a long, hostile stare before she turned and disappeared into the avenue.

I went slowly up the stairs. My heart was beating violently and I felt an anxiety which seemed out of proportion to its cause. At each step I reasoned with myself. If Mair had discovered my relationship with her brother, it was disagreeable but not catastrophic. She had no power to harm us. She must have intended me to see her in the square, believing, no doubt, that her disapproval would weigh on my conscience, not understanding how thoroughly I was free of her.

When I opened the door, I saw that Idris was busy mending the flex of an electric lamp, frowning as he twisted the cord in his long, thin fingers. He looked at me sharply and said: "You look queer! Has something happened?"

I suppressed a strong impulse to tell him the truth and said that the journey in the heat had tired me.

"Well, have a rest before lunch. You're always getting upset about nothing. What's the use?"

And he turned to his mending again while Mair's face grimaced in my brain, a menacing little image which, in the days to come, would keep me incessant and unwelcome company and obsess me with the nagging question: "What can she do to harm us?"

It was at the time of this second apparition of Mair that the first doubts began to creep into my mind. They took root gradually. They were like a hand which, stretching out one after the other its icy fingers, was scratching gently at the roots of my happiness.

I could not have defined this creeping doubt. In appearance nothing was changed and this very calm disturbed me. I knew that Idris was resolute in his determination to refuse all responsibility, to live entirely in the present. For the moment, no doubt, he was happy to live beside me but tomorrow his attention might be diverted to some other interest, then he would be off, on principle, without giving himself time to reflect, and if he felt remorse he would hate me for it.

One evening when we were standing on our little balcony, enjoying the cool breeze that had risen up after the oppressive heat of the day, he said to me:

"All human relationships are really a sort of treachery. To choose out one special person and to reject all the others… When I see all that is going on around us, the progressive en-slavement of mankind, the injustice and misery of modern life, and then I see how the very people who are most aware, who are most needed, exhaust their energies in the wear and tear of personal relationships … it makes me sick with disgust."

The evening air seemed suddenly chilly on my skin. He was speaking of us. He appeared to be tossing off an idea, a theory, but I knew that it was of us he was speaking. I groped for words to check him.

"Man is an individual as well as a social being. I cannot see why he should deny half his nature."

He shrugged his shoulders.

"Because that half is worthless. The individual you are so keen on is nothing but a romantic idea that prevents man from becoming efficacious. Every reasonable person should try to root out that part of himself."

"And have you … rooted it out?"

"I'm on the way, I hope."

I turned and walked through the window, back into the studio. A few minutes later Idris followed me. He switched on the light, for the room was already filled with shadow, then he lighted a cigarette and lay down on the divan, smoking and staring moodily before him.

"Come and lie down," he said. "Why are you so nervous?" I lay down beside him and lighted a cigarette in my turn and the smoke rose up in twin columns that spread and mingled in a hazy cloud. As I turned my head to look at him, it struck me how greatly he had changed from the youth I had known. Now that he was approaching thirty his nervous, dislocated movements had frozen, by his will, into a sort of rigidity. He held himself stiffly, as if constantly checking in himself some instinct for disorder. Already some mental strain had etched deep lines along his cheeks. It was easy to imagine him, black-clad, striding along a village street, towards a villa of red brick, towards… .

His voice sliced off the image.

"You have never asked me why I wanted to live with you here. Does nothing ever surprise you, or are you inviolably discreet?"

I made no answer and after a time he said:

"I suppose I owe you some explanation, yet I can hardly give it to you since I do not really understand myself in this matter. It never occurred to me till we came here that day by chance that I could put up with and even desire the continual presence of a woman in the house. Sometimes I think I was acting almost against my own will."

"Do you regret it?"

"I don't know. I needed someone I could love simply without according too much importance to her. I could feel free then, but that could never be possible between us two."

Now he was forcing me to take part in this dialogue from which I only wished to escape. I could not do otherwise than ask him:

"Why is it impossible between us?"

"My dear, you remind me constantly of all that I have most hated in my life. Whenever I see you, for instance, I am obliged to think of my father. It is not because he is dead, you know, that he has ceased to preoccupy me."

He lit another cigarette, blew a long ribbon of smoke into the air and went on:

"It is extraordinary, the way in which he managed to mark you in such a short time. I can see you as you were that day up on the Sugar-loaf. You remember? You defended him with such ardour … and suddenly it seemed to me that it was *his expression* I saw in your eyes, they were full of that austerity, that conscious rectitude I so detested in him. It was as if they reflected his soul instead of your own."

"And you hated me for it?"

He said slowly: "Ah, that's the question. A little, yes. But above all, I hated him a little less. And I didn't want that. I didn't want to be softened, to be persuaded to compromise. You represented a moral danger for me then, and I am afraid you still do so…"

He talked on and each word drove a fresh breach between us. It seemed to me now that our two bodies, stretched side by side and at no point touching, resembled those stone effigies that sometimes mark the ancient tombs of pious couples.

I moved my heavy head of stone to look at him, but his face told me nothing. I said:

"I don't understand. I don't know what I mean to you. I have never known."

"Ah!" he said: "The tug of memory, homesickness, the subconscious attachment to all that reason tries to throw off. You see that I am terribly lucid …"

"Such small things in your life … Hardly worth speaking of…"

"You are mistaken," he said. "These things are far more important to me than they should be. After all, you come from my own country. We have fallen out of the same nest."

His voice had become more gentle now and he turned a little on his side to look at me. I said:

"I did not know you were so fond of that nest."

"Fond! My poor child, I hate it more than you can imagine. Only, hating and loving are so nearly the same thing."

"I suppose so."

I tried to rise but he pressed his hand against my shoulder and forced me down again.

"I said to you once before that we are bound together. Perhaps that is why I sometimes desire so much to liberate myself. Perhaps I was wrong to … accept so easily. Wrong for myself and wrong for you. Especially for you."

"What do you want to do, then?"

"Nothing. You must not imagine that I do not care for you. I wish I was different. I wish I was someone who could say to you: This is for always.

"Mind you," he went on, "I am not trying to tell you the contrary cither. I simply don't know. There are certain things in my life that will never change—the stable core, if you like.

You don't come into that. Then there's the uncertain element, that may develop in one direction or the other. I love you with all that side of myself that I distrust."

"I, too, distrust my love for you," I said. "But what I distrust in myself belongs precisely to the stable core you speak of. There is nothing I can really be sure of."

Now he kissed me and said lightly: "Don't let us take all this too seriously. Let us just go on and see what happens. I only wanted to be honest with you, so that you should not … count too completely on me."

And now, because the last year had taught me so much, I was able to take a tone as light as his own and say:

"I never count on anything. We shall see…"

AFTER this conversation I felt myself vulnerable on every side and the vague anxiety left by the appearance of Mair in Montrouge changed to an almost superstitious fear of her. I was annoyed with myself for this unreasonable obsession and a few days later, on a radiant summer afternoon when it seemed imposs-ible that any unpleasant thing could happen, I decided to clear the matter up once and for all. So I waited until Idris had gone to work, then I left the house and made my way to the rue Jacob.

The frail notes of the piano floated down the staircase and became gradually clearer as I mounted from floor to floor. Mair was practising an Italian piece and already I could hear her voice repeating a series of trills beginning on a very high note which she sang over and over again, eternally unsatisfied. When I reached her door, I remained for several minutes in the passage, listening to her, drawing reassurance from that pure voice which still recalled so vividly, for all its full round-ness, the child I had known in Pont-y-Gibby.

Presently I knocked on the door and Mair's voice stopped, detached abruptly from an F-sharp.

"Come in!"

I lifted the latch. She was sitting on the piano stool, swivelled round so as to face the door. She regarded me without surprise, eyebrows raised questioningly. Then she waited for me to speak, but I could discover no hostility in her polite, stranger's stare.

"I wanted to see you... ."

"Did you?" she uncrossed her legs, rose nonchalantly.

"Sit down. I'll make some tea."

She busied herself at the spirit stove, prepared the thick china mugs from which we had so often drunk together, poured out the steaming tea. We drank in silence and it seemed to me that she was enjoying herself. A small smile played at the corners of her mouth. She was waiting for the moment when my nerves would get the better of me and oblige me to speak.

"How are you getting on?"

My voice sounded artificially careless. A point to her.

"As you see. I'm always hard at work. The radio has offered me a contract and I think I'll accept while I am waiting to give my recital."

"When is that to be?"

"I'm in no hurry. I shall want it to be perfect."

A heavy silence fell between us once more. This time it was she who broke it.

"What about you?"

There was a note of defiance in her voice. She was not at her ease, in spite of the impassive face she presented to me.

I said: "You ought to know."

She regarded me attentively: "Yes, I do know. You are living with my brother. I need not tell you what I think about it."

"Why must you think anything. It just happened. We fell in love."

She smiled: "Do you believe Idris is capable of loving anyone?"

I made no reply and she continued: "You think that I am heartless because he is my only near relation and I never want to see him again. That shows how stupid you are, how un-imaginative."

"I don't interfere in your concerns, Mair."

But now she was away, riding her hatred like a horse, happy in it almost, pursing her lips with a disapproving air, and suddenly she resembled the vicar's wife, Mrs. Williams, the mischief-maker.

"I dream about it every night," she said. "Every night since it happened. That scene ... all those people staring and whis-pering. What can they have said about us? I've never stopped feeling ashamed."

Her voice trembled. "I took so much trouble to hide father's ... weakness ... from everyone. No one would ever have known."

"You think too much about other people's opinion," I said. "We are talking about your father and your brother, about you and me. The opinion of the postman and the grocer at Pont-y-Gibby has nothing to do with any of us."

"Well, the opinion of people one must see every day counts a lot. Scandal is a terrible thing. Father used to say, before... (She could not bring herself to pronounce the words. She left a gap in her sentence and that gap was Mr. Howells' death)... He used to say: 'Woe unto him who scandalizes my little ones'. He used to repeat it all the time. He would sit there on his chair, with his hands on his knees and never move. He never went out, he did nothing at all, he didn't even read. When he did open his mouth, it was nearly always to say the same thing: 'Woe unto him who scandalizes my little ones.' He was thinking of himself but it was Idris who caused the harm. He was really the guilty one." She was crying now and in spite of my determination to remain objective, the old affection swept over me and with it the infinite tolerance that had always led me, in the old days, to forgive her everything in the end, because she was Mair.

"And you," she said. "You have lied to me. You have gone off with him in secret, like a thief. Now I have no one."

I took her hand. It was useless to speak. She was too far from reality, nothing existed for her beyond the narrow limits of her own imagination, and that imagination itself was a deforming mirror.

"Sing something for me," I said, knowing the one way to console her. "Sing that piece from the Messiah. The one you used to sing at home."

She understood at once and thanked me with a rather tremulous smile. "It isn't meant for a solo, you know, and it doesn't even suit my voice."

"Never mind. It reminds me …"

She rose, struck a chord on the piano. Her chest, which ordinarily seemed so flat and narrow, swelled, expanded, as the lungs drew air in preparation for sound. She smiled, a radiant, unreal smile which seemed to address itself to a vast and invisible audience, and began.

"Worthy is the Lamb that was slain …"

Through the clear notes I seemed to hear the voice of the child, still unconscious of its power.

"And honour… And glory …"

When she had finished she waited for a moment as if for the clamour of applause to die down. Then she came to sit demurely beside me.

"What a lovely voice you have!" I said sincerely, for her singing never failed to move and enchant me.

She made a slight gesture with her hand, as if to brush away the valueless compliment of the uninitiated, and said:

"It's ridiculous to sing it like that. I wouldn't let anyone else hear me doing it." She laughed. "Do you remember those Welsh choirs, alternately bellowing and whispering their way through the Messiah and the Elijah! What a long time ago it seems!" Then she asked suddenly, taking me unawares: "What do you intend to do now?"

I did not understand her at once and she repeated the question aggressively.

"Do?" I said. "Nothing special. My work at the Sorbonne … write … go on as I am now."

"But Idris?"

"Well, just go on too."

She clutched my arm: "You have no right to say that. It's disgusting! Is he going to marry you?"

There was no need for me to reply. She regarded me with a gleam of triumph in her eyes.

"You see! I told you he was a beast! You'll regret it."

"Perhaps I shall," I said. "But I cannot think so now and anyway it is too late to draw back."

"How can you let a man who isn't even your husband do … that … to you? A man who is as good as a murderer…"

The horror in her eyes was sincere, I could not believe otherwise. The words hissed out between her lips. The whites of her eyes were swallowed up now by the black, glowing pupils, so that they were all black, like coals set in her small, pale face.

I rose.

"There's nothing more to be said, is there? I'm sorry this upsets you so much."

"That isn't the question. You are living an immoral life." I shrugged my shoulders.

"I'm afraid there is nothing I can do about that."

"But there is something I can do," she said. "I can tell your parents. It's my duty."

And suddenly I read the spiteful satisfaction in her eyes. A terrible fear stabbed somewhere in my chest.

"You wouldn't do that?"

"I've done it already. As soon as I knew the truth I wrote to your mother."

And she added proudly, as if repeating a phrase learned from a novel. "An anonymous letter."

"It isn't true!" I was making a great effort to appear calm, but I recognized the panic in my voice.

She shrugged her shoulders. "You'll see for yourself." For her, the conversation was at an end. She had produced her effect and now, transformed into a perfect hostess, she pressed me to take a second cup of tea.

On the staircase, I had to stop and lean against the banister because of the nervous trembling that shook my body. I seemed to see with extraordinary clarity the dining-room at home. My parents are having breakfast, seated one at each end of the heavy mahogany dining-table. My mother is helping porridge from the great silver porringer, engraved with the

Gethryn arms, surmounted by a conceited-looking cock. My
father pours coffee, helps himself to the bacon that is warming
over the hot-plate. My mother bends to speak to the terriers
that crouch at her feet; my father brushes with an uncertain
hand a crumb from his moustache. Now a little red-faced
servant girl, shaped like a bun, enters the room, bringing
letters on a silver tray. "Here's a French stamp, Mam. News
from Miss Laura it will be, no doubt."

"No, Gwynedd, this isn't her writing. I hope she is not ill."
She slits the envelope, draws out the folded sheet.

"Dear Madame...

I forced my mind away, but the scene had appeared so
vividly that I was almost surprised to find myself still at the
turn of the dimly-lit staircase with its worm-rotted steps and
sculpted, crumbling balustrade. Mair had gone back to the
piano. She was striking single notes, one after the other, and
after each note her voice rose in a sort of scale, mounting very
high then falling suddenly towards the bass and remounting
immediately. She must have been in fine form, congratulating
herself on the dramatic outcome of our talk.

Yet now the notes ceased abruptly, to be succeeded by utter
silence. They had lasted, it seemed to me, just the time that I
would normally have taken to leave the house. And now I was
certain that Mair, leaning forward upon the keyboard, her hair
streaming over the keys, was weeping.

I kept my papers in the drawer of a deal table that served as
my writing desk and as soon as I arrived I began to sort my
mother's letters out from among the miscellaneous collection
of unfinished poems, bills and lecture notes which I had
crammed into it during the last three months. She never dated

her letters and there was little variety in their contents. I tried to remember when I had last heard from her, but the days and weeks had been melting so swiftly away that I had no exact recollection. I spread the letters out on the table, compared them. They told of nothing but golf-matches and trouble with a thieving cook. There was certainly no hint about anonymous letters. Then, just as I was beginning to feel reassured, to say to myself: "Another of Mair's lies!" I noticed that the most recent letters contained an omission. My mother no longer sent her kind regards as she always used to do to the girl companion who was supposed to share my lodgings.

Idris came home late that evening. He looked tired and told me briefly that he had been detained at the office. I knew that in this mood my presence easily irritated him. If I confided in him, it might break the thread, whose strength was so impossible to judge, which still bound us together. He must not know that he was perhaps now my last resource.

He soon fell asleep and I remained wakeful beside him, constantly aware of his body touching lightly all along my own. When dawn came and the room was filled with half-light, I watched his face appear gradually, with uncertain contours, as if seen through a grey veil, and it seemed to me that this was already his absent face, as I should see it in memory after the passage of many years.

We were having breakfast when the concierge brought up the morning post. We still seemed to be in her good favour, although by now she must have put us in the same class as the Slavs, parsimonious with their tips. She held out three letters. Two were for Idris, post-marked from Paris. The third was from my mother and she continued to hold it, turning it between her red, swollen fingers as she explained:

"It's the stamp that interests me. My husband collects them, he's mad about it. All my tenants give me theirs and I don't know how many times he's said to me: "You ought to ask that little English lady!" Only I kept forgetting and then, it's quite a time, isn't it, since you've had a letter from home."

"Do you think so, Madame Boucard? I was just wondering."

"Quite a time, it's been. I was saying so to my husband only yesterday."

"Give it to me, please, Madame Boucard."

She held it out rather unwillingly, relinquishing an excuse for lingering to gossip. I noticed how she was beginning to bulge beneath her flowered overall. This would be her fifth.

"You'll let me have the stamp?"

I tore off the corner of the envelope and there appeared a morsel of paper and a few words written in my mother's firm, well-rounded writing. The disconnected fragment revealed nothing. I put the letter in my pocket and waited to read it until Idris had gone.

I had so prepared myself for the worst that I had to read the letter twice over before I could understand that it contained none of the allusions that I had feared. It was an ordinary letter, in the rather abrupt style affected by my mother, a list of small events in an uneventful life. Yet it was a little longer than usual, since it contained a postscript which ran:

"It is nearly time for the summer holidays and of course we are expecting you home. In a few days I will send, instead of your usual monthly allowance, enough money for your journey and for your hotel bill in London. You will not find a great deal going on here but we will try to arrange some tennis parties for you. Your father says he will be glad of your help as he is building a rock-garden down by the shrubbery."

THE SUMMER holidays … The thought of them had not yet entered my mind and indeed I had hardly realized that the passage of the months was bringing me inevitably to this holiday season. Now, as if to underline my mother's phrase, a heat wave descended on the city. The thermometer shot to record heights and each morning the newspapers headlined the previous day's sensational temperatures. When I went out into the streets, I felt that I must surely stifle, for the air was so heavy that it seemed too solid to flow into the lungs. This was summer in the African style, proper to great sandy spaces, but destructive here, trapped between the high blocks of houses. The soles of my shoes stuck in melting tar. The stout matrons of the market streamed with sweat, their faces like dripping, purple plums. The children trailed listlessly in the shaded garden and the apprentice gangsters from the Zone paraded in suits of imitation tussore.

Yet I enjoyed this heat, whose very violence suited my mood. I enjoyed the siesta after lunch, with its confused dreams, and the long, languid strolls in the evening when the falling dusk brought an illusion of relief, though it was still so hot that we must stop at every café encountered, to refresh ourselves with iced *Vichy-menthe* among the exhausted workmen who crowded round the counters, swearing and mopping their streaming faces. It was already the month of July.

"My mother wants me to go home for the holidays," I said to Idris.

He yawned, overcome by the heat which he detested. "You'd better go. I wish to God I could get away too. The office has promised me a fortnight in August and I suppose I shall have to roast in this furnace until then."

"How will you get on here without me?"

He made a vague gesture.

"One can always get on somehow. I'll eat out. It will be like the old days."

"Very well," I said. "I will go at the end of the month." He smiled—a reassuring, friendly smile—and said:

"It will do you good to get a rest. You look as white as a sheet these days."

So I began a letter to my mother. Dates… trains… As I wrote the memory of Pont-y-Gibby began to take on a more solid reality in my mind. I seemed to feel the moist coolness of the lawn against my cheek, to breathe the garden smells— the spicy, exciting smell of pine-trees, the sugary fragrance of rose-beds, the smell of cut hay drying in the sun. And with that smell of hay came a sudden and almost overpowering desire to bury myself in an odorous stook in the new-mown paddock, among the prickly, tickly stalks, tepid with sun, to burrow among them and be there motionless and hidden, drunken, really, and drugged with the intoxicating smell of sun-baked grass. Then I thought of the flocks of sheep, herded by attentive sheep-dogs along the lanes, between dripping hedges. Then I thought of the galloping streams in the hills and of all that slow, country life, moving in the unchanging rhythm of the seasons, where man is at all times submissive to nature. And as these thoughts and images formed themselves in my mind, words were forming themselves almost unconsciously beneath my pen: "I am glad to be coming home." Then, gazing at them with a sort of astonished anxiety, because I could not have dreamed that I should ever write such words, I asked myself whether they were true or false, and was unable to find an answer.

Towards the end of the afternoon it seemed to me that the air was freshening a little. It was Idris' day off from the office and I suggested that we should go into town. I posted my letter at the corner of the square, then we took the bus for the Porte d'Orleans. "Let's walk down to Montparnasse!"

The Avenue d'Orléans seethed with a good-humoured crowd. People were fingering the workmen's overalls and rayon petticoats that hung along the front of a great clothes store; street hawkers were offering artificial pearl necklaces and tendering rose-pink letter paper; purposeful women clutching long sausage-loaves of bread, pushed perambulators from shop to shop. From far off came a noise of music and shouting and as we approached the Place Denfer Rocherau, we saw that the annual fair was in full swing. Here the crowd was so dense that it was difficult to cross the square. We pushed our way forward, between the houp-la stalls and the caravans of the fortune-tellers. Suspended against a sky of Reckitt's blue were the steel loops of the scenic railway, where cartloads of squealing men and girls hurtled down slopes of false snow. Then a powerful stench of ill-tended caged beasts told us that the menagerie was near, and indeed, a moment later, there was a painted clown gesticulating in front of a great tent, boasting of the ferocity of his lions.

"Let's get out of this," gasped Idris, and we plunged resolutely through the crowd, skirting the round-about and the boxing booth, and thus arrived at the fringe of the fair.

Here, opening on to the *Place,* was a small public garden, frequented by the children of the district and by aged men, inflicted with various infirmities, from the hospice across the road. Close by its barrier, a troupe of acrobats was performing before a small group of indifferent spectators. It was evidently a family affair. The father was a massive and brutish creature, whose muscles rose in unsightly hillocks over the surface of a squat body, mounted on short, knotty legs. Two or three large iron balls lay at his feet and he was roaring the praises of his coming feats of strength. We paused, from exhaustion rather than from interest, to listen to him. "A hundred pounds, that one weighs! And I lift it with one hand! Ah, my friends! It isn't often you'll get a chance to see something like this!"

He bent down, his back braced for the effort, but even before his fingers had touched the ball, he had straightened up again and, glancing around the scanty audience, selected a young sailor to whom he held out his arm, bracing it so that the muscles sprang up like clenched fists beneath the sun-reddened skin.

"Feel that, old man! Hard as stone, eh? I was a wrestling champion—a heavyweight—in the old days."

The sailor touched the knotted muscle gingerly and said: "Not bad!" in an embarrassed voice. His small, vicious face, rose-tinted like that of a very young child, had taken on an expression of mingled curiosity and disgust. His companions laughed scornfully and one of them said:

"Well, when are we going to see something?"

The acrobat's face split in a monstrous smile.

"You're in a hurry, eh? Well, gentlemen, I won't keep you waiting any longer."

He turned back to the middle of the ring and seen thus from the back, with his heavy, shambling tread and the long arms that hung almost to his knees, he resembled nothing more than a gorilla clothed in a vest and bathing drawers.

Now he bent again, lifted the ball an inch, groaning, and let it fall to the ground again.

"You don't expect me to do all this for nothing, do you? In this heat, too! If you want me to kill myself, you must make it worth my while."

A woman advanced, listlessly beating a tambourine decorated with grimy ribbons... . A puffy, white face, surmounted by an orange wig... . The audience dropped coins into the tambourine because they had not the energy to escape, then, having paid, felt obliged to wait for their money's worth.

At last the man set to work in earnest. He raised one of the balls, with a great cracking of muscles, and held it aloft, his arm upstretched above his head. His face was the colour of port-wine now and his eyes bulged, starting from their sockets with the effort of the body.

"It's faked," explained someone behind me. "Those balls are hollow, really. He holds his breath to make it look hard."

But already the ex-wrestler had lowered the ball to the ground again. He sponged his dripping forehead, then clapped his enormous hands to gain attention.

"Look out! Look out! Here's the biggest event of all!"

Three chairs were placed now in the form of a pyramid at the centre of the ring. The woman reappeared, pushing before her two unwilling children, a boy and a girl, who seemed like two little old people, shrivelled, undoubtedly terrorized, with sunken cheeks and fragile bones ready to pierce the skin of their narrow little chests. Docilely they bent, with arched backs, till their hands touched the ground behind their heads.

"Hup!"

Now they climbed to the summit of the chair-pyramid, reared themselves up on their hands, balancing dangerously, the slender arms trembling beneath the weight of their bodies. The two frail pairs of legs wavered uncertainly, like antennae in the air, made precarious contact and enlaced each other beneath the implacable eyes of the parents. The grinding music of the fair swelled around us, the heat was like a weight at the back of my neck and suddenly I felt immensely tired.

"There'll be a storm soon," said Idris.

He passed his hand over his forehead, which shone with sweat. He had the haggard eyes of his bad days.

We pushed our way through the sweating crowd and came at last into the Boulevard Raspail, where the plane trees threw long, cool shadows on the ground. I was feeling a little dizzy, so I leaned on Idris' arm. In the distance we could hear the bleating of hurdy-gurdies and the shrill cries of the girls on the scenic railway.

The terrace of the Café Dôme, invaded at this season by tourists, was relatively cool beneath the green awnings. We found a free table and installed ourselves thankfully. The ice tinkled in the tall glasses of lemonade and the cold prickle of the drink in my throat seemed to extend itself in a sudden shiver that ran the whole length of my body. We drank in silence, stunned with heat and noise. I was thinking vaguely about my approaching journey, projecting myself forward into the coming months, trying to savour them in advance, so that I might divine whether they were destined to make me suffer. It was easy to live them thus in advance, since I knew that life at home would be absolutely unchanged. It would be enough to take a single backward step and I should find myself at precisely the point where I had been a year ago, at the time of my departure. That point itself would hardly differ from the remotest recollections of my childhood and they, in their turn, would prefigure the future and my own old age. Yet I knew that I could never take that step, however much I might wish to do so. I could never become again the Laura who had packed her trunks and been gone. I had made of myself an irrevocable stranger.

A hand on my shoulder drew me from my thoughts. Jean-Pierre Carré was standing beside me, his face glowing with the heat, his clear, grey eyes shining with unfeigned delight at our meeting.

"I haven't seen you for ages, Laura! Where on earth have you been hiding yourself?" I introduced him to Idris and invited him to join us. He hesitated.

"Are you sure I am not interrupting you?"

"Of course not! Sit down and tell me what you have been doing."

He installed himself and ordered an ice. Idris, watching him from the corner of his eye, suddenly decided to like him and began to make himself agreeable. We exchanged news, talked of our plans for the holidays. Jean-Pierre intended to go with a party of friends for a bicycling tour in Italy.

"We haven't a penny between us, of course. We shall sleep in youth hostels when we come across any, otherwise we'll camp wherever we happen to be at nightfall. No fixed itinerary ... we just plan to see as much of the country as possible. One can't go wrong in Italy; everything is worth seeing, so it doesn't matter where one lands up."

Idris listened to him with interest. "It sounds a terrific idea! You'll be absolutely free. I wish I could do the same thing!"

"Why not?" said Jean-Pierre. "It doesn't cost more than it would to stay at home and one brings back a stock of memories to keep one going for the rest of the year."

"Too late!" said Idris. "I'm stuck in Paris. A steady job and a monthly salary are as good as any ball and chain for keeping a man in prison."

"When are you leaving?" I asked Jean-Pierre.

"As soon as the exams are over. That is, in about ten days. I'm glad to have seen you before I go, especially as I have a message for you that has been weighing on my conscience for a long time."

"From whom?"

"From Professor Sougny. He would like you to call on him again. He's tremendously interested in that schoolmaster you knew when you were a child and who turned out to have been his friend and pupil. It seems he has found some notebooks— a sort of diary this man kept when he was a student here. He wouldn't show them to me, but he says they are extraordinary and they will help you to understand a lot of things. … In fact, he seems to think it is important for you to see them."

Idris' face was expressionless. I could not even guess whether he had been paying attention to our conversation.

"Very well," I said. "I will go to see him. Thank you for telling me."

After that we spoke of other things and presently Jean-Pierre rose, saying:

"I must be going now. I shall see you next term, shan't I, Laura? You are coming back to the Sorbonne, of course?"

"I suppose I shall," I said.

He shook hands with Idris and turned away. I watched him as he picked his way among the close-set tables, stopping here and there to greet an acquaintance, bending his fair head to greet a young girl who laughed vivaciously up at him, waving to a distant group of bearded art-students. His simplicity, and the joy he took in living had, as ever, calmed and reassured me and it was not till several minutes had passed that I began to feel uneasy about Idris.

We left the café without exchanging a word and began to wander quietly down the Boulevard in the direction of the Gare Montparnasse. Our silence might have been that of peaceful accord or of gathering storm. I could not yet determine its quality. Idris seemed a little absent. Perhaps he was thinking of Italy, of Jean-Pierre, who would soon be riding along the dusty roads, aimless and careless among miraculous landscapes.

We stopped in the velvety shadow of a high wall, just opposite the church of Notre-Dame-des-Champs. I had the feeling that this halt, in this precise and somehow essential décor, had been ordained long ago for some special purpose. We stood there in the shade and watched the banal building of the church, still drenched in a pale yellow sunlight, and it seemed to me that both of us were awaiting some event which must inevitably take place within a little time.

A few moments passed, then out of the church door came two little old women. They were very small, very shrivelled, all muffled in rusty black. They paused an instant, crossing themselves, then, leaning one on the other, they began very slowly to descend the steps.

It was as if this was the signal for which we had been waiting. Idris said slowly:

"You leave for England next week, don't you?"

I nodded. My throat felt dry and I wished that I could have another long, cool drink. Idris went on:

"Listen, I want to say something to you, quickly, while I have the courage. We must not come together again."

"Because of what Jean-Pierre said?"

"Perhaps Jean-Pierre made me understand how urgent it is that I should say this to you now, before you go, above all, before you come back. But sooner or later, we should have had to recognize the truth. We must separate because of your influence on my life, because you will never let me forget. I want to destroy the past and you hold me to it. You force me, not to return to my vomit, but never to leave it. So long as you are beside me, I am enveloped in the sight and sound and smell of the past. You must go before we do each other harm which can never be repaired. When you are gone I shall have broken the last link. I know now that that is what I must attain."

I had always known that this moment must come and almost I had known the words he would use, yet now that they had been pronounced, I heard them distraitly, as if they did not concern me, or as if they had been spoken by some unknown passer-by. My mind was fixed on the image of two pallid children twisting thin bodies in the pitiless heat for the pleasure of an indifferent crowd. I said to myself: Idris has spoken. I must speak, too. But it seemed that my mind had stopped at that image like a motor-car suddenly arrested in an unintended place. At last I said: "What shall I do then? What will become of me?"

"I don't know," he said. "I don't know what is to become of either of us. You are going home for three months. Perhaps I shall be elsewhere by then, or perhaps neither of us will care any longer…"

Then he cried angrily:

"But I refuse to be concerned about this. I refuse to feel scruples or remorse. I am saving my own life. I can say nothing more."

He spoke very quickly, without looking at me. The two little old ladies had just reached the last step and were peering suspiciously and insecurely into the road, leaning on each other's arms.

PART III

THE TRAIN rushed across England, the green Wiltshire fields streamed past like sea cleft by a swimmer's passage. We plunged into the Severn Tunnel. Sparks flashed past the window in the thick darkness. A dim light glowed in the carriage. The noise of the roaring train was immense. Then suddenly we emerged into the daylight again. Newport Station. Walls plastered with texts. Porters calling to each other in their sing-song voices—little, dark men, extraordinarily alive in comparison with the slow-moving, silent-staring Saxons of the English stations. And a voice calling over the megaphone: Platform number four for Cardiff, Bridgend, Carmarthen, and West Wales.

I drank tea, black and bitter with tannin, in the shabby buffet. Everything seemed strange and far-off like a remembered dream. The ham sandwiches beneath the glass dome on the counter, the sizzling tea-urn, the half-familiar face of the untidy waitress, belonged to distant memory rather than to the immediate present. I told myself—It is less than a year since I came away—but it was impossible to reduce this great separating gulf to a distance measurable by the calendar.

Soon, though, it was time to catch the local train for Llanglaslyn. Dreamily, after the manner of such trains, it wound among the hills, stopping for long halts at apparently uninhabited spots. I munched a sandwich and refused to think of Mair's letter. As for Idris, he seemed already very far away. I felt no special pain at our separation, yet I was uneasily conscious that the pain was there, held at bay by some psychological anaesthetic, but ready to spring and take possession when a little time should have passed.

My mother was waiting at the station. I caught sight of her immediately, standing squarely in front of the bookstall and holding a nervous terrier on a leash. She was scanning the coaches as they drew in and now came forward purposefully as I stepped, encumbered with suitcases, on to the platform.

We kissed. "You look very thin," she said. Then, when I had handed over my ticket and the porter was stowing luggage in the car, she remarked:

"I'm afraid you'll find it very dull here. We haven't much excitement to offer you."

This oblique reference to my life in Paris was the last which she felt called upon to make. We drove unhurriedly along the familiar road, inspecting the spot where an oak had been torn up in the great gale last spring, catching a glimpse of Bayliss' new filly as she cantered behind the hedge-row, commenting on the ugly new villa built by a retired cloth-merchant from Newport.

"Miss O'Gorman is failing fast," said my mother. "Her poodle died and she has never been herself since. She was always a bit queer, I thought."

"And have you seen Lady Wynn-Evans?"

For a moment it seemed to me that a strange expression, which might almost be one of secret pleasure, flashed in her eyes. It was gone in a moment and, looking again at her calm, handsome face, I was astonished at the trick which imagination had played on me. She said:

"I saw her a few days ago. I had to drive to Abergavenny to fetch the new house-maid and I dropped in to see them on the way."

"Did she ask after me?"

"I suppose she did. I remember she asked after you last month at the flower-show."

We drove in at the gates and drew up in front of the house. The Virginia creeper was just turning colour and the walls were almost hidden beneath the thick curtain of pale crimson leaves. The roses were as fine as ever I remembered them, but the house itself seemed to have shrunk a little, so that it was less imposing in reality than it had been in memory—or was it, I wondered, that I was seeing it for the first time with the eyes of an adult?

My father came out of the door and shook hands with me.

"You look as thin as a rake! I suppose you never got anything decent to eat out there."

He himself was shrunken and brittle as a dried branch. For the first time I saw him as an old man, a fragile old man with wavering, guilty eyes. He could not have been more than five or six years older than my mother, yet they appeared almost to belong to different generations.

"Your father has not been really well for some time," she remarked as we mounted the stairs, preceded by Gwynedd and the new maid, carrying the luggage. The room was unchanged, very clean and swept-looking and the dressing-gown I had forgotten to pack last summer was still hanging from a peg behind the door. I noticed how small and narrow the bed looked—a young girl's bed, a bed for the young girl I had been.

"You must unpack for yourself," said my mother. "One can't ask these girls to do a thing. It's hard enough to persuade them to stay at all in a place where there is no cinema."

She was standing just inside the room, with her hand on the

latch of the door, continuing to make a few unimportant remarks as I opened my cases. Suddenly I realized that she was watching me closely, with a sort of piercing and almost hungry scrutiny, as if she was trying to read some secret that I might betray at any moment by a word or a gesture. I was so startled that I stood quite still, my arms piled with under-clothes. Our eyes met for a moment; she flushed and, turning, stalked out of the door, closing it with a firm, decisive click that should, to complete the gesture, have been followed by the classic grinding of a key in a lock.

As the days and weeks wore by, I surprised this same expression more and more often on my mother's face. It was as if she suspected that some stranger had returned in place of her daughter and she hoped, by this continual, secret scrutiny, to uncover her real identity. She was polite to me, as she would have been to a visitor, but she refused to discuss my stay in Paris or to listen to any talk of my experiences there. If I happened to mention any event of the past year, her face would harden, she would fix her eyes on some object in the room or on the landscape seen through the window and watch it intently, with an expression of impatient disgust on her face, until I had finished speaking. Then she would immediately begin to talk to my father about the crops or the prospects for the point-to-point season, or, if we were alone, she would pick up a newspaper and begin to read ostentatiously. Sometimes it seemed to me that it was more than irritation that tightened her lips to a thin line when some remark, some attitude, a more sophisticated manner of dressing or arranging my hair, re-minded her that I was no longer exactly the same Laura who had left a year earlier. It was hard to understand exactly what it was in me that irritated her so constantly and sometimes it was no longer mere irritation, but a sort of horror, a sort of furious contempt that I divined in her expression when she noticed, for instance, how one of my old dresses, cut for the flat figure of my schoolgirl days, strained now over my breasts. And certain attitudes, and even perhaps tones in my voice, were enough to cause her to avert her eyes and send a flame of dusky red sweeping upward over her neck and face.

Once or twice it seemed to me, too, that she was anxious to discourage me from contact with the village. Several times, during the first few days, I mentioned my intention to call on some old acquaintance, and each time she produced some reason against the visit.

"Colonel Musgrave has been very poorly lately. I don't think he would feel up to seeing you just now."

"Miss Morgan has been away staying with her sister. She'll be hardly settled in yet."

I had no special desire to see Colonel Musgrave or Miss Morgan and had considered making these visits only from a vague desire to do something, to find some activity which would awake me from the curious state of unreality in which I found myself, so I allowed myself to be convinced and found it easy to renounce my projects. Indeed, I soon realized that the people of the village had hardly noticed my absence, or, rather, that they behaved as if they had hardly noticed it. They enquired after my health and asked whether I had enjoyed my stay abroad, then they took my presence for granted. Yet the old intimacy had been broken. I was no longer one of themselves. They regarded me uneasily, as if I was a stranger come among them, yet sometimes it seemed to me as if their eyes followed me with a sort of avid curiosity.

So it was simpler to stay in the garden, reading in the swing, while the mulberries from the overhanging branches plopped on my head and shoulders, or to stroll aimlessly along the sanded paths in the kitchen garden, plucking raspberries or plums from the laden bushes.

One day, my father suggested that we would begin the rock-garden and the announcement that had filled me with such ennui when I had received my mother's last letter in Paris, now seemed a promise of activity if not of pleasure. I spent the afternoon arranging stones under his direction, piling them in a subtly balanced pyramid and filling the cracks tightly from a sack of earth and leaf-mould. By the end of the day, however, he lost interest and wandered off. I came upon him a little later, seated in a deck chair and polishing a golf club while he hummed to himself an air from *H.M.S. Pinafore.* The unfinished pile of stones remained as a monument to our un-fruitful labour and soon groundsel was flowering in the freshly laid earth where gentian and saxifrage should have grown.

When Sunday came round, I prepared automatically to ac-company my parents to Church. The bells were ringing for morning service and the familiar, monotonous chimes vibrated softly through the open window as I made the familiar gestures of "getting tidy". The memories they evoked called me to lean on the window-sill, where I could feel the soft dampness of the wind on my checks and listen to the birds that twittered in the trees. It was the same uncanny Sunday stillness, broken only by the sound of birds and bells, that had marked the rhythm of my life as inevitably as the tides and the moon. Soon we shall be walking decorously up the steep village street, passing the black-clad chapel members returning from their interminable service, waving greetings to the churchgoers who emerge, clasping prayer-books, from front-door or garden gates. Inside the church, we settle ourselves in the family pew, just beneath the pulpit. Behind us there is the rustle of unseen arrival, the sound of heavy boots clumping in the aisle, the rustling of stiff old-ladies' skirts, coughing, dropping of prayer-books and pennies, whispered admonitions to restive children. Presently Mr. Williams appears—the Sunday Mr. Williams, wearing a cassock and a shinily white surplice, quite different from the week-day Mr. Williams who overcalls at bridge and is known as an inconsiderate thruster during the hunting season. Psalms ... "Rejoice in the Lord, O ye righteous ..." My father stumbles out of the pew and up to the lectern. A wide ribbon of red silk marks his place in the huge Bible that a man could hardly lift alone, but even so there is a good deal of fumbling and some false starts at the wrong verse before he gets properly going. "Here beginneth the First Lesson ..." My attention wanders. Coloured shadows play from the stained glass window over my mother's firm brown cheeks. Beneath the window there is a marble plaque: In proud and loving memory of General Osbert Gethryn, d. 1862. Two of the choir boys are sucking sweets and Dewi Jenkins—the only decent tenor out of Chapel—leans over the stall to pinch their ears. Mr. Williams' sermon is a droning accompaniment to my thoughts. He starts with a clipped, careful Oxford accent but his voice, as the twenty minutes wear to an end, unconsciously yields to the monotonous up-and-down, hillocky rhythm of his native Swansea. Now we sing ... hymns A. and M. ... accompanied by Mrs. Williams, erect and noticing at the organ. My mother sings firmly, unaware that she is always half a tone flat. A final blessing, and we stream decorously out to commence, on the church steps, the social business of the day. "So Laura is back with you, Mrs. Gethryn. How pleased you must be!" "You must tell me all about your adventures, my dear Laura! I suppose you can chatter away in French like any thing now … !"

The bells changed to a slow, single-noted tolling which warned that time was growing short. I drew my head in from the window and began to scramble my drawer in search of gloves. A scarf twisted around my head completed the Sunday disguise, and I ran downstairs, anxious to create a good impression by my punctuality.

My mother was standing in the hall, explaining to a troop of eager dogs that this was no outing for them. She wore a felt hat of sage green, jammed uncompromisingly on her head, and carried a very shabby prayer book under her arm. From a sort of alcove beneath the staircase, my father's voice could be heard telephoning to the vet about a horse that had been seized overnight with the colic.

When she saw me, my mother raised her eyebrows in surprise, as if my appearance was unexpected and even in some way provocative. Cautiously she asked if I meant to go to Church.

"I supposed you would want me to," I said.

She hesitated. For once she appeared to be at a loss.

"Your first Sunday," she said. "I thought you would be tired."

"No, I'm not tired at all."

"Well, if you want to …"

My father emerged from beneath the staircase, saying: 'Rees will be over this afternoon. He says this colic is all over the place. Some sort of bug… ."

"We must let Owen know," said my mother. Her face cleared, at last she knew what should be done.

"Laura can just run up and tell him. He'll be home from chapel by the time she gets there."

My father looked doubtful.

"She's all got up to go to church, isn't she?"

My mother tapped her foot impatiently.

"She can come in late and sit at the back. We must get Owen down this afternoon."

I had no special desire to go to church. Indeed, I desired nothing, or at least nothing that Pont-y-Gibby could offer. I was ready to be as docile as even she could wish, since I had no incentive to refuse anything she asked.

Owen was old now and, with only two horses in the stable, we had no need of a groom. For the last year or so, he had come to us only from time to time, to lend a hand in case of need and for the rest of the time he remained at home, working in his garden and listening to the Welsh programme on the wireless.

I walked past the quarry, climbed the stile into Colonel Musgrove's top field and took the right-of-way that led into the main road. Then the way led past the sawmill, past the virtuously closed Red Lion and up the path that led to the cottage at the edge of the common. As I walked, I thought about Owen and the calm, lonely life he led since the death of his wife and the departure of his children. Although he had been faltering for some years now into old age, I thought of him as I had known him when I was a child when he was still only middle-aged—a small, spare man with a shiny bald skull and legs bowed by a lifetime spent in the saddle.

"Bump the saddle, Miss Laura, bump the saddle!"

The muscles of my legs ache, the tugging rein has left a sore red patch on the palm of my hand, but Merryleg's trot no longer flings me about like a packet on the saddle. I am in control, I can really ride.

Then I reflected that Owen, though we had seldom exchanged more than ten words at a time, had truly been my friend. He had never made me feel in the way, though he often cursed me, with fine swear-words both in Welsh and in English, when I forgot to close the stable door or left the oat-bin open, inviting rats. Certainly, now I came to think of it, we had never exchanged an idea, or even a remark on any subject other than horses or the weather, but he had been part of my life for as long as I could remember, a solid, comforting figure in the background of my existence.

When I reached the gate I could see him sitting on a bench, resting his back against the wall of the cottage and reading the *Methodist Recorder.* He wore black, which made him appear even smaller and more shrivelled than usual. As I came up the path he rose politely, knocked out his pipe and stared at me with calm interest.

"Well, Miss Laura, you're back again!"

"Yes, back again, Owen. You look very well."

"Can't complain, Miss. Will you take a seat, please."

I sat down on the bench and he remained standing, his legs a little apart, looking down at me with bright shrewd eyes shining in his puckered, parchmenty face.

"What can I do for you, Miss?"

I told him my errand and he said discontentedly:

"Mrs. Gethryn knows I don't hold with work on the Sabbath."

"Patsy is ill, Owen."

"That horse is getting old, like a lot of us are. Well, it'll be this once but not again."

My message was delivered. There was no reason to stay. Owen was waiting to return to his pipe and the *Methodist Recorder,* but I felt a strong desire to talk, to tell him about Paris, to associate him in some way with that year that lay behind me. There was a moment's silence then seeing that I made no move to go, he said politely:

"Well enough, you look, Miss Laura."

"I had a wonderful time abroad, Owen."

"Did you, Miss?"

"Don't you ever wish you could go … somewhere else, Owen ?"

"What would I wish that for, Miss Laura! No good there is in gadding about."

There was disapproval in his face. For him, I had been wasting my time, pointlessly. It was useless to try to move him, but a wave of irritation had seized me, I felt that I must wring some sign of interest from this wooden man, that I must force some word of recognition from him. So I asked. "Do you disapprove of travelling, then, Owen?"

"It isn't my business, Miss."

"But why do you feel like this?"

He shook his head, perplexed and annoyed at such un-accustomed questioning.

"An *estron* they've made of you, Miss Laura. A foreigner. Not the same at all, you are."

"But I am, Owen. Just the same. Do you remember when you taught me to ride?"

"Very well indeed, Miss. Very quick on the uptake you were."

"And now I am changed?"

"They've made an *estron* of you, Miss Laura."

It was no good. I rose. My body felt heavy, unwilling to forego the comfort of the bench. Owen accompanied me down the narrow garden path and held the painted gate open for me to pass.

"We'll expect you at three, then?"

"Very well, Miss. But it's the last time on the Sabbath, vet or no vet."

I walked back by the same way I had come. The Red Lion, the sawmill, Colonel Musgrove's top field... . I was a foreigner. Owen had understood. He knew that I had been changed and remade. I could not take him in or make him believe that I was merely the child he knew, grown now to a woman. No one, indeed, would be taken in for long. If I stayed here for the rest of my life, I should still be an *estron,* a foreigner. I could not get back. I was no longer part of my own past, a single year had been enough to cut me off for ever.

ONE DAY, when the early Welsh autumn was staining the trees, my mother consented to drive me to Llanglaslyn. It was the weekly market day and she had decided to replace the old rooster, who was beginning to feel his age.

We set off early, driving over the hills through a veil of mist. By the time we reached Llanglaslyn, the town was full of the lowing of cattle and complaining of sheep. In the centre, in the square dominated by the granite block of the Town Hall, workmen were winding ropes round staves, fencing in the ring where the beasts would be paraded. Two farm-hands were tugging on the cords that bound a huge red and white bull who stood, snorting stupidly, dazed with his journey and unwilling to leave his van. Women were piling eggs and butter on the stalls. Farmers in breeches and flat felt hats stood on the steps of the pub, tapping their thighs with their riding crops and speaking of livestock prices and weather prospects. A hen broke loose and scudded in a whirr of dust and feathers, desperately clucking, between the legs of the crowd. From the church steeple broke nine resonant chimes, sowing panic among a herd of cows.

A crowd had already gathered round the ropes, but my mother took it for granted that a place would be made for her and indeed the farmers, all of whom knew her well, if only by sight, respectfully made way for her. We had just time to take our positions and to buy a Roneoed catalogue before the auctioneer waddled to his stand, and a moment later a purposeful collie was bundling a flock of frightened-looking sheep into the ring.

"What am I offered? ... Fine, plump ewes ... Sweetest Welsh, mountain-pastured mutton ... What do I hear . . ?"

Sheep, pigs, cows, hens. My mother bought her cock—a fine creature with glossy russet feathers and a plump vermilion comb who would surely be a success in the barnyard. Imprisoned in a crate, angrily ruffling, he was installed in the back of the car.

"Just time for a cup of coffee," said my mother, pleased with her purchase.

The Tylwyth Teg was crowded with farmer's wives from the outlying villages, enjoying their weekly treat. They sat squarely at the flimsy tables, bundles and parcels on the ground between their legs, drinking cocoa and discussing the morning's prices.

"Oh, dear!" said my mother. "There's Miss Pugh. We shall never get away now!"

Miss Pugh it was, waving excitedly from a discreet corner

table. We edged our way towards her, while a waitress flipped crumbs off the cloth and snatched an extra chair.

"Well, Mrs. Gethryn! Laura! What a lucky chance! It's not often I find time for my elevenses these days and just today I had a feeling I must drop in here. Well, Laura dear, what a lot you must have to tell me."

"We haven't time to stay more than a minute," said my mother, and to the waitress she said:

"Two coffees and some buns. As quickly as you can, please."

"You're always so busy, dear Mrs. Gethryn. I don't know how you keep on the go as you do."

"There's a lot to be done," said my mother. I could see that this meeting annoyed her. She put down her bag and gloves beside her plate and began to tick off the items on the catalogue.

Miss Pugh was staring at me intently, her eyes liquid with pleasure.

"You've got a little thinner, dear. I find you …" she hesitated for the word, "changed".

"It's a year since we last met, Miss Pugh."

"And what a lot has happened since then! Paris! Ah, Laura, what a privileged person you are! The Louvre! Versailles! The concerts you must have heard! The exhibitions you must have seen!"

She clasped her hands tightly before her. Magical visions were surely passing before her eyes.

"You should come and visit me there, Miss Pugh."

"Ah, if I only could."

"I don't think the visit did Laura any good," said my mother. She swallowed a last gulp of coffee, pushed back her chair.

"We must be going."

Miss Pugh turned to her pleadingly.

"Oh, Mrs. Gethryn, do let me keep Laura for a little while. We have so much to say to each other."

"I'm afraid we must get back," said my mother firmly, signalling to the waitress.

"I would like to stay a little longer," I said. "There is a bus for Pont-y-Gibby in about an hour. I will take that."

"That would be lovely. Will you spare her, Mrs. Gethryn?"

"Laura does not consult my wishes nowadays," said my mother. She pushed back her chair, placed three pennies beneath her plate and stood up, drawing on her gloves. Miss Pugh looked distressed.

"Oh, Mrs. Gethryn! I'm sure Laura wouldn't dream…"

"It's of no importance," said my mother. "Please be back before nightfall," she said to me sarcastically, and was gone.

"Oh dear," said Miss Pugh, "I wonder what can have annoyed your dear mother so much? Perhaps I should not have asked you to stay."

She began to collect her parcels, a frown of worry puckering her brow. Out in the street, we walked for a little while in silence, oppressed by the weight of my mother's absent anger, and it was not till we reached the house in Church Street, where Miss Pugh lived in a converted flat on the second floor, that she began to regain confidence.

"You will find a few changes," she said as we climbed the stairs. "Just some little things I have been able to collect." The first of them was a brand new reproduction of the Mona Lisa on the sitting-room wall.

"When I think that you have seen the original!" sighed Miss Pugh. "When I think that you have only to step down to the

Louvre and you can sit there and gaze at it for hours—the very painting as it came from the brush of that miraculous Leonardo!"

Then there were the latest novels to be examined, and Miss Pugh was secretary of the new society for the preservation of Welsh poetry. She darted about, happy and excited, while I tried to recapture the enthusiasm she had been able to inspire in me in the old days, tried to crush down a creeping doubt, the feeling that this was a scene that was being played on a false note and that, anyhow, no longer concerned me.

"So much to say, isn't there?" cried Miss Pugh, boiling the tea kettle. "If only I had dared to ask you to stay to lunch! I thought your dear mother seemed a little nervous. She worries so much about you."

"I don't know why she should."

"Well, mothers will be mothers, dear. I must say, I do think Mrs. Gethryn works herself up more than she need. Last time I saw her—not so long ago, it was—she almost seemed afraid you might be living, well, quite a wild life. Not at all like you, as I told her, but she has such a mind of her own, hasn't she? It's a job to convince her."

"It is indeed."

Ruffling the pages of the *Times Literary Supplement,* I wondered in just what terms my mother had conveyed to Miss Pugh that I might be leading a "wild life", and to how many other, less well-disposed listeners she had given the same impression. And now a whole series of rapid images passed through my mind, images of moments that had seemed at the time so unimportant that they had left no immediate mark … Maggie's haughty, "How-do-you-do, Miss?" in reply to my greetings on my first visit to her shop, and now, turning away, she volubly serves Mrs. Jenkins with a cream cheese and a quarter of butter.... . The assistant teacher's curt nod—though she had begged me, before my departure, to remember everything for telling on my return... . Mrs. Williams, watering a potted fern at the foot of the war memorial, who happens to turn her back just as I pass. And Owen, too, who perhaps meant outcast when he called me foreigner. And Bron, eyeing me with such cunning curiosity as I ask news of her brother away in Pontypridd. Had my mother even waited for the signal of Mair's letter before taking revenge for flouted authority? That letter, in whose existence I was beginning to believe at last, may have done no more than give a face to the shadowy figure whose presence at my side must have long obsessed her imagination.

"You will see a tick beside all the titles I have put on my Times Book Club list," Miss Pugh was saying.

"They look very interesting."

"You must borrow as many as you like, dear. It will be quite like old times."

I looked at my watch. There was just time to catch the bus that would bring me to Pont-y-Gibby in time for lunch. Miss Pugh accompanied me to the stop in front of the Post Office, where a crowd of people, encumbered with parcels, was already waiting.

"Oh dear," said Miss Pugh. "I'm afraid you will have a very uncomfortable journey. Will you even get a seat, I wonder?"

I did not get a seat and the road was blocked with slow-moving carts driving home from market, so that lunch was nearly over by the time I reached home.

A congealing plate of mutton awaited me.

"I suppose it's no good asking you to be a little thoughtful for the servants," said my mother acidly.

"Perhaps you had no regular meal-times in Paris," said my father. "But here you are expected to be punctual. Gadding about with that silly woman! Disorganizing everything!"

He pushed the food away to the edge of his plate, peevishly.

"I've had enough. How much longer are we to sit about here?"

"Don't wait, dear, I've finished too. We won't stay for Laura."

But she lingered, pretending to polish a silver cup, when he had shambled out of the room. I waited for her to speak and presently she said:

"I am afraid Miss Pugh is a very silly woman. I am beginning to feel that she has been encouraging you all along in these foolish notions you have got in your head."

"What foolish notions do you mean?"

"You know quite well. Leaving your home. Leading this ridiculous, rackety life abroad. Coming home like a skeleton and moping round the place."

"You asked me to come home," I said.

"Of course I did. I am your mother and I hope I do my duty by you."

She paused, a hint of caution crept into her eyes and she went on:

"I hope you quite understand that there is to be no more of this nonsense. I should not dream of giving you any more money to waste."

"What do you expect me to do then?"

"Stay here, of course, in your own home."

"Do you want me?"

The question surprised her. It seemed to imply a criticism. She said:

"Naturally I want you. This is your home and it is my duty to look after you and keep you from doing foolish things which you will regret later."

"There is nothing for me to do here. I have no friends, no occupations."

"You must not be surprised," she said. "If people don't exactly fling themselves at you. I told you that it would not be considered right for a young girl to go off on her own as you did. People wonder what you have been up to. It is natural and the people here are decent, old-fashioned folk."

"Would they have wondered if. . ?"

"If what?"

Her eyes met mine, challenged me. They were full of such hostility, such desire to wound, that I suddenly felt defeated in advance, incapable of giving battle. We understood each other too well. We had no need of words. Tacitly she was telling me: You have touched me in my most sensitive part. Without power I cannot exist, if I can no longer dominate I am as good as dead. You have dealt me a wound, the scar of which will always remain to harass me. When I had almost surrendered, when I had weakened and let you go, I was given a second chance. Now I consider that any weapon I may use against you is used in legitimate defence.

"If what?" she repeated.

"It doesn't matter. And I do not specially want to go back to Paris."

"You see!" she said. "All this trouble has been for nothing. What has your obstinacy gained for you in the end?"

As the question was purely rhetorical, I made no answer and contented myself with leaving untouched a slice of jam tart—proof of a parental solicitude which would not allow me to starve however trying my behaviour might be—and walking out into the garden.

Already a pool of freshly fallen leaves lay at the foot of each of the trees. The deep crimson of rose petals was fading to purple, but chrysanthemums flamed like brass in the borders. The grass was paling already, its juicy summer-green had been washed away and, although the air was soft and warm, it was heavy with unshed water. The dahlias, my father's chief pride, were as fat as cabbages, light as feather-dusters. They reminded me of the dahlias in the Luxembourg Gardens, blazing at the feet of marble queens in the shadow of the Senate House. A child leans far over the rim of the great pool, gazing at his own image, while the white sails of his boat scud across the water. A girl and a young man sit beneath a tree, enlaced, enraptured, while leaves drift lazily down on to their heads and shoulders. A troop of little boys shout and ges-ticulate, kicking half-heartedly at a football but absorbed really in some secret game of their own, while a young priest dashes, clutching his skirts, between the unthreatened goals. At the gate, where the traffic of the Boulevard St. Michel crashes by, the chestnut seller is back and the air is pungent with the smell of chestnuts as they blacken and crackle on the red-hot grill… . The holidays are nearly over. Soon the students will be flowing through the great entrance to the Sorbonne. Professor Demarest takes his place on the dais, his short grey beard bristling, clearing his throat from permanent hoarseness, exuding his irreducible hatred against Mazarin. Jean-Pierre is late as usual, tiptoeing in with a grin of apology on his face. His fountain pen has run out of ink again, he leans over, whispering to a young girl sitting just in front of him, and gravely she drips ink from her pen on to his own.

I had said to my mother: I don't specially want to go back to Paris. It was true. That year, that too-brilliant flash in the pan, already seemed so far away that I could not imagine taking up the thread that had been so sharply, so definitely severed. Idris stood between me and all those charming images. Each of them, if I allowed it to linger too long in my mind, led to him and at that point, lost its clearness and brightness and fogged over with a cloud of bewilderment and distress. To return now, even if I had the energy, even if my mother had not held the final trump in the form of a closed purse, could never restore the happiness of that first, marvellous autumn. Speculation as to the future was equally impossible. There was only the present moment, the smell of rich, damp earth, the barking of a dog, impatient to be taken for a walk, the distant cries of the children at play in the schoolyard... .

NOW IT was mid-October. The mild weather continued. In the early morning, wreaths of mist curled above the lawn, and wrapped the summit of the trees in a veiling of pearl grey. Soon after breakfast, the mist lifted, a distant sun began to shine in an uncertain way and patches of crisp blue opened between the clouds.

"Now what are you going to do today?" my mother would ask briskly.

What indeed? I could ride a solitary ride on Starlight, or wander in Glenmawr Woods, where the nuts were hanging ripe in thick clusters on the bushes. I could rake the fallen leaves from the lawn and wheel them to the compost heap. Or read in the drawing-room, among the forest of glacé flowers that bloomed over armchairs and sofas. These occupations seemed to exhaust the possibilities offered by Pont-y-Gibby, since there was no longer any suggestion that I should work off surplus energy in parish work or renew my activities with the Llanglaslyn girl guides. From Gwynedd I learned that Miss Pugh, visiting Pont-y-Gibby one afternoon on the business of the Welsh Poetry Society, had called to see me.

"The mistress told her you was out, though well I knew you was only at the bottom of the garden," said Gwynedd. "Very short with her, she was."

I said nothing to my mother of this incident. The very idea of an argument tired me now. I knew that she would be so convinced of the rightness of her own action that she would almost convince me, too. Sooner, then, than acquiesce in the breaking-off of relations with Miss Pugh—for surely this was the tacit decision my mother had taken that morning in the Tylwyth Teg Tea Shop—I preferred silence.

One afternoon, my parents had driven up to the links for a round of golf. It was a fine day and my mother had stood in the doorway, sniffing the crisp autumn air. There was a glow in her cheeks, her eyes shone with some unsatisfied craving. I could see the nervous rippling of the muscles of her arm beneath the sleeve of her close-fitting jumper. She looked at this moment like a young, eager woman.

"Edward!" she called. "Edward!"

He came to the door.

"What is it, Molly?"

"We can't stuff indoors on a day like this. A game of golf would do you all the good in the world."

My father looked doubtful. Any exertion tired him nowadays, he would return from his game haggard, irritable, with drooping shoulders and dulled eyes. Yet my mother refused to see his exhaustion. She took pride in his play, triumphed over his scores rather than her own, reminded him constantly of the compliments he received from the professional attached to the clubhouse. I suspected that he himself was no longer interested in or cared for the success he still won.

"It gets dark very early these days, my dear," he said.

"There's plenty of time for nine holes if we start at once. You know you've been having trouble with your liver, Edward. It will do you all the good in the world to get some exercise."

They drove off. I noticed that my mother no longer pressed me to accompany her and I knew that, if I had suggested doing so, she would have found some excuse to refuse me. I almost regretted it today, for the windy, open links would be like an escape after the months spent in the encircled hollow of the village. Yet I knew that she would reply to such a suggestion with some vague excuse, not troubling even to convince me, glad enough, perhaps, that I should divine beneath her words her refusal to condone, even in appearance, the unspecified crimes of the past year.

I was walking up and down the drive, wondering how I should spend the rest of the day, when a car turned in at the gate. It was a dashing sports car, painted an elegant vermilion, quite unlike the sober four-seaters owned by the more prosperous families in the district. The driver was bareheaded and I recognized him at once, by his very handsome mane of chestnut hair, as Mervyn Wynn-Evans.

He drew up beside me and jumped out.

"Hullo, Laura! What ages it is since we met! You *have* changed!"

"In what way?"

I was regretfully conscious that I must be looking my worst, since my tweeds dated from schoolgirl days and I had not troubled to powder my nose. Mervyn was looking at me critically, head on one side, with the conscientious scrutiny of an amateur seeking for the right phrase in an art gallery, but he only said:

"Well, you look more grown-up."

"So do you, as a matter of fact."

We regarded each other gravely, each a little astonished to discover a man and a woman where there had been a boy and a girl. Then Mervyn said:

"I'm home on leave, you know. I've been lunching with a chap in my regiment and motoring back, I suddenly realized how near I was to Pont-y-Gibby and I thought I would drop in to see you. I'd heard you were back."

"It's very nice to see you," I said, and indeed his appearance brought a sensation of relief, as if it sufficed to create a link with the fading outer world.

"Well, my idea was this," Mervyn went on. "The hard courts are in quite decent condition and I thought you might come on back with me and have a game if you aren't doing anything else."

Why not? Ten minutes to change, a scribbled message to my mother, and I was free. It was the easiest thing in the world. I had been imagining prison bars where none existed. I had been hypnotizing myself. Glancing at the mirror in the hall as I dashed out, I caught a glimpse of my Paris face, alive and eager, ready to reflect any pleasure the coming hours might offer.

"You look fine," said Mervyn, handing me into the car. "That lipstick makes all the difference."

We whirled along the village street. There was hardly time

to enjoy Mrs. Williams' indignant astonishment and flurried skip to the safety of the pavement. The wind snatched the scarf from my head, sent my hair dragging back from the scalp, spreading on the air like sea-weed on water. Half an hour later we were hooting our way through Abergavenny and in another ten minutes we were speeding between the rhododendrons that bordered the Manor drive.

Lady Wynn-Evans was coming down the front steps as we drew up. She wore an old-fashioned green loden cape and carried a flat rush basket on her arm. She looked surprised to see me but she welcomed me kindly, asking after my mother and enquiring how I was spending my time.

"Robert is sorting out his books, I believe," she said. "His term begins tomorrow, you know."

The butler was hovering in the hall. "Please tell Mr. Robert Miss Gethryn is here," she said to him. She twirled her basket on her arm.

"I was just going to say a word to the gardener… . We must have a little chat, dear, before you go. Now you had better get your game while the light lasts… ."

Down came Robert, four steps at a time, taller and weedier than his brother, more loquacious, more easily influenced by any passing, fashionable idea. Although he was six months older than myself, he seemed to me very young, almost childish and still fluid, as if there was no saying what final form his manhood might take.

"Hullo, Laura! How was Paris? You *are* a lucky devil!"

"I expect Laura is glad to be home," said Lady Wynn-Evans. She turned, with a little wave of her hand and walked off in the direction of the kitchen gardens, stopping now and then to snip a dead chrysanthemum head from its stalk.

Tennis at the Wynn-Evans' was not taken too seriously but I was no match for either of the boys and after a little while I sat out, watching their strenuous singles and throwing back any balls that rolled in my direction. When they had finished, the light was already growing dim and a chilly dampness was beginning to rise from the ground.

"We'd better take the net down," said Mervyn. "It'll be the last game this season." He sniffed the air, with a cunning, countryman's look, and said:

"It'll rain to-morrow. Winter will be here in no time now."

Sir Thomas was in the drawing-room, standing square and heavy and rubicund in front of the fireplace. He greeted me boisterously.

"Well, well! So you're back again! *Parlez vous français?* Quite a Parisian, aren't you, my girl? *Très chic,* what!"

"Don't be silly, Thomas," said Lady Wynn-Evans. "She is just the same as ever."

Sir Thomas winked. His kind, stupid face shone with the pleasure of having someone to tease.

"I wonder! She looks a real Mademoiselle to me… . But seriously, Laura," he said to me, "I don't know how you stood it so long. I had plenty of leaves in Paris during the war—and I bet your father had too if the truth were known— but I wouldn't live there for a fortune. Talk, talk, talk, and not a decent armchair in the place. The food's all right at first, but everything's got up to taste like something else—enough to ruin a man's digestion. No wonder you're so thin!"

Lady Wynn-Evans was pouring tea.

"Do you like China, dear? Pass Laura the muffins, please, Robert."

It seemed to me that for once she was a little uneasy at her

husband's exuberance, that she would have liked to check
him, but it was too late, he had had his head for a quarter of a
century and was not, anyway, accessible to such fine-drawn
hints as she might bring herself to give. He went on:

"Well, everyone to his own taste and of course, you young
people will never admit a mistake, but I bet you'll stay at
home now and be glad to."

"Perhaps I shall, Sir Thomas."

"Not that they'll keep you for long, eh, Lena? She'll be
married before we know where we are now."

Lady Wynn-Evans rose, saying:

"I just want to take a look around the greenhouses before
Jackson goes. Will you accompany me, Laura dear?"

"I should love to."

"In that case," said Mervyn, "I'll go and get the car filled
up. Then I'll be ready to run Laura home whenever she wants
to go."

He was already at the door. Lady Wynn-Evans made a tiny
gesture of her hand to check him.

"There are people coming to dinner, dear. They'll be here
early and you'll have to change. If you don't mind I'll get Ellis
to drive Laura back."

Suddenly I understood the determination behind the softly-
spoken words, the implacable decision in the gentle eyes.
Mervyn hesitated, said: "Oh, well. ..." Sir Thomas gave one
of his loud, meaningless laughs and we passed out into the
garden.

Dusk was beginning to fall and we advanced through deep
pools of shadow beneath a rustling arch of beech trees. A soft,
heavy smell of leaf-mould rose from the ground. Lady Wynn-
Evans guided me, her hand lightly laid on my elbow and

presently we came out on the lower lawn that stretched before us, pale and wide like the sea, so that, walking or floating across this apparently immense space, I was surprised to find myself so quickly at the barrier and to see the glass houses looming before us.

"Here we are," said Lady Wynn-Evans. She opened the door, switched on a light. Immediately I found myself in a tepid jungle, roofed over with thick, dark foliage from which dripped great clusters of ripening grapes. Pots of azalea and hydrangea stood on trestles that ran the whole length of the greenhouse and there were feather-light ferns and tomato plants, heavy with ripe fruit, tied to light stakes. The air was so heavy with warmth that a languid well-being began to creep over me, mingled with a sort of disquietude caused by the sensation of isolation from the ordinary world outside the greenhouse. We were like fishes in an aquarium filled, not with water, but with bright, hard light, while all around us the surrounding dark pressed in against invisible walls of glass.

Lady Wynn-Evans reached up and cut a cluster of grapes that hung in a purple cone from the leafy roof. She detached one grape, holding it between finger and thumb, and put it in her mouth, crunching it while an attentive, appraising look crept into her eyes.

"I think they will do. Grapes are always such a gamble ..."

She handed the cluster to me, saying:

"Try them, Laura. We only use a few for ourselves, of course. The rest go up to the hospital."

We moved slowly up the aisle, between a double row of flower-laden trestles. She poked her finger into the earth round a pink and mauve azalea.

"Too dry. Jackson doesn't understand them."

Under her downcast eyelids she shot a desperately embarrassed glance at me.

"Laura …"

"Yes, Lady Wynn-Evans?"

"It is perhaps a little my business, since I, in a way, was
responsible for your departure. All this has made me very
unhappy, it has distressed me so much. Your mother came to
see me some time ago… ."

"What did she tell you. I don't understand."

"She was in such distress. I felt so sorry for her, and indeed,
so guilty, as if it was all my fault."

The thick, warm air seemed to be swelling inside my head.
The light shone harshly on her puzzled, reproachful face.
Suddenly I saw with horror that tears were gathering in her
eyes.

"Please, Lady Wynn-Evans. . !"

"I had always thought," she said, "that Mervyn … Perhaps
some day … I should have been so pleased . .."

"Will you not tell me what my mother said to you?"

"I only wish it might all be untrue, but she was so sure—
so unhappily sure. She said that there were … men …"

"Men? Are you sure she said that?"

"Of course, she would not care to give details but I could
not mistake her meaning."

"It is not true. She could not have said that…"

"Oh, Laura, could you really promise me that it is not true?
I know people are only too willing to speak evil, but she
seemed to think there could be no doubt, that you had really
taken advantage of your liberty to … if I must say it … to
debauch yourself."

"It is not true! It is a wicked lie that she is glad to believe!"

She started back. The shadows of the vine-leaves blotched her face and she regarded me with such anguish that I wished the words unspoken. Indeed, I had only at that moment been certain of their truth. Now she whispered:

"Laura! You are speaking of your mother. You get on badly perhaps, but Molly is incapable of such feelings as you imagine her to have for you."

"I don't know How can I know what to think of her ?"

"You say all this is untrue, Laura. Forgive me if I question you, I only wish to understand. Was there not some man— some man from your own village . . ?"

"Yes, there was a man. One man. And I ..."

I was going to say: I loved him, but it seemed impossible to express by a word made so meaningless by usage the inexplicable necessity which allowed me to feel comfort and happiness only in Idris' presence. Lady Wynn-Evans had turned away. I could see a quarter of her bent profile as she plucked nervously at the pollen-dotted fronds of a fern.

"A common man." The frond fluttered, scrap by scrap, to the ground. "A man whose reputation is notorious. Think of the shame it has brought on your mother, my dear."

"No one need have known."

"Of course, she would have told no one but me. She felt she must confide in someone."

"I cannot make you understand, Lady Wynn-Evans, but I assure you, all this was quite different to what you imagine."

She was dabbing at her eyes now with a very fine cambric handkerchief.

"My dear child, do not think that I am condemning you. It is so easy to make irremediable mistakes when one is very young and I blame myself so much for the advice I gave to

Molly. It was by my fault that you were left alone without any older or wiser person to counsel you."

"I don't see why you should blame yourself, Lady Wynn-Evans. All this started a very long time ago. I can't explain, but it had to happen."

From somewhere in the surrounding night a clock chimed softly. She lifted her head, gave a final dab at her eyes and crumpled the handkerchief back into her pocket. Already her face had taken on its usual expression of distant and courteous sweetness.

"How late it is! Your parents will be worrying."

She hesitated.

"Please forgive me, Laura. It is because I am very fond of you that the disappointment has been so great."

At the door, she stopped to verify the thermometer.

"The night frosts will be beginning soon. We must be careful."

We went out into the darkness and walked quickly over the lawn, guided by the lighted windows that glowed in the black mass of the house-facade. The car was waiting in the drive by the front-door and Ellis, as we approached, slipped from his seat, touching his cap.

"Mervyn and Robert must be dressing by now. Shall I say good-bye for you, dear?"

I got into the car. Sir Thomas' figure loomed in the doorway.

"Just off, Laura? Good-bye my girl! *Au revoir*! *Parlez vous français*?"

MERVYN HAD been right when, with that wise sniff of his, he had said: Winter will be here in no time now. One morning I awoke to see the sleety rain pouring down like a curtain before the window. By noon the lawn was a bog; by the following day the last chrysanthemums were lying tattered and torn in the muddy borders. A fire was lit in the drawing-room, the damp logs crackled and hissed, pine cones sent their transient flames glazing high up the great chimney. Then the sleet turned to a light snow that faded quickly from the ground except in the hollow places where it lay in patches, marked with the watery hollows of footprints. A sort of muteness fell on the village. People were no longer to be seen strolling in their gardens or gossiping on their doorsteps. Snow and rain and early darkness were like a siege round their homes and when they came out into the streets, they had the air of braving an invisible enemy, proclaiming in loud, aggressive voices how healthy was this fine cold, how enjoyable a brisk walk in the face of the wind.

"You might take the dogs out for a run," my mother would say to me, and generally she would add: "You had better go down by the woods, but don't let them go rabbiting. There are traps."

These woods, which I had hated and feared in my child-hood because of their dark solitude, were becoming my favourite retreat. There was a sense of primeval mystery in this strange, shadowy place, where the great, naked trees towered all around and the bushes creaked and whispered and the rutted path led through black hollows, where thorns leaned across the way and knotted roots seemed to move and curl beneath the feet. Sometimes a shadowy figure would slip across the path—a poacher with a ferret in his pocket—and sometimes I would come on the clearing where mad Emily lived in a rotting cabin with her idiot children, in a vague, mindless retreat of her own, safe from the visits of school and sanitary inspectors. Otherwise the woods were deserted and it occurred to me that my mother's insistence that I should walk here whenever I left the house, was the symbol of her desire to conceal me. We had had no need of words on my return from the Wynn-Evans'. Everything was understood between us. It was no longer necessary for my mother to say: "Miss Morgan is not properly settled in yet." Her silence itself was a tacit comment: "Miss Morgan would not care to meet you", or, indeed, "I cannot allow you, as my daughter, to risk a rebuff."

Sometimes I wondered whether she regretted the insidious confidences, born of rage and jealous misery, that she had scattered, or planted, indeed, where they would bear most fruit. Did they not reflect on herself, on my upbringing, give birth to the very humiliating pity which it had been her life's preoccupation to avoid? But reflecting on these things with one eye on the restive dogs ready to plunge into the dangerous undergrowth, I understood that, when I had wrung from her the admission of my independence, I had destroyed the link of pride and possession by which she felt herself bound to me. She had accepted the inevitable, it is true, with apparent calm, but gradually the idea must have been born in her that this independence might have consequences which she had long refused to foresee. Gradually I had come to understand my father's insufficience and the devouring energy of her own temperament. Life had not been able to tame her. She would never find peace from the inward cry of rage against fate. Her revenge on me, surely, had been almost unconscious, a mere *pis-aller* for revenge against the world. Then I wondered whether I had perhaps come to represent for her the youth and strength which were so unemployed and so painful in herself and which she would no doubt have been glad to crush down and stifle.

Although I was at last beginning to understand these things, the understanding brought no incentive to action. It seemed rather to grow at the same rhythm as the inertia which was gradually invading me. I had tasted at life, for a whole year, but it seemed to me, in retrospect, that that year had brought me nothing. It had been a bright, quickly fading dream and now I was resigned in the same way that, after a night of happy dreams, one soon resigns oneself to waking to a monotonous reality. I was back at the same point and now I accepted the retreat my mother imposed on me because neither imagination nor desire proposed an alternative. I was no longer even unhappy. It seemed to me that this was the life for which I was destined and that no other had ever been really possible.

Sometimes I turned the pages of the notebooks that I had filled so enthusiastically in Montrouge. Certain phrases, certain images, astonished me. Surely they had been written by someone very different from my present self. Yet they had been written only a few months ago. A scribbled drawing— that had filled, no doubt a gap when my mind had wandered in pursuit of some word or idea—showed a corner of the studio. The divan, with the striped cover we had bought from an Algerian merchant in the rue Lepic; a shelf with books and an effective lamp from Uniprix; a tooth-glass and a fountain-pen, encumbering a chair placed at the head of the divan, where Idris must have set them down a moment earlier … this was the décor of an alien moment in my life. Towards Christmas, my mother said to me:

"You don't look well. I shall order some malt and cod liver oil for you."

Her words and a scrutiny of my face in the glass convinced me that she was right. From mental indifference had followed physical change. I became aware of a perpetual lassitude. Crouched by the fire, with cold limbs and a heavy head, I read novel after novel, counting the hours which separated me from the relief of bedtime.

"You never ride nowadays," said my mother. "And times are so hard. These foreign investments... . We have decided to sell Starlight."

Old Dr. Johns came from Llanglaslyn, tapped my stomach, sounded my chest and looked puzzled. I could hear him whispering with my mother in the corridor. The name of Uncle Herbert, who had died of consumption, wafted through the keyhole.

That night, on the point of awaking from an uneasy sleep, I had the clear impression of some future time, an unspecified year that had carried me forward into middle-age. At the same time as a vision of myself, similar yet faded, as if hair and features were obscured by a cloud of invisible dust, I heard a very distinct voice—which might have been that of Mrs. Williams—pronounce the words:

"Poor Mrs. Gethryn's invalid daughter."

At the last syllable I awoke and lay, in that dim borderland before full consciousness is regained, feeling my arms, uncertain whether my fingers were still caressing the skinny sticks that had been the limbs of that future self. Time was not yet revealing its normal, waking facet when I slipped out of bed and, groping for the light, stumbled to the mirror. There I was relieved to see the reflection of my accustomed face, but a vague disquiet accompanied me all through the night and far into the next day.

My mother became kinder to me at this time and I remembered how, in my childhood, illness had always softened her and how she had cared for me devotedly through various childish diseases. I could see that she was touched by my helplessness and exhaustion. She took the trouble to procure books for me and installed a wireless set in my room. Each morning Gwynedd brought my breakfast up on a tray. She would set it down on my knees.

"The mistress says you're to be sure to eat it all up and not to forget your cod liver oil."

Then she would linger, retailing the gossip of the village so that, although I seldom went out, I knew more of its hidden life than ever before. The new Methodist minister was so poor, people were leaving parcels of food on his doorstep at night, and they said his young wife had died from undernourishment. Rhys the Farm's second girl was expecting. Her parents had put her out and it was said she had gone to Cardiff (Caer-deef, pronounced Gwynedd, turning the hard English syllables to liquid honey). Miss Jenkins could tell the cards and she had told Gwilym the Post, the day he brought a registered parcel from her nephew in India, how the ace of spades was threatening her with death and the very next day came the news her sister had been taken... .

Gwynedd's soft voice talked on and on as I lifted the lid from my fresh-boiled egg. She had lit a bit of a fire in the grate and the flames danced pleasantly. I had an interesting book on hand and later, when I went downstairs at last, my mother would enquire anxiously whether I had spent a good night and recommend me to stay quietly by the fire in the drawing-room. Only my father grumbled sometimes about trouble for the servants, but for once she hardly listened to him.

The winter passed thus in a sort of contentment, and at last the air softened and snowdrops began to pierce through the black earth, foretelling spring.

One afternoon, when my parents had driven off on some business of their own, I was resting on my bed. Reading seemed too much trouble and I had let my book slip to the ground while I lay, half-dreaming, half-listening to the Bach concerto that issued softly from the radio. Presently there was a knock on the door and Gwynedd appeared.

"The post's just come, Miss. Here's a letter for you."

I took it with surprise, for my correspondence was rare indeed and confined chiefly to Christmas time. The cheap yellow envelope bore a French stamp and a typewritten address. I tore it open. It contained several sheets of typewriting paper, scrawled over with a difficult hand and I had no need to turn to the signature to know that the letter was from Idris.

"My dear Laura,

"A letter from me may perhaps prove as unwelcome as it must be unexpected; in that case it will be simple for you to throw it in the waste-paper basket and forget that it was ever written.

"In case, however, you care to read what I have to say to you, I must explain something of my state of mind so that you may understand why I am writing. I must tell you first of all, quite frankly that your departure was a relief to me—a physical relief, like the lifting of a heavy weight off one's shoulders or the ceasing of a nagging pain. I had feared—although I was careful not to mention this to you—the loneliness I should feel when you were gone. I am not incapable of sentimental regrets and I had imagined nostalgic returns to an empty studio. Even—though you may doubt this after your experience of my fundamental egoism—I had feared my own eventual remorse and the thought that you might be unhappy through my fault.

"Actually, none of this happened and your train had hardly steamed out of the platform before I was seized with an extraordinary lightness and exhilaration. Everything seemed easy, simple. I felt that I had been living in a world of false complications and I was astonished and delighted to realize that a single outburst of energy had been enough to set me free. This state of mind continued for a certain time, perhaps for several months, but I cannot say at what moment I began to realize that this freedom I had desired so much was not freedom at all but merely its pale reflection. The first step, I suppose, came with the realization that this was by no means the first time I had felt exactly the same exhilaration. I recognized my relief at your departure as the same feeling of exultant liberty I had known when I left home for the first time (I was fifteen then, it was before the Pont-y-Gibby days); then after my father's death, which left me less indifferent than you may imagine but which, all the same, lifted a load from my life; and at various other moments of a somewhat eventful career. It was rather like being in love—or rather, like falling out of love. On such occasions one invariably imagines that the exultation induced is something new and unique. Then, after a time, one remembers feeling exactly the same exultation over other women, and immediately the enchantment is destroyed.

"Well, Laura, the enchantment of freedom was destroyed in the same way. I remained, and still remain, clearheaded enough to realize that you and I will never make each other happy. The thing is, can either of us find happiness elsewhere?

For my part, I am inclined to believe that my need of you is greater than my distrust of your influence (You know what I mean). It is impossible for me to guess what you, after the passing of all this time, will feel on the subject. Perhaps your life has taken a new direction and I no longer represent anything of importance to you. In that case, as I said before, it will be easy for you to destroy this letter and think no more of it. If, on the other hand, you still feel the same need for me as I feel for you, perhaps you will consider returning to Paris. I am still living in Montrouge, so everything is ready for you.

"If you will come, you have only to send me a wire. In case the parents (if you are living with them) make difficulties, I have deposited a small sum of money in your name at my bank in London.

"In these doubtful circumstances, I prefer not to classify my sentiments by one of the usual forms of greeting. You may choose whichever suits you best.

Idris."

I read this letter through three times. At the first reading, I felt nothing but annoyance. I had forced the memory of Idris so far back in my mind that it had almost ceased to intrude on my waking thoughts. Now he was taking shape again, becoming solid, intrusive. A few sheets of paper had been enough to shatter what I had believed to be solid ramparts of peace. At the second reading, a flood of memories swept over me, so insistent that I seemed to be transported, in the course of a few minutes, through hundreds of events, scenes, landscapes, conversations. A sudden trick of mental perspective restored in an instant the clarity of these images that had sunk away into the dimness of half-memory, while the intervening months became in their turn grey and distant.

Then I read the letter a third time and, as I read, I realized with astonishment that my decision was already taken. An instant of revolt against myself, the fear, well-inculcated, of "making myself cheap", could not resist the force of emotion and energy that had just been released. I jumped up from my bed, confusedly conscious of a new rush of vigour through my body. The table encumbered with medicine bottles, the radio still softly playing seemed the comic accessories of a charade. As I brushed my hair it seemed to me that even, my face was changing moment by moment, as if a mask of dull indifference was slipping from it. The charade had been played out. I no longer belonged to this décor, which it was time to bundle out of sight without more delay.

My parents had not yet returned. The servants were no doubt enjoying their afternoon sit-down in their own quarters. I slipped into the niche beneath the staircase, lifted the telephone receiver.

"Operator … I want to send a foreign telegram…"

A little while later, my mother returned. Absorbed in a brush with the golf-club committee, she noticed nothing. She poked up the fire, rang for tea. My father huddled in his armchair. He held *The Times* before his face but I knew that he was not reading. His legs, stretched out before him, with a glimpse of long, white pants showing above his socks, were so thin and frail it was surprising that they could bear his upright weight. As I passed near him, I caught a glimpse of his profile behind the shelter of *The Times*. In my mind I attempted to fit over it, like a stencilled pattern, the image of the dashing young Guardsman of the old photograph. Nothing remained. At no point could the two images be made to coincide. The years had eaten him away, leaving nothing but this poor, fragile carcass, in which must linger a few memories of parades, with regimental bands and fine uniforms and horses stepping high to "Weel may the keel row"; of marriage with a radiant girl, the loveliest girl and the finest horsewoman in all South Wales; and of promotion and the praise of his chiefs and Kitchener saying: "Mark my words, Gethryn has the makings of a general in him."

My mother was pouring out tea, her face bent over the silver tray with its cups and plates of scones and sandwiches. Here, the much-courted girl, the bride and young mother were still recognizable in the coarsened, weather-beaten face and thickened body. Too often recognizable, indeed, and too often a turn of the head, a movement, a momentary softening of the eyes, recalled memories of a young woman which I should have preferred to suppress. She, at least, had never admitted defeat. She would go down fighting, valiant and pitiless, dragging down with her all who came within range of her devastating need for power. Yet defeat was there, recognized or not, and perhaps it was more complete even than that of my father... .

"Why are you staring at me?" she asked sharply.

I could hardly tell her that I was trying to expunge from her face all that recalled the time of my early childhood and to fix in my mind the sole image of the woman who had done all in her power to harm me. Nor could I tell her how hard it was for me to deny the past.

I spent most of the night packing and writing a letter which, ten times recommenced, diffuse and voluminous with explanation and excuse, was reduced, as the sky whitened with coming dawn, to a single sheet and a dry statement. After breakfast, as soon as my parents had left the house, I dressed and, dragging my two suitcases, arrived at the dairy just in time to catch the bus for Llanglaslyn. At the moment when the last houses disappeared round the bend and only the empty mountain road stretched before us, I was seized with veritable panic at the thought that I should never, whatever my need or whatever trials the future might hold for me, take that road again. I was cutting myself off, this time, for ever and irrevocably. And in front of me I seemed to see the tall figure of Idris, with his tormented face and the controlled disorder of his gestures.

PART IV

WHEN I opened my eyes that first morning, I remained for some time in that state of vague anxiety when, floating between sleep and waking, it seems as if one had been transported during the night to some alien world in which memory can no longer serve as guide. Struggling to pierce the fog of sleep, I became conscious of a patch of dingy wall, then of a glass-fronted wardrobe, whose mirror returned a blurred image of my own face. The room remained anonymous, but I raised myself on one elbow and caught sight of two suitcases which I recognized at once as my own. They evoked the word: journey, which, in its turn, unveiled another: Paris.

This "Paris" was an anchor. Gradually my head cleared. Now I knew that this was no dream, that I was indeed lying in bed in an hotel in Paris and that I had come here on an impulse so sudden that I had some difficulty in explaining it even to myself. People were moving about the corridor. A clock struck nine. I had slept late but I was in no hurry to get up and indeed I shrank from the moment when I should be obliged to ask myself: Now what shall I do ?

So I lay back, pulling a fat red eiderdown up to my shoulders. Yesterday, I thought, at this moment I was leaving London. The boat train was just pulling out of Victoria. I was on my way to Idris and it would not have occurred to me that I should awake next morning elsewhere than by his side in the wide divan of our studio.

Then, gradually, the details of my journey reformed

themselves in my mind... . The boat chugs into the harbour, leaving a trail of white foam along the pale blue water. The expanse of sky that dips to the horizon is of the same pale, innocent blue, flecked with a few plumes of white cloud. We can see the row of cafés along the street that borders the waterside, with their signs: *Ici on peut apporter son casse-croûte* or *Friture,* and the vegetable shops with great baskets of fruit piled outside the doors and the crowd of porters in their blue overalls, waiting to dash on board. A few children hang over the railing on the pier, waving and shouting greetings. The people look happy and nonchalant in the warm sunshine, hurrying about their business along the quay, so that it is as if the boat was steaming straight into the centre of a gay, ancient and rather grubby village.

The crossing has been good and the passengers, alert and well-disposed, crowd the deck, impatient to land. The engines cease throbbing as we glide along the wall of the quay, then the gangway drops with a clatter of chains. People in the street shift their shopping bags to wave at us; sailors hurry along the deck shouting, *Attention! Attention!* and the passengers grasp their suitcases more firmly, elbowing for position, intent on being among the first to land.

Then I remembered how, holding out my passport, I had had a moment of fear lest I might be turned back, lest my parents might have sent out a warning to the ports. Then I had realized, feeling foolish, that I had reached my majority and had the right to go where I pleased.

Presently I was settled in a third-class carriage in the train that was waiting for us at the siding. I had procured a corner seat and had time to buy some bananas and a newspaper, so I looked forward to a comfortable journey. In three hours' time,

I had thought, peeling a banana and watching a vociferous argument over tips that was taking place just below my window, I should be in Paris. Idris would not be at the station, since I had not been sure of the exact day of my arrival. I would take a taxi—it would cost a lot, but impossible to drag my luggage through the *metro*—and go straight to Montrouge. The concierge would have had her baby by now, perhaps, at the rate she was going, another would be on the way. She would give me the key. I would let myself into the studio and make myself, first of all, some coffee. Then I would unpack and hang up my clothes. The place would be terribly untidy, Idris would have made a chaos of it during all these months. If I had time, I would sweep the floor and make the kitchen look nice and polish the taps in the wash-room. There would probably be no milk, I should have to run across to the dairy. People would be surprised to see me, they must have thought I was gone for good ... *"Tu sais, la petite dame anglaise est revenue..."*

The train had started while this domesticated thread of thought was running through my mind. We were passing through flat, green country, dotted with farms and pollarded trees, where well-fed cattle grazed in fields intersected by straight, white roads. In the carriage itself a stout woman in black was lamenting to her husband about the injustice of some deceased relative's will. A harassed mother was peeling oranges for two restless children and a young English girl sat prim and incurious, gazing straight in front of her with an expression of faint disgust. I turned my attention to my paper, but it devoted most of its space to the previous day's football match ... *Roubaix beat Lille* 4-0. ... There were some murders and a rape and an article entitled: Can Molière be filmed?

I had begun then to realize that I was very tired. Excitement had sustained me through the long journey to London, through the crowded day, a second sleepless night and another day of travelling, but now I was forced to admit the insistent ache in my back and the abnormal dryness of my eyes. Perhaps, I thought, instead of sweeping the studio and cleaning the kitchen, I would just have a good wash and lie down for a little sleep before Idris came home.

At this point, I had realized with a certain astonishment that, however far my mind might wander into the future and however exactly it pictured my arrival, it always stopped short at the moment when a step would sound on the stairs and a key turn in the lock. Idris, the motive and mainspring of this terribly decisive journey, was absent from its final image. In memory, he seemed singularly distant, as if his presence had been greatly anterior to the décor in which we had lived together. Perhaps it was the desire for sleep that was gradually creeping over me, that made it so hard to reconstitute his figure. Yet I felt sure that this reconstitution was necessary and even, for some reason, urgent. To the blurred accompaniment of plaintive and irritated French voices, I began to build him up, feature by feature, limb by limb. Strangely enough, this mental picture refused Montrouge, or Montmartre, or indeed any part of Paris, for its background. It seemed to exist in no special place, to form itself in front of a sort of misty curtain. Here he comes, very tall, very thin; long, nervous hands which refuse to twitch; a measured walk which refuses to become an impatient, staccato stride. Here is the long, narrow face with the hollow cheeks and eyes so dark that they are surely the legacy of some marauding Spanish ancestor. These eyes, a little veiled by heavy lids, are extraordinarily sad. They have an expression of intense suffering, yet at the same time of a sort of unquestioning resignation. Now he stands close beside me. He bends to speak to me and the eyes suddenly become warm with kindness. The misty curtain drops away. We stand beside a table covered with a red plush cloth... . "I hope, my dear Laura, that you enjoy your lessons here... ."

"Tickets, please!"

And there had been the ticket-collector standing over me, holding out his hand.

Thoroughly awake now, scrambling in my bag to find my ticket, I had not been able to deny to myself that Mr. Howells had taken the place of Idris. It was not enough to say that I had slipped into a dream and dismiss it at that. I sat up, tensing my muscles to throw off the temptation of sleep. I felt troubled and confused and suddenly I understood that some turmoil in my mind had got to be straightened out and that, since we were already passing through Rouen, there was little time in which to do it.

A little loosening of consciousness had been enough to operate the substitution of father for son. It was a warning that had been given often enough before, but this time I could not allow myself to ignore it. On my way to meet my lover, after breaking so irrevocably on his account with the past, I was forced to realize that it was the reflection in him of Mr. Howells that I had been seeking. Idris himself, more lucid than I, had been aware of the situation for a long time. Now I knew that he had been right and, realizing this, I was forced to suppose that my flight had not, after all, been determined by my desire for him. Indeed, it seemed to me now that he had never really existed for me except as a reminder of the past.

But Mr. Howells, I thought, has been dead for many years. If, in going to Idris, I am only seeking for him, I am going back to the dead past at the very moment when I thought I was breaking with it for ever.

If I am only seeking for the past, I thought as mistletoe-hung woods flashed past the window, I might as well have stayed in Pont-y-Gibby. All this revolt has been for nothing. I am more bound and shut in by myself than ever I was by my mother. I, and not she, am responsible for this situation.

The impact of these thoughts was so violent that I had felt rather as if, walking by a calm sea, I had been suddenly engulfed and inundated by a tidal wave. It seemed to me that everyone must be aware of my agitation, but the couple were still arguing over testamentary clauses, the children had gone to sleep at last and the English girl was moodily reading the *Strand Magazine*.

I told myself: This is just an idea. I am tired. I shall go back and tonight Idris will take me in his arms and I shall forget all about it. One does not change the course of one's life for a mere fancy.

Then I thought: If I do not go back to him, what shall I do? Where shall I live, and how? This is impossible. I have no alternative.

A panic of uncertainty was taking hold of me. "I must have time to think." The houses were growing thicker now, we were thundering through the Northern suburbs. The man opposite rose and began to lift suitcases from the rack. The English girl closed her magazine and took a powder-puff from her bag. The train pounded out: Time to think … time to think… .

Now the houses formed a solid wall along the line, shutting out the sky. Mechanically I put on my hat, picked up my gloves. "Within five minutes I shall have taken a decision and I have no idea what it will be."

The train drew up. Doors flew open and people began to jump down on to the platform. A porter reached up for my luggage. "Taxi, Mademoiselle"" On the platform, people were meeting, embracing. They had purpose, a destination, an address on the tips of their tongues. Electric trolleys dashed along, piled with trunks, their bells pinging madly. It was impossible to linger. The flood of travellers surged towards the exit, carrying me along with it, ridiculously lost and unreal, belonging to no one and without any idea where I was going.

Now I was settled in a taxi. The driver, his hand on the brake, was looking back at me enquiringly. Something had to be done. I said to him:

"Please take me to an hotel. Somewhere quiet and cheap."

Street after street, and night descending slowly on the town.... An hotel, after all, I thought, would do as well as any other place as a perch on which to alight and reflect. An hotel *Ça n'engage à rien,* one might as well not be there. A day in an hotel would be not so much a day as an interim, a pause or break in the continuity of life. Nothing can be better when it becomes necessary to think things out.

When we drew up, I had no idea of our whereabouts. The street, uniformly grey in the twilight, was sedately quiet, with an air of respectable poverty. The inscription painted above the door had flaked away so that I could make out the word "hotel", but the preceding word was illegible. This detail increased, for some reason, the impression that my life had somehow come to a standstill, like a clock that has run down and is waiting to be rewound.

Inside, a dim corridor, a counter with an open register …

"For how long, Mademoiselle?"

"I am not sure. A day, perhaps two… I shall see. …" And so I had come to this room. I remembered staring at a little ball of hair-combings that the previous occupant had let fall behind the wash-stand and reflecting how accidental, how for-tuitous was my presence in this room. Then I remembered dropping into the bed, and the way the mattress had heaved beneath me with the slow motion of the sea until I had fallen asleep.

I HAD SAID: "A day, perhaps two…" but the days passed and this provisional regime began to take on an air of spurious permanence. The very emptiness of the days, and the solitude in which they passed, seemed to make the idea of time meaningless. They slid one into the other; it was as if I was being carried along on the silent and imperceptible drift of a tide.

Although the days were lonely, they did not seem long. Everything I did seemed to have an importance which I could not explain or justify to myself. In the mornings I used to write in my room, without any definite idea of composing a novel or other work, but for the pleasure of words and because I hoped that certain aspects of my life might thus reveal their true visage. I concentrated so well on seizing the fugitive images of the past that I was able to forget that I was hungry until well on in the afternoon. Then I would lunch on a *café-crême* and bread and cheese and afterwards I would stroll in the streets, enjoying the mild spring weather, but avoiding the quarters frequented by Idris. I even avoided Montparnasse and the Boulevard St. Michel, having at present no desire to meet the friends of my student days. The Jardín des Plantes, the charming and populous Place de la Contrescarpe, the quays of the Seine beyond the Gare d'Austerlitz, were safe territory and I would linger in such quarters until a hunger which was by now irresistible drove me back to dine at one of the cheap workmen's restaurants near the hotel.

Each evening, retiring early to my room because I had no money to go to a café or a cinema, I asked myself with astonishment how it was possible that I had come here and why I found myself here rather than anywhere else. I would lie on my bed, watching the pattern of the wall-paper, blurred by the feeble electric light, and reflect how utterly I had delivered myself over to uncertainty. Tomorrow I might be elsewhere; within a week or two, the simple and fundamental problem of how to find the next meal would crowd out all other preoccupations. Yet I knew that I regretted neither the step I had taken nor the step I had refused to take. I felt no melancholy and little anxiety, but rather a pleasurable excitement, as if I had been a snake that was shedding its skin and wondering what it would look like when the process was completed.

There were moments of panic it is true. Once, as I was walking near the Opera, a bus for Montrouge drew up immediately beside me. The sight of it jerked me suddenly back to other spring days which it was in my power now to recreate by a simple gesture. It would be enough to step in and allow myself to be carried off. A home was waiting for me, company, and relative security. I could not float for ever, rootless, about this inhospitable city. My hand was stretched to grasp the rail, I was ready to leap on to the platform, but I drew back, for the phrase that had imposed itself so brutally in the train had formed again in my head, no longer as a mere doubt, but as an affirmation, reached after serious reflection: By going to him, you will be going back to the dead past.

After this experience, I avoided certain bus routes. Sometimes I reflected that I was like those pious men and women who used to withdraw into the desert in order to avoid temptation.

On my way to and from the hotel, I frequently found myself in the rue St. Jacques. It held vivid memories for me and I had not forgotten that, on a certain day in summer, Jean-Pierre had said to me: "I have a message for you from Professor Sougny." The street, and the sight of the ancient house with its peeling facade, never failed to raise the question of a visit.

I should have liked to see the Professor again, for I felt vaguely that he might be able to advise me in a situation that was fast becoming a predicament. Chiefly, though, I was tempted by the thought of Mr. Howells' diary. The memory of my old schoolmaster was strangely insistent at this period when I was just beginning to realize how important a part he had played in my life and how that part had prolonged, and was indeed still prolonging itself into my adult life.

On the other hand I was held back by a sort of shyness and because there was also an indirect connection between the Professor and Idris, and on this subject I preferred to close the door of my mind, to shut out an image which, in moments of loneliness, was still dangerously appealing.

The problem was solved for me. One morning I was passing before the Deaf-Mutes School when I met Madame Sougny walking along the pavement from the opposite direction. Seen in the bright daylight, outside her own home, she resembled any of those shrivelled little old women, dragging too-heavy bags, whom one meets in the streets during the morning shopping hours. She resembled them, in fact, so closely, that I hesitated for a moment, but she recognized me at once and greeted me with casual kindness, as though we had been old friends, used to frequent meetings. The Professor's health, she said, was failing, but he would be glad to see me. I left her after promising to call on the following day.

The prospect of the visit caused me an agitation which nothing seemed to justify. To calm myself I went for a long walk and presently, after crossing the river, came to Auteuil. Airy, prosperous, vacant of meaning, the quarter oppressed me with that air of satisfaction and security which is agreeable only if one is in the mood to share it. Near the *Conservatoire* in the rue de la Pompe, a poster announced a forthcoming concert. I scanned it idly and saw that the name of Mair Howells was among the soloists. It looked as if she might have been right when she had prophesied, long ago, out in the street in Pont-y-Gibby, with the rain driving the notes back into her throat and foretold her future glory.

"Worthy is the Lamb that was slain…"

Step by step, she would fight her way to success. One day, surely, in place of the unharnessed carriage drawn by fanatical admirers, she would drive in a sleek Cadillac and receive the homage, if not of kings, at least of rich industrialists.

I thought now how Mair would pity me if she could see me standing there, with an empty stomach, nothing achieved and no prospects, staring at her name on the poster. She would love me again, surely, as she had loved me at certain moments of our childhood, as she had loved me that day when I had witnessed her triumph at the Eisteddfod, and during the first months after my arrival in Paris. I reflected, staring at the

name which evoked nothing but an angry child singing with
all the force of her lungs against the rain, that she would,
objectively speaking, be right to pity me: it must have been
out of sheer inconsequence of mind, that I could feel no pity
for myself.

Yet I thought of Mair all that day, comparing the well-laid
lines of her life with my own vague wandering, and the
contralto solos from *Orphée* formed a background, during all
that afternoon, to the noise of the Paris streets.

When the time came to ring at the Professor's door, I felt
vaguely uneasy, as if I might, in some unspecified way, be
inviting trouble. Madame Sougny let me in and led me into
the sitting-room, where the Professor sat in his rocking-chair,
peering at a leather-bound volume held close to his eyes. The
stove was lit in spite of the spring warmth and the same
marmalade cat was purring on his knees. It was as if he had
not moved since our last meeting.

He half-rose to greet me, clutching the cat against his chest
to save it from slipping to the ground. I thought he looked
smaller and more frail than when I had last seen him.

"It is a long time since you last visited us," he said kindly.
"Mademoiselle Gethryn has been away in England," said
Madame Sougny.

"Yes, yes, I remember. Our friend Carré told us so."

"I should like to see him. I will write to him… ."

"I hear he did well in his examinations. His father was here
a little while ago."

This visit, after all, was to be of no importance. It would
pass in trivialities, in a polite exchange of news. The magic
link had snapped.

"I am going to make you a cup of tea," said Madame

Sougny. "I always like to do so when we have visitors from England."

When she had gone there was a silence. The Professor stroked his cat and appeared to be searching for something to say. The cup of tea classified me as a stranger, a being apart for whom special provision must be made.

Presently he said: "Did you not tell me that you wished to be a writer? Have you made progress during the time you spent at home?"

"No," I said, and it seemed to me that the admission must destroy any interest he could feel in me. "I did not write at all in England and I am only just beginning to do so again. I think I may have been mistaken and that I am not really capable of writing anything worth while."

He looked at me shrewdly and said:

"You are too young to be sure of that as yet. But suppose it is true, what do you plan to do? I suppose you will get married and perhaps that will satisfy you?"

This comfortable view of my future seemed so far from reality that I laughed aloud. He looked surprised and I said quickly:

"Perhaps I shall get married some day, but there can be no question of it at present. I do want to write and perhaps some day I shall find out what I really want to say, but apart from that there is nothing in my life, nothing at all."

As I said this, I realized that it might sound like a complaint, which was the contrary of my meaning, but at that moment Madame Sougny came in, carrying a tray with cups and a teapot. She said:

"Nothing at all? What a strange thing to say, Mademoiselle. How can there be nothing in your life?"

"It is perhaps very strange," I said, realizing for the first time just how surprising it was. "Yet it is the truth."

"Are you sure?" said Madame Sougny. "It is so difficult to be sure of the truth at your age."

"Age has nothing to do with it, my dear," said the Professor. "I suppose there comes a moment in many lives when the past has entirely dropped away and the future has not yet taken shape. It may happen at any time. The thing is, to recognize such moments which are—if one has the courage to face them—the richest of our lives."

"You mean that they must be complete," I said. "No half-measures, no palliatives... ."

I waited expectantly, for it seemed to me that the Professor's last remark had been an introduction to something very important which he could tell me if he wished to do so. In the slight pause that followed, I realized that I had always considered Professor Sougny as the guardian of some secret which could solve all my problems if he would consent to reveal it... . Now we had reached the point at which this secret must be told if it was to be told at all. My attitude must have revealed my eagerness, for he looked at me sharply, his eyes flickered; it seemed to me that they were crossed by a shadow of annoyance, and I understood at once that I had been asking him for more than he could give.

"My dear child... ." he said... . Then he muttered, m ... m ... m ... as very old men do, looking down at his shoes, nodding and mumbling into his white moustache.

"I am a rationalist," he said a moment later. "A rationalist," he repeated, then: "On this particular point I may have got on to common ground with the mystics, but it is by chance. You mustn't make me mean more than I say... ."

A frail hand gestured away an undesired burden.

Madame Sougny had been pouring out tea. Now she said briskly:

"I think you should tell us exactly what you have been doing and all that has happened to you since we last met. It is all very well for my husband to talk of the richness of what you and he call moments of emptiness, but they are dangerous too. There is a practical side to these questions. You were the pupil of our dear friend Howells, formed by him. It seemed to us, after our talk with you last year, that you were almost his daughter—more like his daughter than that little girl who is really his child."

"You are perfectly right, my dear," said Professor Sougny. "Abstractions are all very well in their place."

His eyes brightened, he was alert again, a wonder for his age.

"Do tell us everything you can," he said to me. "And allow us to help in whatever—surely limited—way seems possible."

When I had completed my story, the Professor said:

"I am an old man, a man formed by a certain sort of mental gymnastics and I really doubt whether my experience could be of any use to you. The only important things are those that one discovers for oneself.

"If you decide to return to this man," he went on, "to the son of our friend Howells, it will at least be no unconsidered step. It will be because you feel that the need for him is the most important thing in your life."

Madame Sougny interrupted him.

"My dear, have you not understood? That would not be a solution at all. They would always make each other miserable... ."

"If you feel that," he said to me. "We must help you as far as we can. As far as we can," he repeated, as if he knew that the help he offered was not that which I had hoped from him. "I can procure translations for you, and send you pupils if you wish to give English lessons. Since you feel that a period of independence is so necessary for you, this will make it materially possible for you and I shall be happy to help you for the sake of my friend Howells. You must not let yourself be rushed into taking any unconsidered step. The thing is, to gain time."

"Do not answer at once," said Madame Sougny. "All this seems to me so very uncertain. You must reflect and let us know what you decide to do."

The Professor was looking very tired and seemed indeed, for his forefinger tapped gently, in the manner of impatient old people, against the arm of his chair, to be hoping for my departure. I rose.

"You are very kind. I will think for a little longer, then, if I may, I will come and see you again."

As I said this I was thinking of the manuscript of which Jean-Pierre had spoken and which had been the real reason for my visit. At this moment, Madame Sougny said:

"Was there not something which you wished to give to Mademoiselle Gethryn, my dear?"

"Of course," said the Professor. "I had not forgotten. It is up there, on one of the shelves, if you will be so kind." Madame Sougny had already opened a cupboard in the wall. It revealed a number of folders, neatly stacked and labelled, pamphlets and piles of notebooks. Standing on tiptoe, she peered through her steel-rimmed spectacles into the recess and drew out a flat parcel, carelessly wrapped in brown paper and tied with coarse string. She handed it to the Professor and he held it, balancing it in his hands, palpating it, and I was surprised at the sudden vigour with which he spoke.

"I think you know already what this contains," he said. "It is a diary kept by our friend from the time when he first left home up to the day when he disappeared so suddenly from Paris. It was among a number of things he left with us, on a pretext, since he gave us no warning of his departure. It was only after your first visit, after you had told us how tragic had been the manner of his death, that we felt justified in reading it and both of us felt at once that it belongs to you rather than to anyone else."

He clasped the parcel to his chest, gazing fixedly at me with his tired blue eyes and I realized that he was reluctant to part with it.

"What a remarkable, what an extraordinary story," he said, half to himself. "Really, something should be done with these diaries…"

"But, my dear…" protested Madame Sougny, softly. "Yes, yes. We should not allow sentiment to stand in our way. There was no stipulation of privacy and Howells' case is probably unique. These diaries should be edited and published."

He handed me the parcel and said:

"If anyone does so, it should be you. Edit them, put them into publishable form. It will be your first literary work."

"But only if you wish it, of course," said Madame Sougny. "It is a matter for your own judgment."

"That is understood," said the Professor. "She must do as she thinks best, since the diary is now her own property."

"We wish you good luck, my dear," he said to me. "Come back soon and tell us what decision you take."

His eyes were still fixed on the brown-paper parcel that I clutched beneath my arm and as Madame Sougny accompanied me to the door, I heard him murmur:

"An extraordinary case, a unique case... ."

THAT NIGHT, as soon as I had eaten dinner, I hurried back to the hotel and up to my room. The parcel, awaiting me on the chipped deal table that I used as a writing desk, seemed vaguely menacing, since I suspected that the reading of it might force me to the definite decision before which I still hesitated. The string was tightly knotted and I picked at it with my nails, obscurely glad of the delay. Then I reflected that a year ago, I should surely have cut the string, torn the wrappings apart and plunged straight into the manuscript.

When the parcel was open at last, it revealed a number of variously coloured notebooks, of the kind used by schoolchildren. Some of them bore labels in English, while others had evidently been bought in France. I began to turn them over slowly, one after the other. They were neatly numbered and the first bore the words: "Maths. Prof. Goodwin, Tuesday IO-II," and these words, written in an unformed and almost childish hand, had been crossed out and replaced by "Diary", printed right across the cover.

I opened the book at hazard. The ink had yellowed with age. I began to read and found myself at once uncomfortably transported into the heart of a problem that had culminated long ago, so miserably, before my eyes.

Here was Mr. Howells at London University. An effort of imagination brought to life that figure in a photograph in the schoolhouse parlour ... a thin boy with a lock of hair hanging dankly across the brow, a boy who had sung baritone in his father's choir and who moved warily now, like a man astray in a jungle full of snares and pitfalls. His companions are as incomprehensible to him as men from another continent. Their presence is a continual irritation, a continual challenge. In the evening, returning to the stuffy room in a cheap Bloomsbury boarding-house, he writes sternly of their impiety and frivolity; then, awakening at night, he rises, lights the dim gas lamp and records his remorse, denounces his own lack of charity. A few months later the tone changes suddenly and he is writing joyfully of an encounter with a group of students who appear to share his own interests. They question him on the condition of the miners in North Wales, listen eagerly to all he tells them. For the first time, he is encouraged to talk by people who refrain from laughing at his clothes or his accent. He is asked to give a lecture at one of the student societies. Then comes the discovery that these young men are Socialists. Immediately the conclusion follows —they are interested in the miners less because they are poor and oppressed than because they furnish arguments for a godless thesis, for the improvement of conditions by the overthrow of the social order rather than by a change in men's hearts.

I closed the book quickly, with a feeling of embarrassment. Mr. Howells could never be for me the callow student who, at his first contact with the outer world, had confided the turmoil of his mind to these pages. By reading them, I felt that I was in some way betraying him. This violation of his secrets seemed almost a denial of his right to my respect. The adolescent of this first diary seemed, although I refused as ever to allow my mind to dwell on the subject, inextricably connected with the image of a final humiliation.

Yet, even while I was reflecting in this way, I was turning

the pages of another book. A year passes, a year of scruples and moral agitation; another year, the same isolation, the same furious intent to learn. It was as if I was watching, page by page, as Mr. Howells shed the outer signs that distinguished him from his comrades. The writing was becoming more even, more controlled, the expressions that of any young Englishman set aside by intellectual attainment from his humble origins. Alternating with details of the reading and lectures of the day, were comments on the chapter of the Bible read each morning on waking. I felt sure that this custom must have seemed to him as inevitable a part of the day's routine as dressing or eating his meals and I understood that the prophets and patriarchs of those ancient Hebrew tribes were for him a more living reality than the fellow-students whose names were mentioned more and more rarely in this chronicle of intimate preoccupations. More and more, this young Mr. Howells was withdrawing into that closed world from which he had never really emerged.

Now, a note: "Today I was informed that I have been awarded a scholarship to X college, at Cambridge. This is the first scholarship to be given by that college to a student from a grammar school. I telegraphed to my parents, but now, the first feeling of elation passed, I ask myself what trials and temptations lie before me and how I shall comport myself among men of a type that I have never yet had occasion to meet."

The Cambridge notebooks were thick and glossy, covered with a writing that could hardly be recognized as the same unformed hand of the earlier diaries. A new assurance has taken hold of Mr. Howells; he is aware of his power. A few dry phrases reveal that his intellectual capacities have impressed brilliant young men from brilliant homes, his reputation

spreads, he is listened to with respect. Behind the reserve of
the words I sensed a new, more worldly Mr. Howells who was
preparing for himself an enviable career. As the months pass,
the Bible quotations grow less and less frequent. They are
replaced by speculation. Mr. Howells has discovered Darwin,
then the German philosophers. He questions, compares,
speaks against the theory of evolution at a Union debate, but
admits the possibility of doubt. There are many references to
discoveries in the domains of physics and psychology. Mr.
Howells analyses, discusses. It is as if he were engaged in an
uneasy dialogue between his past and present selves.

My eyes hurt from straining at the faded writing and my
throat felt dry. I rose, stretched and poured water into the tooth
glass. It was nearly midnight and the sounds and rustling of
life in the hotel had ceased gradually while I read, so that all
was now as silent as if I had been alone in a deserted place.

As the cool water trickled down my throat, I thought of Mr.
Howells so intently that I seemed actually to see the young
student, avid to learn, bewildered at all the new perspectives
opening before him, asking himself: if *this* is true, how can
that be true? I saw him so clearly, indeed, that the physical
details seemed to build themselves up, atom by atom, to
integrate and move. Yet for some reason, this clear and
detailed image remained merely an image. I saw Mr. Howells
with the same vividness with which I had sometimes pictured
characters in books—Julien Sorel, for instance, climbing the
ladder to Mathilde de la Môle's window in a tumult of
ambition and desire. He seemed no more a part of my life than
such personages could be. I thought of him now as a character
developing before the eyes of my mind, rather than as a person
I had really known. Indeed , the clearer the figure of the young

student of the diaries became, the dimmer grew the memory of the middle-aged schoolmaster.

I crossed the room and leaned out of the open window, hoping to see some living figure—a beggar, perhaps, furtively rummaging in a dustbin—to relieve the oppressive emptiness of night. But not even a cat was visible in the dim, grey street. I could only turn back from its emptiness and stillness, to the room where a pile of coloured notebooks still awaited me on the table.

The labels of these notebooks told me that they had been purchased in France. I opened one of them at hazard and read with astonishment the name of a famous philosopher of the period, quoted in familiar conversation. Mr. Howells had talked with Alain, perhaps with Bergson, with other men whose names Jean-Pierre and his comrades had quoted with awe; he had lived with them in a strange world of abstract ideas. Into this world I could no longer follow him. The brilliant philosopher, the disciple and friend of M. Sougny, the "thinking-machine" described by the Professor, was too far from the grave schoolmaster who had taught the children of Pont-y-Gibby to read and write. Here, neither memory nor imagination could attain him.

Yet I continued to read, although the meaning of what I read no longer, in the state of mental fatigue in which I found myself, penetrated my brain. This story of the growth and destruction of intellectual power no longer touched me. It was impossible for me to concentrate sufficiently to follow the difficult phrases. Yet gradually, as I read, I began to imagine that Mr. Howells had written them in a room exactly resembling that in which I now found myself. ... I thought of him returning here at night, pale and weary already with the day's work. I thought of him as sitting down at this very table and drawing towards him the thin, paper-covered book that I held now in my hands, beginning to note the conversations of the day, to build up with their aid the philosophical system he is gradually devising. He works far into the night, till his eyes grow dim with exhaustion. Then, as the exhilaration of thought begins to fade, his father's figure forms itself gradually in his brain. The room fades, he feels the soft, damp air of the hills on his skin and looming behind him, immense and overshadowing, the stern minister evokes his warrior God, calls on Him to send the unrighteous to eternal flames. *"Consume them in wrath; consume them that they be no more."*

And now Mr. Howells lays down his pen. His hands cover his eyes but he cannot shut out the vision of the past. The mighty singing in the chapel beats like waves in his brain and he is gripped again by exultation and sacred fear: *Let the ungodly perish… . Consume them in wrath… .*

How insistent, how imperishable that fear must have been to have driven him back to Wales, to have sent him seeking a refuge in the schoolmaster's villa in Pont-y-Gibby and to have brought him to that sad and lonely death, despised and rejected by those whom he had tried so hard to love.

There remained many more notebooks, but I knew they could tell me nothing more. I understood Mr. Howells now as well as I should ever understand him. The thought of this long conflict inspired in me an immense lassitude. I knew that Mr. Howells too had not dared to escape from childhood, that that very excessiveness, that "frenetic desire to penetrate the farthest possible into the domain of pure thought" of which Madame Sougny had spoken, had grown from the consciousness of the strength of the chains that still bound him. He must have felt obscurely that only total revolt, total denial, could free him. So he had never been free for an instant. Every step forward had been guided by those childhood memories from which he imagined himself to be escaping so completely.

I thought of Idris whom, I knew now, I should never see again. He, at least, had been clear-sighted from the beginning. He had understood himself, and me. "The tug of memory," he had said. "The sub-conscious attachment to all that reason is trying to throw off... ." When he wrote me that letter, that letter that had torn up for ever my roots in Pont-y-Gibby, he had been acknowledging defeat.

"Are we all like that?" I asked myself. "Can none of us live otherwise than in the shadow of our own childhood?"

But I knew now that I was free. Mr. Howells would never haunt me again. I had no more need to recreate him and I thought sadly of the years I had lost through seeking him and, through him, for the comfort and security my mother had given me before my father's return. Then I reflected with joy that there was still time, that I was ready now to create my own, adult happiness, to live the life of the woman I had become, instead of that of the child I had been.

Now I took the pile of notebooks in my hand and held them, thinking of the years of futile revolt and progress towards ultimate defeat that they traced day after day. I knew that I should never read them again and that they could have no more meaning for me.

I began to tear the pages of the first book. To do so, I had to strip off the cover, then tear through four or five pages at a time. It was hard work and my fingers were stiff before I started on the second book. I tore each page into tiny morsels, as though I had been tearing my own past. I wanted nothing to remain and the sentences in the yellowed handwriting dissolved between my fingers and became meaningless as a thick carpet of paper gradually covered the floor around me.

As I tore, I thought intently about Mr. Howells. It seemed to me, although in a very uncertain way, that I was rendering him a last service and that he would, if he could see me now, approve of what I was doing.

I thought, as my tired fingers twisted the tough paper: Now the joys and sorrows of the past will be memories, good or bad, but no longer invaders of the present. Minute by minute I am taking leave of sad and beautiful childhood. Minute by minute I am approaching the gates of life.

The scraps of torn paper floated down and settled like snow all around me. I felt very tired, as if after a long physical strain. I stood up at last and stretched my cramped fingers. There was so much torn paper that the waste-paper basket would not hold it all. I undressed quickly, then I got into bed and switched off the light. As sleep began to creep upon me, I thought how I should awake when morning came to a difficult and unknown world, full of problems, but in which a place was surely waiting for me. The prelude was over at last. Life was about to begin.

ABOUT HONNO

Honno Welsh Women's Press was set up in 1986 by a group of women who felt strongly that women in Wales needed wider opportunities to see their writing in print and to become involved in the publishing process. Our aim is to develop the writing talents of women in Wales, give them new and exciting opportunities to see their work published and often to give them their first 'break' as a writer. Honno is registered as a community co-operative. Any profit that Honno makes is invested in the publishing programme. Women from Wales and around the world have expressed their support for Honno. Each supporter has a vote at the Annual General Meeting. For more information and to buy our publications, please write to Honno at the address below, or visit our website: www.honno.co.uk

Honno, 14 Creative Units, Aberystwyth Arts Centre
Aberystwyth, Ceredigion SY23 3GL

Honno Friends

We are very grateful for the support
of all our Honno Friends.

For more information on how you can become
a Honno Friend, see:

https://www.honno.co.uk/about/support-honno/